MW00709345

Diane Morris failed.

I will soon become enmeshed with her life and death.

This is to be a therapy day of blasting holes in paper targets with my two detectives—Gary Horton and Joseph Malone. The three of us conduct criminal investigations for Elko County. Our jurisdiction is the size of the state of Maryland. The Elko City Police cover the much smaller city area. Yeah, I'm bitching a little.

We arrive at the shooting range and remove our gear from the car. A blazing sun bakes the valley floor as ominous black clouds begin to gather over the jagged Ruby Mountains. With a wary eye at the skies, my thought is, *please, not today*. One afternoon away from the office is all I ask.

Our county range is inappropriately located next to a pungent sewage treatment plant. As further evidence of poor government planning, an Elko City park is located on the opposite side of the sewage facility. Great place for a picnic, when the wind isn't blowing. Ahhh, rural Nevada.

With the sun reflecting off his shiny black pony-tail, Joseph gazes up at the azure sky. "Must be something dead out there."

Two vultures circle overhead.

Cold But Not Forgotten

by

RJ Waters

Cold But Not Forgotten

Cover Art by *Abigail Owen*

The Wild Rose Press, Inc.
PO Box 708
Adams Basin, NY 14410-0708
Visit us at www.thewildrosepress.com

Publishing History
First Mainstream Suspense Edition, 2019
Print ISBN 978-1-5092-2649-8
Digital ISBN 978-1-5092-2650-4

Published in the United States of America

Dedication

This book is dedicated to my wife, Penny, who is responsible for me becoming a writer. She said I had led an interesting life and should write my memoirs.

I wrote down a few incidents from my past. The coy little imp said, "This is good, now write a book." I protested. I am told, since I'm full of BS, humor, and sarcasm, this is the perfect mix for being a writer.

I had never thought of being a writer. It took off from there. Her proofing and suggestions have been invaluable to me, always there to support and encourage me as I struggled.

My love for her is unbounded.

Chapter One

Elko, Nevada

Diane Morrissey died today because her cell phone failed.

I will soon become enmeshed with her life and death.

This is to be a therapy day of blasting holes in paper targets with my two detectives—Gary Horton and Joseph Malone. The three of us conduct criminal investigations for Elko County. Our jurisdiction is the size of the state of Maryland. The Elko City Police cover the much smaller city area. Yeah, I'm bitching a little.

We arrive at the shooting range and remove our gear from the car. A blazing sun bakes the valley floor as ominous black clouds begin to gather over the jagged Ruby Mountains. With a wary eye at the skies, my thought is, *please, not today*. One afternoon away from the office is all I ask.

Our county range is inappropriately located next to a pungent sewage treatment plant. As further evidence of poor government planning, an Elko City park is located on the opposite side of the sewage facility. Great place for a picnic, when the wind isn't blowing. Ahhh, rural Nevada.

With the sun reflecting off his shiny black ponytail, Joseph gazes up at the azure sky. "Must be something dead out there."

Two vultures circle overhead.

"Damn, Joseph, your Native American instincts never cease to amaze me," Gary jabs.

Ignoring his partner's characteristic sarcasm, Joseph scrambles up the tall dirt berm that runs along the side of our range.

"Guys, come here," he shouts.

Gary and I start running. A surge of wind blows past us—a dust devil. It races up the berm enveloping Joseph's large form in a shimmering cloud as he points, statue-like, toward the city land. For a moment he vanishes within the cloud, then suddenly it's gone, leaving Joseph still there, still pointing. Truly an eerie almost mystical sight. Bone chilling in fact.

Blinking my eyes, I look toward the area Joseph indicates. Approximately seventy-five yards out in the barren, sun-lit field, between the park and the berm, is a body. My experience tells me the person is dead. I hope I'm wrong.

The vultures circle lower.

Skidding down the berm, we run across the field to the prone form—a female on her side, dressed in athletic pants, tank top, and running shoes. Her left arm is stretched out with her fingers dug into the loose dirt, as if she had been desperately clawing her way forward. Her right arm rests at a crooked angle by her waist.

Immediately dropping to my knees, I shout, "Ma'am, ma'am." There is no response. Her eyes are wide open, the pupils fixed. Placing my index and middle fingers on the side of her thin neck over the carotid artery, I can't find a pulse. I try the other side, still nothing. She's not breathing and there's no heartbeat—the woman is dead. Warm to the touch, she has not been deceased long.

We look at each other and then back to the body, each man lost in his own thoughts. What if we hadn't eaten lunch first? Left earlier? Driven faster? Maybe we could have saved her. The damned 'what ifs' can haunt a cop forever.

Since this is the City's jurisdiction, Gary radios the Elko Police, alerting them they have a D.B.—dead body.

To my shock, there are extensive blood stains covering her shirt and pants.

"There's so much blood it looks like it was poured on her," I say.

"Jesus Christ, that's not what I expected to see," Gary blurts out.

Her face and arms are encrusted with dirt. Once manicured fingernails are broken and split from clawing the ground. Her blonde hair, partially in a ponytail, is now caked to her suntanned face. She appears to be in her mid-thirties. There are also blood smears on her neck and arms. The shirt and pants are blood soaked, but the woman's clothing is intact, no tears or cuts, no knife or bullet wounds, not damaged in any way. Slowly I roll the bottom of the tank top up, looking for the source of the blood. I find no signs of trauma or cuts, not even any bruising. It appears the blood was on the outside of her clothing and soaked through.

I wonder out loud, "How could someone have this much blood poured on them and not be harmed? Was it a ritual?"

Judging from the area behind her, it appears she crawled twenty feet or so. There are uneven tracks coming from the park. Was she running away, then staggered, fell, crawled, and died? To one side of where she first began to crawl is a small puddle of thick, greenish liquid. Vomit? The fluid is beginning to solidify.

Looking down at her lifeless body, I can almost sense her panic. She was urgently trying to get away. But from what? From whom? My mind is a jumble of possibilities; did she fight off an attack? Human, animal, or back to my first thought, was she a victim of some psychotic murder ritual?

I stare into the park; it appears empty. There are no people, no vehicles, nothing. What the hell happened?

Beseechingly, we look at each other. Joseph gets a fogged-over look in his eyes.

"You all right?" Gary asks.

I put a finger to my lips and shake my head. I have been around Joseph long enough to know when he is getting one of his *feelings.* His grandfather, a shaman in the Shoshone tribe, taught his grandson many of the ancient ways. Having benefited in the past from Joseph's *feelings,* I know better than to interrupt him.

In a deep trance-like voice, Joseph intones, "This is all wrong. Many things going on here. Her spirit was taken from her."

"You mean she was murdered?" I query.

He jolts to reality; he is back with us now.

"Yes, Bob. Her spirit was taken," responding in his normal voice. "She was murdered. I do not know how. But I do know she was killed."

He scans the area, staring into the silent park and

then down at the trail the woman left in the dirt.

"We are missing something. I cannot see it, but I feel it. I know there is something here we need to find."

The sun disappears behind that growing bank of dark, heavy clouds; there is a sudden chill to the air. It feels as if those clouds have ripped open, releasing an icy fog, the wind biting at us. As a shiver of apprehension snakes down my spine, my hand instinctively hovers over my weapon. After a silent glance at each other, we fan out and start walking toward the park, eyes straining and senses at a fever pitch.

We are jarred to an abrupt halt by the sound of approaching sirens. "Guys, let's go back. Remember, this is not our jurisdiction." They both stop and rejoin me, Joseph expressing something I do not want to hear.

"This may not be our jurisdiction, boss, but it is our case. I know it is."

Chapter Two

First on the scene is an Elko City police officer, followed by paramedics. Pointing to the bloodstained clothing on the seemingly uninjured victim, the puzzled officer looks up. "What happened here?"

"No idea," I say, lowering myself down beside the body. "This is how we found her. It appears she was running from the park." I point out the tracks in the dirt. "She must have tripped or fallen and then started to crawl toward our range." I turn and gesture toward the shooting range.

One of the paramedics looks at us with wide, troubled eyes. "I can't find any trauma that would cause all the blood on her."

Next a fire truck arrives and the crew sprint toward us.

"My god, it's Diane Morrissey." The Elko City fire captain releases a ragged gasp. "She was one of the volunteers who played a victim in our disaster drill this morning. She's a dentist's wife."

That explains the bloodstains.

"She car-pooled with another participant."

That explains the empty parking lot.

Captain B. Howard—per his polished nametag— six feet, solid build, trimmed reddish mustache, continues, "After the other volunteers were gone, I noticed Mrs. Morrissey in the park doing stretching exercises. I asked if she needed a ride. She was going to run the exercise course and then call her husband to take her to lunch. 'I do it all the time,' she said."

His freckled, suntanned face stiffens. He gazes upward, eyes blinking, then turns away.

"Not your fault, man," I offer. "She was an adult, made her own decisions."

He chokes back his emotion. "I know, but we are the *Fire Department*. We're supposed to save people. Not abandon them. We left her here. What happened to her?" He gives me a pleading look.

"At this point, I have no idea. The coroner will determine the cause of death. It may be medical and would have happened anyway. You did your job by checking on her. It's not on you." I reach out and give his shoulder a squeeze. He gives me a somber nod and tells his crew to pack up. The coroner and crime scene investigators will take over now.

The three of us county boys step out of the way so the city police officers can go ahead with their work. The grizzled patrol sergeant comes over to me and mutters, "All right, Lieutenant Carson, what is this? We in police work try and imply the crime occurred in someone else's area. But this appears you were trying to *drag* the victim into your jurisdiction. If you're hurting for cases, I'm sure we can give you some." The sergeant and I have worked together in the past and we always rib each other. Dark humor helps us in emergency services handle the horror we encounter all too often.

"Honest, Sarge, this is how we found her. She was trying to get away from the park, trying to find help."

He directs his officers to search the park area. An

Elko City detective arrives. I brief him on what we observed and the action we took. He asks us to write our statements for the case file. While we are doing that, one of the officers comes from the park with a cell phone and hands it to the detective.

The phone is dead. No wonder she was running away. She had no way to call for help. But help from what, from whom? Damn it, there are still so many unanswered questions.

After completing our statements, we head back to the office. On the way, I ask Joseph if he has any more thoughts.

"It doesn't feel right, Bob. Nothing in the park except a dead cell phone. Not right."

"How about that cell phone? Could that be what you felt was missing?"

"No. It's not the cell phone. Something else. I know it." Joseph stares out the window; I can feel energy radiating from him. Having partnered with the big guy since arriving in Elko, I realize that I am getting *feelings* too. One thing is clear. The last thing we need to do is to spend our time, talent, and energy solving someone else's case.

Chapter Three

So why did we need shooting range therapy yesterday? We learned that William Randal Weaton, whom I shot to death on a rain-soaked street in Portland, Oregon, was not the person responsible for a cold case that has haunted me for years. This morning a headache also haunts me. I drank too much last night.

Weaton *was* a serial killer. It's impossible to know how many years his reign of terror lasted. I went to Portland to arrest him on several outstanding murder warrants. The documentation of his involvement was clear-cut—statements from multiple witnesses, DNA, and a lengthy trail of evidence screamed his guilt. God only knows how many young women he had beaten and dumped along the highways of America. I investigated the death of three of these women and assisted other agencies with their inquiries. To conceal his identity, he stole IDs from fellow truckers of similar appearance. Murdered two and left another for dead.

I tracked him as my law enforcement career moved from California to rural Nevada. Now it turns out Weaton was in an Oklahoma hospital when *my case* occurred. I have always referred to it as *my case*. Why? As a young police officer, I discovered the body of a woman who may have been one of his victims. It is possible I watched his truck drag her body past me without being aware of what was happening. All I saw

9

was the silhouette of a passing truck.

I could never let it go.

Weaton lost his prosthetic eye when his last victim tore it out of his socket. The woman had been fighting for her life on a highway outside of Elko, Nevada. Joseph and I were the investigators at the scene of that crime.

We had finished the initial examination of the body and allowed the coroner to remove it. The other emergency responders were gone; it was just Joseph and me. A full moon illuminated the roadway and its surrounding shoulder. I told Joseph this would be our last chance to find evidence while the crime scene was still secure.

An odd expression appeared on Joseph's face, and he slowly walked down the shoulder of the road. He stared up at the moon and then down. "Come here. I feel something." He waved his hand toward the side of the road.

I'm on a deserted highway with a brand-new partner. He is acting weird and waving at the darkness. I have read the Tony Hillerman books about shaman and medicine men, but this is a Native American kid from Elko, not a gray-haired seer from New Mexico.

"I know you don't drink much, Joseph, but how about peyote?"

"No. Sometimes I get *feelings*."

I began shining my flashlight around the area he pointed toward, then I walked down to the drainage ditch, at the bottom.

"Keep going."

I glanced back at Joseph, and he was still pointing in my direction.

I continued to shine my light around the ditch, then I saw something flash. I went over, and it was—what the hell—it looked like an eyeball. I leaned down closer. It sure looked like an eyeball, with blood on it. An eyeball, come on. What would a real eyeball be doing here? Then it hit me. The victim we released to the morgue had blood and flesh under her fingernails.

"Joseph, get down here."

I am not sure if I wanted a witness or just company.

Putting his hand over his mouth, he stammers, "Is that what I think it is?"

"I think so. Turn your head away if you're going to puke."

Retrieving an evidence bag and using gloves, I carefully pick up the eye and place it in the bag. It must have been quite a sight. Joseph, holding the evidence bag, is shaking so much I could hardly get the eye inside it. To be completely honest, I wasn't doing too well either. I have seen a lot of trauma in my careers, which include EMT, police, and war, but this is a *real* eyeball. Wait a moment. It's hard, not soft like a real eyeball. What is it? It has fresh blood on it. Is it a false eye? I have never encountered one before.

"Joseph, what was all that waving about?"

"I can't explain it, but I was drawn to walk down the roadway. Then I looked up to the moon and I saw the owl dive down toward that area of the ditch. I knew it was a sign."

Fate is a mysterious creature. That eye led me to an ocularist in Reno, who, along with unraveling the clues of the prosthetic eye, eventually became my wife. An ocularist is a craftsman who can fabricate a realistic looking artificial eye; my wife is one of the best. After marrying me, P.K. moved her business to Elko.

Mercifully, quitting time arrives. Home is always an oasis of sanity, love, and much happiness. The emotions of this job can be overwhelming. I'm not new at this game, pretty much seen it all. Unlike many others, I haven't become jaded, at least that's what I tell myself.

As I walk through the door of my home, my wife comes running up, throws her arms around my neck, and proclaims, "Guess what, baby?"

"What, my love?"

She notices my less than cheerful mood. "Uh-oh, what's wrong, Robert, no smart-ass comeback? That's not like you. What happened, bad day?"

"No, you first. You're excited about something. Mine can wait," I protest, knowing she won't buy it.

Narrowing those mesmerizing hazel eyes, "Mine's good news. It can wait. What's going on, my love?"

I tell her about the dead woman we found.

"Robert, I just met Diane Morrissey. It was at lunch yesterday."

I blurt out, "What do you know about her?" I cannot help myself; I am a cop after all.

Pulling herself up to her full five-foot two-inch height, P.K. announces crisply, "Well, Officer, she was about five seven, maybe one hundred twenty pounds. She wore a peach, sleeveless blouse, tailored jeans, and expensive leather sandals. She was very pleasant but was pale and didn't feel well. Elaine expressed concern about her health. Diane told us she was having trouble with her diet. She was taking all sorts of health food supplements. She was into marathon running and was out of balance in her diet, whatever that means. Sir! That is all I have to report, Sir!" She salutes me.

I break out laughing and take her into my arms.

"I did good, huh?" She giggles and snuggles into me.

"You definitely did good. You are the best observer I know. Now what is your good news?"

"After hearing someone I recently met is dead, I don't feel I should be happy about anything. In fact, Diane is part of why I'm happy. You remember Elaine mentioned I should be in an art gallery here in Elko? Good friend that she is, she arranged for me to take a few of my paintings to the gallery for their review. I didn't tell you because if I was turned down, you would be upset." She places her hand against my cheek. "You *are* my biggest fan. The director called me this morning. The Board met and overwhelmingly approved my work and I now have four paintings proudly adorning the walls of the gallery. Diane Morrissey was one of the directors. How bittersweet this is. The three of us went to lunch later. I liked her."

Pulling P.K. closer, I tell her how proud I am of her. We hold each other in silence. It is a tragic set of circumstances; sadly, in my profession, that is often the norm. Good things, bad things, that's life. I think about the lady who died. It's sounding more like a health problem. Still it doesn't set right with me. Not my case, not my responsibility. Something inside tells me differently. I am beginning to pay more attention to my intuition.

Thanks, Joseph!

Chapter Four

The following morning, I'm at my desk when Gary bursts through the door and comes straight to my office, his face taut and serious, not his usual partial smirk.

"Bob, I know it's not our case, but last night when I told Katie about the dead woman, the dentist's wife, Katie went ballistic. She called the dentist a low-life scum. Said she went to him for a filling one time and he wouldn't stop hitting on her. When he tried to send his assistant out of the room, she told him, 'No way, she stays, or I leave.' Katie never went back to the creep. I have never seen her that worked up, even at me. And she has gotten pretty mad at me on a couple of occasions."

"Gary, I know we're all unsettled about this matter, but from what I've learned, the lady did have a health issue. We'll just have to see what the Elko Police and the coroner determine."

That afternoon the Elko City detective called to update us about Diane Morrissey. The woman's doctor had seen her regularly, as she had not been feeling well. He had done blood tests and ordered more testing, to find out what was wrong with her. The doctor was aware of her marathon running and knew she was using various dietary supplements and vitamins. Since was *under her physician's care at the time of death*, no autopsy will be performed. Her husband, the scumbag dentist, didn't push the issue, so it was ruled a death by *natural causes*.

Her funeral will be in a few days.

Later in the week my wife attends the funeral with Elaine, Undersheriff George's wife. Elaine wants company, and P.K. feels an obligation to go. She calls me after the funeral, upset and ranting that Dr. Morrissey had been behaving like a big showboat.

"It was pathetic. I tell you, Robert, it was a huge act."

"Um, he should be upset, right?"

"You should have seen him. It was bullshit. What a show. He had his dentist buddies hovering around him, all their wives consoling him. It was bull."

"I know he has a reputation as a womanizer, but was he that bad?" I dumbly ask, as only a man can.

"He gave me the eye in the reception line. No remorse there."

"I gave you the eye when I first met you, too." *I am losing here and should just shut up.*

"Yes, but you weren't at your wife's *funeral*! I think he killed her, and you should prove it, Robert." She likes to call me Robert.

"We'll talk more when I get home, my dear."

"Bring some wine."

That night, over wine and dinner, I tell my feisty wife I cannot investigate the death of Diane Morrissey.

"Number one, it is not in my jurisdiction, and number two, the coroner went along with the cause of death as degrading health." I sound lame, even to myself.

"Yeah, well *number three*, he killed her. It wouldn't be the first time you took on a case that wasn't in your *jurisdiction*, would it, my love?"

She has me there. I started my manhunt for Weaton when it wasn't in my jurisdiction.

I promise to consider it, discreetly.

"I believe he killed her, and I know my brilliant investigator husband can prove it." She gives me that *determined* look she can get when she has her mind set on something.

I take a big swig of wine.

Chapter Five

Entering headquarters next morning, I observe an elderly Native American gentleman sitting at Joseph's desk. They're talking quietly but I can tell it's a serious conversation. I go directly to my office and don't bother them. In a few minutes, Joseph comes to my door and asks if I will talk with the man.

"He has a problem and I would like to help him anyway we can."

"Sure, I'll be happy to listen and see if we can be of assistance," I reply warily.

Joseph knows the ins and outs of what we can and cannot do. I suspect this must fall under the gray area of cannot do. Besides being intuitive, Joseph is also at times, *conniving.*

The man comes in, shakes my hand, and thanks me for agreeing to listen to his problem. He appears even older than I first thought, his face creased by the wisdom and woes of many years. Harold is his name, and he comes from Joseph's reservation.

"I've known Joseph since he was born and watched him grow up. He had his wild moments when he was younger, but he has made his family proud. He has earned the respect of the community. I did not know where to turn, and his mother said I should ask Joseph. He would know how to help."

Joseph is blushing.

"Well, Harold, I am very fortunate to have him on my team. Now tell me what's going on and I'll see if we can help."

The gentleman seems to age further as he tells me the story of his grandson who has continually gotten into trouble over the years.

"My daughter had the boy, Mathew, out of wedlock, then had two rocky marriages and a few relationships, none of them good. The boy grew up living with turmoil. He got into trouble early on and has kept at it. I can assure you, Bob, Mathew has a good soul and is quite smart, however, always hangs around with the wrong crowd. Old sad story of many upbringings, now and in the past. After he spent time locked up at Juvenile Hall, Mathew did seem to be trying to change for the better. He has a natural artistic talent, and Joseph attempted to channel his gift in a positive way. Got him into an Indian college in New Mexico, majoring in art. It went well for a few months, but then Mathew was kicked out for drugs. He went to live with my cousin in Iowa but got a DUI. So, he came back to Elko and the Rez. His mother is more enabler than parental figure." The timeworn elder is emotional; he stops and wipes his eyes. This is humbling for him. The proud patriarch of the family is requesting our help.

"Where is Mathew now?" I ask.

"He is in Las Vegas, the last place on earth he should be. That place will suck out whatever goodness is left in his soul. We have not heard from him in over a year, but I feel it is not too late to help him. Is there anything you can do, Lieutenant?" Ancient eyes beseech me.

"I'll see what I can do," I promise. "Give Joseph

all the information you have on him." I feel my throat closing and my eyes well up.

In the last few days, I have had 'pleading eyes' asking me to accomplish miracles at the best and the impossible at the worst, or however that damn saying goes.

Harold leaves and Joseph comes back into my office. "Thanks, Bob. I know there is not much we can do from here. I didn't know what to tell him; you were my only hope. The old man's heart is breaking. I like Mathew. I have always felt he could be saved, but he keeps fighting it. He has a good soul, but it is buried. I thought when he got out of Juvie he wanted to change. I got him that scholarship at the Indian college. Well, I conned my sister into it. She's still pissed he didn't even make the first quarter."

"I'll make a deal with you, Joseph. You prove the dentist killed his wife, and I'll help the kid. Winner buys dinner."

"I don't think either one of us is going to win this one, Lieutenant."

Chapter Six

Joseph goes back to his desk and I stay at mine, trying to come up with some ideas to help Harold and his grandson. Gary comes into our office and waves as he passes my open door. And it's then something clicks in my brain.

"Gary, come in here, please," I call out.

With a salute he responds, "Yes, Mon Capitaine, what can I do for you? Coffee, perhaps?" After letting him have a couple days off, he has been very subservient. I remind myself to encourage that.

"Knock it off. You earned some free time, but now that you mention it, coffee would be nice, and bring Joseph back with you."

Pivoting on his heels, he heads out the door. He returns with coffee and Joseph.

Taking the cup from the detective I say, "So, Gary, we have a situation, and possibly you may be able to assist us, well rather your girlfriend, Katie." I then tell him about Mathew and the grandfather's concerns.

"If he's not a juvenile anymore how could she help? I mean, she would do whatever she could for any kid in trouble, that's how she is, but in Vegas?" Gary asks. "Okay, knowing you, Bob, you have something up your sleeve, don't you?"

"Honestly, no. But when I saw you come in, it hit me your connection with Katie and Juvenile Probation might be a place to start."

Joseph smiles. "Boss, you are more Indian than you know. You are feeling it, your mind is running free, and it has directed you to a path to follow. I'm proud of you."

"Oh, you kiss-ass, Joseph. He's just thinking like the good cop that he is." Gary snorts.

"Now who is the kiss-ass?" Joseph retorts.

I enjoy the banter, makes us a strong, cohesive unit, and the humor is just good fun.

I tell Gary to check with Katie and ask if she might have any suggestions on what we could do. Since Mathew 'did time' in the Elko County Juvenile Hall, she might peek at his records and see if anything in there could help us. I know about sealed records and privacy stuff, but maybe she can find something to help the kid. I suggest Gary wander over to her office and see what he can find out.

In a flash he is out the door, but almost as quickly, he comes back in.

Sheepishly he says, "It might help if I had the kid's info. You know, full name, etc."

After our laughter subsides, Joseph gives Gary the information.

"I've started Mathew's case, Joseph. Have you started working on the mysterious death of the dentist's wife? Remember our bargain?"

"Oh, jeeze, Bob, give me a moment." He walks back to his desk grumbling. "You may be becoming too good an Indian."

Shortly, Gary is back from Katie's office. Sliding into one of my chairs, he takes a deep breath. "Tired from the walk or just excited at seeing your woman?"

He reddens. "No, I'm just trying to get my thoughts together."

From the other room Joseph shouts, "I'm betting on seeing Katie."

Gary shoots a side glance toward the other room. "Ignore the rude interruption; let me relay what Katie had to say. It turns out she dealt with Mathew on a couple of his visits to juvenile hall. She believes he is a basically good kid but weak willed. He tends to follow others, especially the wrong ones. In their counseling sessions, he told about his mom and his unsettled childhood. She knows his whole background."

"Does she have any suggestions on what to do next?"

"Well she does have contact with a couple of juvenile officers in Vegas. Seems he isn't the first Elko youth to skip out to Sin City. She is calling them for any help they can offer. The kid is not 21 yet, but if he gets into trouble, he is not a juvenile, as far as law enforcement is concerned. He will be dealing with real cops—not kiddie cops."

With raised eyebrows I ask, "We are assuming he will run afoul of the law, sooner or later?"

"That's been his history," Joseph adds, leaning in my door.

I get another inspiration. Reaching the phone, "I'm going to call Preston at Las Vegas Metro. Ask him to periodically check on Mathew's name, see if it shows up in any of their reports. He'll do that for me."

"I though you said he was a homicide detective?" Gary asks.

"Yeah, he is. Preston is a good guy. I wouldn't mind working with him again."

Preston and I go back awhile, to when I was chasing the murdering trucker. Metro assigned him to help me. I always felt like I was standing next to Danny Glover when I was with him. Black, tall, six-four at least, with a shaved head, but a compassionate face. We connected right from the start. As did our wives when they met.

I give Preston a call. He is happy to assist when I tell him about the heartbroken grandpa.

"So, when are you and your charming wife coming down?" he asks. "You know how Marie enjoys P.K.'s company."

"Well, if you can drum something up with this kid maybe I can wrangle a trip."

"You do have vacation time up there in the wild west, don't you?" he asks sarcastically.

"Yes, we do," I reply. "Apparently Metro doesn't?"

"Touché. We were talking about making a trip up there to see you two, when the weather is good. There is nice weather there sometime, isn't there?"

"More than I thought, but not enough for my liking."

"Come to Vegas. We will occasionally dip into the forties at night in the winter, but that is your *high*, if you're lucky." He jokes.

After a bit more manly banter, Preston agrees to get back to me later, once he has done some checking. If he can locate Mathew before the kid gets into big trouble, it will be a blessing for grandpa.

Chapter Seven

Later that evening, my wife and I enjoy a delightful dinner at one of our favorite restaurants, and yes, they do have great restaurants in Elko. I poke fun at the town, but it has its share of amenities. After dinner as we're getting into our car, my cell rings.

"Joseph, what's up? Your lady didn't throw you out already, did she?"

"No, she didn't," he replies indignantly. "I'm at the park—where the dentist's wife died. You need to come here; I have something important to show you. I know it's late, but we can only do this at night."

"Do I need a wooden stake? You aren't growing hair and fangs, are you?"

"Boss, just get out here. It's my owl."

Before I can answer him, P.K. declares, "Let's go."

"Be right there, Joseph," I calmly say.

Pulling into the deserted, dimly lit park, we spot Joseph's truck, then the glow from a flashlight waving up and down. The light is coming from the far edge of the park. Joseph is standing alongside a trash container under a large tree. Perched on one of the lower tree limbs is an owl. Joseph briefly shines his light on the bird. The fine-looking creature is a soft gray color, with scattered dark markings and, of course, huge eyes. The owl gives a sharp hoot at the sudden light.

"That's him. Doesn't want me to ruin his night

vision."

"He's magnificent, Joseph, but why is he just sitting there? Is he that tame?" P.K. asks.

"I told him you guys were friends."

The owl then rises from his branch, circles above us, and disappears silently into the night sky.

"I asked him to stay so you could see him. He led me to this." Joseph points to a bottle laying on top of the trash.

From the label, I see the bottle once contained some type of vitamin supplements. My mind is trying to follow Joseph's thinking. The Elko detective told me Diane Morrissey was taking vitamin supplements. So, are Joseph, or his owl, connecting the bottle with her death? We need to take the bottle, and have it tested at the lab for fingerprints, contents, whatever.

"I already took a photo, but I wanted you to see it before I moved it." Joseph then produces a pair of rubber gloves and an evidence bag.

"Joseph, do you always carry gloves and evidence bags with you?" inquires my wife.

"Yes, ma'am, and so does your husband. That is my county vehicle. I've got all my stuff in it."

"Of course." Unfazed she continues, "So how did you two wind up here?"

"Us two? Oh, me and owl. Well, I had to go to the store for Esther. When I started driving, he flew in front of me. I knew he wanted me to follow, and this is where we wound up."

I can't help myself. I start to chuckle.

P.K. scowls at me. "Robert, this is serious. He might have found a clue to that poor woman's death. Why are you laughing? You are supposed to be the boss here."

"I'm sorry, dear, but you're acting as *head investigator* just fine. I'll bag the bottle for evidence, and you continue to interview Joseph. You're doing great."

She looks at Joseph. "Is he always like this?"

"Yeah, most of the time. That's why we love him."

Always the consummate woman, she probes. "Did you get to the store for Esther? Does she know you're here? Have you called her?"

Before poor Joseph can answer all the questions shot his way, his cell phone rings.

"Hi, honey, I was just going to call you. Yeah, I'm fine. In fact, I'm with Bob and P.K. We're at the park. No, no everything is fine. I'll be back real soon."

My wife effortlessly slides the phone away from the poor, hapless male.

"Esther, hi. Yes, he's fine. He got sidetracked with work, but I told him he should have called you. You know how these boys are about playing *cops and robbers*. No, no one got robbed. That's just an expression I use."

I'm laughing so hard I almost pee my pants. Joseph looks at me and then up at the sky.

"Owl's not going to help you, Joseph. You're on your own."

P.K. gives Joseph back his phone and says to me, "Come on, we're invited to Esther's to share freshly baked cake. That is when *somebody* returns from the store with the frosting, like he volunteered to do."

Joseph looks at me. "Is she always like this?"

"Yeah, most of the time. That's why I love her."

Chapter Eight

While Joseph goes to the store, we drive to Esther's house where she greets us warmly. She is the area administrator for the B.I.A., Bureau of Indian Affairs. Her job entails keeping both Washington and the various Tribal Councils cooperating and communicating with each other. That can't be an easy task. She is 'all businesses' on the job but a sweetheart off duty. No professional suit tonight, just sweat pants, a T-shirt, and her long dark hair let loose and cascading down her back.

"Is everything okay with Joseph?" she asks, narrowing her deep brown eyes.

"Most definitely. In fact, I'm extremely proud of him. Not many investigators would pass on warm cake to follow an owl."

She shudders. "Him and that *owl*; in my tribe, owls are considered bad luck and evil. When we were children, the elders would warn us not to go out at night or the owl would carry us away. Other tribes, like Josephs', believe the owl is a messenger from the Great Spirit. Joseph has told me of the many things the owl has done for him."

I pull P.K. close to me. "His owl brought us together. What can I say?"

"I can't argue with that being a blessing," she says with a pleasing smile, before waving her hand toward a comfortable couch. "Sit down, and if Joseph ever gets back from the store, we will have some *not so warm* fresh cake."

Joseph does return, as we are enjoying coffee, and Esther jumps up and inspects the frosting. "Good boy—got it right. Now want some coffee? I always have to double check when he shops." She winks at us. "Never know what he will buy."

"Esther, I have the same problem with him; one time I sent him out for coffee, and he came back with an armed robber. Like we needed another criminal around the place. Never did get the coffee."

Joseph grins. "Hey, it was a righteous bust. The fool wanted to hold up the Starbucks while I was standing in line."

Wiping her mouth with a napkin, P.K. says, "Esther, thank you for asking us over. This cake is the best."

"You are more than welcome, but we do have to thank the owl. My people may not believe the owl is sacred, but we have our own spirit guide; the hawk is our guide."

P.K. leans forward. "If you don't mind, I am curious about Joseph's owl."

"He's handsome, isn't he?" Joseph grins.

"How did you find him, or did he find you?"

Drawing himself up proudly, Joseph answers, "Oh, he found me. Plopped his feathered ass right in front of me one night. I had been having some problems and was reaching out to the Great Spirit, as my grandfather had taught me. I hadn't been into that stuff much before. But when we learned our father had been killed in Viet Nam, it all became different. I felt lost and alone. My father had been the heart and soul of our family. Mom was there, but she was a basket case, my sister not much better. I realized I had to become the man of the family, and so I went up into the hills and cried as if my heart would burst with sadness. Then I heard my grandfather's voice, telling me to look up to the dark night sky and ask for guidance. I did. I had never prayed like that before."

Joseph stops his story to wipe his eyes with the back of his huge hands. Esther puts her arms around him, and he returns her gesture with a strong hug.

"Joseph, I'm so sorry. I didn't know. You don't have to tell us anymore." Tears trail down my wife's face.

"No, no, it's okay. I have never told the whole story before to anyone. I needed to."

"Please, Joseph, finish your story," I say.

"While praying, I was overcome with a strange calmness and knew I would be strong enough to care for the family. I asked the Great Spirit to hang around and guide me. Then, right in front of me, landed *OWL*. He looked straight at me, and I swear he gave me a wink with one of those huge eyes. He just sat there while I gazed at him. I felt he was somehow connecting with me. I reached out and with a slow gentle touch, I ran my fingers over his feathers. Then he flapped his wings and rose up, flew around me once, and perched in a nearby tree. Ever since that night, when I need some help, he shows up. Sounds crazy, but you both have seen him."

He turns to Esther. "I've wanted to share it with you but because of your childhood fear of owls, I have been afraid to. I love you, Esther, and I want to spend my life with you; that's why you needed to hear it all."

We are *all* in tears now. Joseph and Esther are hugging, kissing, and crying.

"Did we just hear a marriage proposal, Joseph?' I ask.

"Uh, yeah, I guess you did. We've talked about it, but until now I just never said it."

He squirms, slides himself from the couch to the floor, then props himself up on one knee. This is not an easy maneuver for a man of Joseph's size. He takes Esther's hand in his and looks into her eyes.

"Esther, would you do me the honor of being my wife?"

Without hesitation she replies, "Yes, Joseph. Yes." He reaches for her as she grabs for him, then they both tumble to the floor, laughing like little kids.

"Perhaps we should leave now," the tactful, giggling Mrs. Carson says.

Esther sits up. "Oh no, please stay. We must share this moment with good friends. He needed to get through this, and you were guided to ask him tonight. He needed this. We both did. I felt he was hiding behind some emotional barrier and now it is gone." She looks at Joseph. "And the owl can stay. This is why he came to you tonight. I know."

"I love Owl," states my always-romantic wife, tears welling up 'yet again'. "Would it be acceptable if I painted a portrait of him?" asks my little artist.

Joseph is silent for a moment. "Yes, I think he would like that. He can be a bit of a show-off at times."

"Just like someone else," Esther adds, smiling at Joseph.

We all have to work in the morning, so we say our

goodbyes.

Sliding into our vehicle, I start the engine then turn on the headlights. Sitting on the hood is Owl, his big eyes staring straight at us. Then he hoots and flies off.

We both sit there for a moment not saying a word.

"I'd take that as a *thank you*," I say finally.

"I'd agree. And you thought I wouldn't find anything to like in Elko. This place is mesmerizing."

Chapter Nine

Joseph had already taken the pill bottle to the crime lab by the time I arrived at the office the next morning. They will check for fingerprints, DNA, and identify any residue. The bottle's label is from a health food company. Joseph used good old Google to get a phone number. The company said the bottle contained capsules of over-the-counter legal vitamins, minerals, and a proprietary herbal combination. Nothing sinister there. Now we wait for the lab results.

I ask Joseph if he thinks finding the bottle was possibly Owl's way of getting him to tell his story to Esther.

"I feel the bottle is part of this case. But, yeah, he used it to get me to open up," Joseph smiles and nods his head. "I'm glad he did. Esther and I feel even closer now. It was a good thing."

Gary walks in on the conversation. He looks at both of us and goes to his desk.

A few minutes later, he returns. "I don't even want to ask what you two were talking about. But to *change the subject*, did you guys see the paper this morning?" He holds it up.

Neither of us had.

He slaps the paper. "Well Dr. Sleaze has packed up and moved to Las Vegas to open a dental practice. Didn't mourn too long."

"Morrissey? He moved this soon? Maybe the memories are too painful for him to stay in this area," I offer as a devil's advocate.

Sure enough, the newspaper story is about him selling his Elko practice and opening an office in Las Vegas. Apparently, the sale had been in the works for some time. Therefore, it was not a new idea. It all looked proper until the last line of the story:

'Dr. Morrissey will be taking his present office manager with him to assist in setting up his practice.'

"I'll bet a month's salary the office manager is a female," Gary asserts.

"I wouldn't touch that bet," I respond.

"I know how to find out." Joseph reaches for the phone. "I got a cousin who works for a dental lab in town. Part of her job is to make deliveries to dental offices, including Morrissey's. She has told me before he's a big flirt."

"Joseph, how many cousins do you have?" Gary probes. "You are always calling one of your cousins for information about something."

"Big family."

Sure enough, the dentist's office manager is a female, according to Joseph's cousin, attractive enough but no beauty queen, younger than the dentist's recently deceased wife. The cousin further goes on to say that the dentist's office staff *knew* there was *hanky-panky* going on between the dentist and the office manager.

"Still doesn't mean he killed his wife." I continue as the advocate. I don't altogether believe my side of the case. I've felt uncomfortable about it ever since we found Mrs. Morrissey. My feisty spouse's beliefs, notwithstanding.

Chapter Ten

The completed lab report arrives in a couple of days. The deceased's fingerprints are indeed on the outside of the empty bottle, but there is also someone else's smeared thumbprint. I ask them to check it against the good dentist's prints, which the investigating officer collected while the case was still open. Worth a try. Or, it could be the store clerk's print.

Inside the bottle is where it gets interesting; there is a slight residue of *arsenic.* Not a listed ingredient. The product comes in capsules that could be easily opened, something added, the capsule resealed, and then placed back in the bottle.

Arsenic poisoning, continued over a period of time, could present itself as any number of medical problems. Now the case is getting interesting. The substance is not detectable in routine laboratory testing unless specifically requested by a doctor. The usual method is a hair sample. Arsenic stays in the hair basically…forever.

According to our lab staff, arsenic was the only residue found on the *inside* of the bottle. This type of capsule seldom leaks. None of the listed ingredients were present inside the bottle. If capsules had been removed and something added to them, then residue could be present on the outside of the capsule. That residue could rub off on the inside of the bottle.

I need to identify that thumbprint. Then I must figure out how to make this a county case, not a city one. First some homework. How the hell was that bottle still in the park's trashcan several days after the incident? We do have someone to empty trash, don't we? I call the parks department maintenance head. He tells me this late in the year the park isn't used much, so trash pick-up is lax. At least he's honest. Since the fire department had used the park, he assumed all trash had been removed.

"They make quite a mess and load up our dumpster," he grumbles.

When I tell him the bottle was in a trashcan on the far side of the park, he says quite honestly, they only pick up the dumpster this time of year.

I immediately send Joseph to the park to retrieve that bag of trash from the can and log it in as evidence. We will sort through it later. In this case, sloppy management practices worked in our favor. The fingerprint guy in the crime lab calls and says he cannot identify the smudged thumbprint on the bottle as that of Dr. Morrissey.

Into Undersheriff George's office I go. He hears me out. "Let's go see 'the man'."

In his fifties, the sheriff is around six feet tall, medium frame, still in decent shape despite many years behind a desk.

He listens intently. I like him. He is a politician yes, but underneath, a good old cop. As he leans back in his chair, the old leather sighs; it's tired, too. The sheriff's face bears heavy lines from his years of handling problems and stress. I have just brought him another problem. He rubs his fingers through his full head of salt and pepper hair. Damn, he has more hair than George and I have...combined.

Finally, he looks at us. "Here's what we do." His eyes are clear and his voice calm. "I will call the Elko Police Chief and tell him we would like to take over this case. It will involve extra expense for out of town investigations, and we have the budget. He doesn't."

George and I just nod.

"I'll let you know," the sheriff says. That's our cue; we leave.

Walking back down the hall, I ask George what he thinks.

"It's an election year. Yes, he's getting tired, but your work has brought new life to the old man. I mean it. He's getting the spirit back again; he loves it. You wait. It'll work."

"Oh great. No pressure, just an election year. Why did I get into this case anyway?"

"For the same reason I got into some cases in the past—spousal pressure. Elaine kept after me, 'You can't let him get away with that. You're a detective; you solve it. I know you can.'

"She was always right too. Damn."

"You know P.K. pushed me to 'look into this one'?"

"Yeah, Elaine told me. She said I should help, but I told her you were already on top of it. I think we should give them our badges and go fishing."

"Sounds good to me."

Chapter Eleven

It's not long before the sheriff calls. "Go get that murderer, Lieutenant. Keep me informed."

"Yes, sir, will do. Thank you." *I think.*

I would like to exhume the body for a complete autopsy, including tests for arsenic and anything else that shouldn't be there. The D.A. says there's not enough to go on yet, but she's interested and tells me to keep digging. I want to ask if *she* ever went to Dr. Morrissey. Some things are best left alone.

Where else to dig? Start from the beginning. Go over everything you have. Look for what is missing. Those are *Charlie's Rules*. Who is Charlie? Just the smartest detective I ever met. He was a master of the game. I learned the craft from him in a sheriff's department in California. His close-cropped gray hair and slight build made him appear older than he was. Fifty something at the time I met him, and scheduled to retire, hence the opening for Detective I. Charlie wasn't ready to retire, but Mrs. Charlie was. The dear lady had supported him and put up with his sometimes-cantankerous ways for years.

Charlie is slight of stature and meaner than a junk yard dog. Well not really mean, but he could make suspects think so, when it suited his purpose. I could go on and on about his talents as an investigator, but mainly he was a people person. Not in the usual sense.

He had contacts everywhere. They were developed over the years by talking to and listening to people and remembering. His brain was a computer before we had them.

Following 'Charlie's Rules', I go back to the beginning. My guys and I discovered Diane Morrissey, so I know the scene was properly secured.

Next, I need to look at Elko's crime scene report. Talking with Rick, the detective who handled the case, I can sense his frustration through the phone. He tells me that between the woman's doctor and the husband's information, he had no recourse but to go along with the coroner's finding of 'deteriorating health' as the cause of death. The dentist had no questions about her death. Said she was over stressing her body by training for marathons and taking all sorts of supplements.

Rick says, "I never felt comfortable with this case, Bob. I was looking for a way to get an autopsy performed, but I had no evidence of wrongdoing, so I couldn't ask. I even suggested to the husband that possibly some of the supplements contained harmful ingredients. You know, dangling a 'wrongful death lawsuit' might make him go for it. No such luck. The husband was adamant; he did not want any more damage to her body. Diane Morrissey was buried quickly."

At least she wasn't cremated. That decision just might be the tooth man's cavity.

"Were you able to check the victim's house for evidence?"

"Negative," Rick says. "Completely stonewalled. I asked for bottles of the supplements and any vitamins she was taking, and he denied that too. He actually told me, 'She's dead, what more do you want?' What a sarcastic jerk. Bob, I went into this case with an open mind, but after dealing with the husband, I'm questioning this whole case. If you can catch him, do it. Any assistance I can offer, just ask."

"How about her clothing? Do you have them?"

"Yes, they're still in the evidence locker. The husband never asked about them. I collected them at the emergency room, before she was taken to the mortuary. Come over and we'll look at them. I don't recall anything unusual, except stains from the phony blood the fire department used."

Rick signs the Chain of Evidence form for Mrs. Morrissey's clothing and her cell phone. At his desk, we begin to go over the clothing. The jogging pants are typical, with the maker's logo stripes running down the legs. I stretch out the pants. Running my fingers over the pocket area on one side, I feel a small lump. Donning a pair of gloves and reaching inside the pocket, I find a capsule. It was buried deep into the fold near the top of the pocket. By casually reaching into the pocket, the capsule wouldn't have been felt. The detective curses. Either he or the lab staff should have found this. I bag the capsule as evidence and we both sign as having witnessed it. The remainder of her clothing and shoes are checked. Nothing else unusual is found.

The lab report on her cell phone states the victim's fingerprints and DNA are on it, along with various other smudged prints from at least three other persons. I'm sure a couple of them are going to be cops, I'll bet.

Next, I review their crime scene report which includes a diagram of the area. The cell phone was found on a picnic table close to the area with the trash bin containing the pill bottle. Right where Owl showed Joseph. I'd told Rick about finding the pill bottle, but not how. He's not ready for Owl. The detective is embarrassed as shit now; he oversaw the scene. He may not have done the area search personally, but it was not done properly, that's obvious.

I take a copy of their report, sign out for the clothing and cell phone, then after stopping by the crime lab to leave the capsule, go back to the office. I enter the clothing into our evidence locker but keep the cell phone. It doesn't work, so obviously a dead battery? The way things are developing in this case, I want a second opinion.

We have a computer geek in the county's IT department. (Who else would work there?) Buzz is in his thirties, with a pleasant face, close-cropped black hair, around five-nine, with a medium build. Despite always wearing clean clothes, he looks like an unmade bed. Of course, he's into computers and electronic gadgets. I take the phone to him. He loves this kind of stuff. We call him *Buzz* after the character on a TV crime show. He liked the name so much he even made an unauthorized name tag that reads *Buzz*.

Gently taking the phone from my hand, as if it were a delicate work of art, he scrutinizes the exterior, then placing it on his workbench, he cautiously pries opens the case.

"No wonder it doesn't work," Buzz exclaims. "The battery terminals are corroded. It almost looks like an acid was applied to them. Here, take a look."

He shows me the inside of the case. The terminals are partially destroyed, and the plastic is melted around the terminals.

"That is *not* how these batteries behave, no matter how old they are. The substance was applied on purpose," Buzz states with authority. "There's fingerprint powder on the inside. Apparently, whoever did the dusting didn't think the terminals looked weird." He shrugs. Geeks make no allowances for human shortcomings.

Removing the battery, he tests it. "It's not dead. The phone failed to operate because the terminals were degraded to the point of non-conducting," the voice of the expert announces.

I ask him to make a report on his findings for me, in layman's terms. Taking the phone, I enter it into our evidence locker.

Is it time go home? I could use a drink.

Despite my best efforts, I might have a murder on my hands. I admit I was uncomfortable with the case from the start. It just didn't *feel right* to me. Now, after digging below the surface, it is beginning to look like a story right out of a New York Times Best Seller murder mystery. It can't be as simple as an unfaithful husband? Or can it?

Just keep digging, that's what Charlie would tell me. Speaking of the old grump, I haven't heard from him in a while. He wasn't ready to retire, but he began a motorhome tour of the USA at his lovely wife's insistence. He hates it. He has been in thirty-some states at last count. Hates it with a passion, but his wife stood by him through all the years of his irregular hours as a detective. He knows he owes her, big time. Still, he hates it. He will call me every week or so to see *how I'm doing*. But he actually calls to bitch, complain, and spew his dislike for whatever part of our great land he is presently visiting.

Love that guy.

Chapter Twelve

First thing this morning I call a unit meeting. With only three of us, it's not a decision that requires much planning.

The guys grab coffee and settle in my office. I do this at least once a week, if the caseload permits. Each of us will verbally go over our present cases and then we all brainstorm suggestions. Usually it's helpful, three minds focused on one problem. It's been a useful tool. We have helped each other out a lot. "Why didn't I think of that?" "Great idea." "What about if you…"

Of course, being who we are, sometimes it degrades into, "Esther let you out of the house dressed like that?" "Need more coffee for your cream, Gary?" "Joseph, does your owl have a badge? He should have a badge. He solves half your cases."

This morning we behave ourselves and stick to the files we're working. Getting around to the murder, I lay out what I have. We discuss all the aspects and kick around various ideas. Nothing I haven't already thought of, but that in itself is reassuring.

The meeting is breaking up and as the guys head back toward their desks, my cell phone rings. Speak of the devil, it's Charlie.

"Charlie, where are you? What miserable scenic wonder are you berating now?"

"I need your help, wise ass." Yep, it's Charlie.

"Parked the motorhome and can't get it out, right?"

"Will you shut up and listen, for once. I'm on I-80 west-bound coming into Elko, and I want you to stop the car I'm following. There is something seriously wrong going on inside. I think someone is being kidnapped."

"Why?" A reasonable, fact-finding question from a police officer to the citizen reporting a possible crime.

"Because the man driving keeps reaching back and hitting someone in the backseat with an object. The woman in front is yelling too. Get out here before they kill whoever is in that back seat."

I get Charlie's location and notify the highway patrol. As I'm heading out the door, Joseph and Gary are standing there, like two little kids.

"Can we go too, Dad? It's been quiet lately."

"Come on."

We race out of the parking lot, lights flashing, sirens blaring. *God, I love this stuff.*

As luck would have it, a highway patrol trooper finds the car first. We slide in right behind him. The trooper is on the driver's side and Gary moves up with him. Joseph and I take the passenger side. The highway patrol officer has ordered the occupants to keep their hands in sight as he looks inside. Joseph goes to the front passenger side as I ease up to the rear seat area. Inside are two little girls. They are laughing and waving at me. The trooper is talking with the male driver. We are still on alert, not knowing what is going on. The driver reaches between the front seats and brings up an object. We yell, "Freeze—Don't move!"

The trooper hollers to us, over the noise of the freeway, "It's okay. It's only Woody." The driver is holding an eight to ten-inch stuffed Woody doll from the movie, *Toy Story*.

Apparently, the young lady in the right rear seat had been misbehaving, annoying her sister by taunting her with the doll. The mother had tried to intervene but to no avail. Then with frustration at a peak, Dad, while driving, reached back grabbed the soft stuffed Woody doll and proceeded to whack at the kid, who had been using the doll as an instrument of torture. The girl would squeeze herself into the corner by the door and keep poking at her sister. Dad would continue to try to whack the miscreant with the toy. This was what Charlie had observed from his perch high up in the motor home. Having missed the initial transgression by the big sister, he only saw someone being repeatedly struck with a fearsome looking object. He was unable to see into the rear seat and thought someone was getting a beating.

Considering all the giggling we hear from the guilty sister, it would appear she thinks this is all great fun. There are no visible marks on her. Woody is unaffected by the 'wear and tear'. With an advisory to pay attention to the road and not the children, the embarrassed father goes on his way.

It's quite a sight for the motorists travelling on the Interstate. One marked highway patrol car, three unmarked cars with lights flashing, and a motorhome, all parked on the shoulder. As the family pulls away, we begin laughing. Charlie is mortified.

He just looks at me and hollers, "Call me when you stop acting like a fool, and we'll take you to dinner tonight and hopefully, finally, meet your wife." With that, he storms off to his motorhome.

By now, I am doubled over with laughter. The trooper says, "You know him? What's his problem; he did the right thing by reporting it."

"You would have to know him to understand," I manage to get out. "Thirty-five years as a cop. He never makes mistakes."

Chapter Thirteen

After I regain my composure, I call my bride and tell her Charlie and his wife are in town and want to have dinner with us. She's thrilled; she can't wait to finally meet them. I'll fill her in on the *incident* later. I'm driving back to the office now. If I start laughing again, I might run off the road or something.

Back at the office, I call Charlie. He should be calmed down by now.

"Charlie," I say as cheerfully as I can. "P.K. can't wait to meet you two. Tell us where and when."

"Don't play cutesy with me, you jerk. You didn't have to laugh. You all looked like a pack of hyenas on the side of the road. Unprofessional. Meet you at the same restaurant we went to last time. Seven o'clock. I'm hungry and tired. Don't be late."

Same old Charlie. He's not going to let retirement take him down.

We meet them in the parking lot of the restaurant and introductions and hugs follow. Mrs. Charlie looks great. Her gray hair is neatly coiffed, and she is wearing a trendy blue running suit. Charlie is stuffed into a green polo shirt and is wearing khaki walking shorts.

"Charlie," I exclaim loudly. "Shorts. I didn't know you had legs. Hairy ones at that."

"Honey, be quiet," scolds my wife. "He looks cute in them."

Charlie looks like he wants to take a swing at me but then turns to P.K.

"Thank you, my dear. At least someone here has taste *and* manners. Let's go eat."

My wife and Mrs. Charlie get along right from the start. Charlie is well behaved and very gracious to the woman who stole his only son. Well, not really, but he calls me his son sometimes, probably not today.

After dinner we go to their motorhome at a local RV park. The ladies can chat in a separate area, so as not to interfere with Charlie's critiques of my crime solving abilities. He is intrigued with the Diane Morrissey case.

"You got something there, I can tell. But be very cautious not to tip your hand too soon. Sounds like he's a cagey one. This was planned out in advance. Too bad the local cops couldn't get into his house for a search." He stops and thinks. Charlie does that a lot. Then, just like the old days, his eyes light up.

"You said he was moving to Vegas, right? What about the house? I'll bet he's selling it. Get in there as soon as you can. If he's still there, put an eye on it. Once he's out, hit it. Legally of course. If you know a good judge, get a warrant. If you can't, ask George or the sheriff if any of those bastards owe them a favor. As long as those two have been cops up here, I bet they've saved the ass of one or two judges. Try and be the next one in after the dentist is gone, before any cleaners or workers. Check for residue, look the place over, yard too."

Joseph may have Owl—but I have Charlie.

Charlie's my owl? That's funny.

The evening turns late and *some* of us have to work

in the morning. Charlie is not wearing down.

"I thought you were tired?" I ask hopefully.

"Got my second wind."

Bless her heart, Mrs. Charlie intervenes and tells her husband that these 'kids' have to get up early for work, so they need to go home and sleep. He starts to argue but she overrules him and tells him they are having dinner at our house tomorrow night. That works for him and we are allowed to leave.

On the way home P.K. says, "He's just like you described him. I always thought you were exaggerating, but you weren't. His wife is quite the lady. She has put up with him for years and loves the heck out of the cranky old grump. I'm going to pick her up when I'm finished seeing my morning patient, and we're going to spend the day together. I like her and since both of us are cop's wives, we have a lot to share. I'll be making my famous lasagna for dinner. You bring French bread and wine. Deal?"

"Oh God, you're spending the day with Mrs. Charlie, which means Charlie will be haunting the sheriff's office all day. Maybe George will take him to lunch."

My fears are realized. I walk in the office the next morning and I find Charlie holding court with Gary and Joseph.

"Whatever this man has told you is either a complete fabrication or was taken out of context," are the first words out of my mouth. "How long have you been keeping my crew from doing their work, Charlie?"

"Long enough to determine you have a couple of good cops here, loyal also. Damn, they won't give me any dirt on you."

We all talk for a bit, then Charlie says he's going to roam through the station and find George. "I'm going to make him buy me lunch." He wanders off down the hall. I observe he is wearing long khaki pants today. I decide to not mention this. Sometimes I can behave.

Standing up, Gary grabs his coffee cup. "Charlie's a remarkable guy. You can tell he was one hell of a cop, like you told us."

Joseph slowly rises to his feet. "He thinks the world of you, Bob. He said you are like the son he never had."

"Come on, don't get me gushy this early in the day. He's been like a father to me. I love the old fart," I acknowledge.

"Now, Joseph, since I have been working *your* case, I need you to do something for me."

"My case? The murder? You ran right over me on that one. What about *your* case, the kid, Mathew? Huh?"

"Well, I've done all I can on that case for the moment. If he's in Vegas, my buddy will hopefully turn up some information on him. You got any more ideas?" I throw it back at him.

"No," he says softly.

"Come into my office please, Joseph. I need you to handle a special assignment for me."

"I can't hear? What's so special that I can't hear?" Whines the Long Beach boy from the hallway.

"You'll find out later."

I give Joseph specific instructions and send him on his way. Joseph goes out the door and says in a loud voice, "You can count on me, boss." He looks at Gary and grins.

Like brothers…*Ha Ha. Dad likes me better*.

Later Joseph has completed his assignment and is back doing his real cases. Gary keeps asking him questions, probing, but the wily Joseph won't give.

In the evening, we have a great dinner party. The girls have had a good day comparing notes and generally having fun, at Charlie's and my expense. I know they did. I can tell when I ask how the day went and they both just giggle. After another late night of cop talk, Charlie is finally coerced into going back to the RV Park.

We have an emotional farewell. Each of us saying we must get together more often—all that stuff. They are going to leave in the morning to go home to San Jose, California.

The next morning as I am getting ready to leave for work, our phone rings. P.K. answerers it and I hear her say, "He's getting dressed. What's wrong, Charlie? What? You found what? Oh, that's funny. Who would do that? My husband? Why would he do that?"

I am now standing next to her, snickering. She looks at me accusingly, then says, "Here he is," and shoves the phone at me.

"Top of the morning to you, Charlie. Sleep well?" I am now laughing so hard I can barely talk.

He is yelling so loud I can't understand him. Finally, his wife gets on the phone. "Bob, I love it. Just what the old grump needed. He'll be fine."

I ask her to keep him in Elko for a little longer until P.K. and I can get there. My little woman is now standing right next to me and I am getting the *what did you do now* look. I had told her about a surprise I wanted to give Charlie this morning before they left, but I only told her half of it.

"Robert, what did you do?"

"Come on, baby, you can see for yourself. Then we can give him the real surprise." Getting ourselves together quickly, we drive to the RV Park.

Charlie is standing on a step ladder at the front of the motorhome. "Here, Charlie, don't hurt yourself. Let me get it." His wife stops him, and I climb up the ladder and remove the object of his concern. Hanging from his windshield, right in front of the driver's seat, is a *Woody* doll. I hand it to him. He immediately grabs it and starts to hit me with it.

"You jerk. Asshole. Damn you!" Then he starts to laugh. He throws his arms around me and gives me a big hug. "Proud of yourself? You got the old man. But you're still a jerk. I love you, son."

Then, on cue, Gary and Joseph pull up. Charlie says, "No wonder crime is rampant around here. No one works."

Joseph comes up to Charlie with a box and hands it to him. "Charlie, this is for you, from the Elko County Sheriff's Department." Charlie looks at me. I nod, and he begins to open the box. "If this blows up on me, I'm going to chase all of you all the way to California."

He reaches inside the box. "What the hell?" He keeps pulling something out.

It is an *owl*. It's not real, but it is made from real feathers and around its neck is a small Elko County Sheriff's Detective badge.

"You are *my* owl, Charlie." I had told him about Joseph's Owl, and he said he wished he'd had an owl when he was working.

"Now you have one."

He's crying, hugging me, P.K., the guys, all of us. His wife is bawling her eyes out. It's quite emotional. More than I could have hoped for.

"That's for all you've done for me. I wouldn't be here if it wasn't for your guidance. Thank you, Charlie." Then I hug Mrs. Charlie. "And thank you for keeping him in line."

"Now we have crimes to solve and you have a long trip." Another round of hugs and we all leave.

My wife is still teary eyed as she looks at me. "Woody. Really?" Then she laughs. "How did you pull that off? Oh, of course, your boys did it for you."

"Yes, ma'am. Joseph said he could get an owl doll, and the badge was from one of our youth programs."

"Where did you find a Woody doll? Do they still make them?"

"They do. Joseph said he had no problem finding one. Woody and Buzz Lightyear are still *in*."

I take my wife back home, so she can get to her office, and I go to mine.

I now have a plan of action, thanks to My Owl (Charlie).

Chapter Fourteen

Using my current case as justification, I ask the sheriff if we can acquire an old public works van for surveillance operations. He immediately calls the County Manager and a van is mine. We will have to scrounge equipment to outfit it. Charlie, of course, gave me this idea. My agency can't afford a new one but, he pointed out, every public agency has old junkers sitting around not being used.

I go to our IT department and ask Buzz if he would be interested in becoming a part-time electronics guru for the investigations unit. I'd already cleared it with the sheriff.

Buzz jumps at the suggestion.

"You mean like the real Buzz on the television show? Yes, I would, Lieutenant. I would love it." He removes his glasses and wipes his eyes. Geeks do show emotion.

"First, call me Bob. Next, what would it take to make an old van into a proper surveillance unit?

I can see the gears turning, well in his case, probably electrons pulsating. He starts to spew out a list of electronic components. Then he stops.

"We have a surveillance van?"

"Well, sort of. We *do* have a van, but all it has inside are the two front seats, nothing else. It was a public works vehicle. It is wired for a radio, but they took it out. Think of it as *a blank canvas*."

"Can I see it?"

"Let's take a ride to the motor pool."

On the way, Buzz babbles like an excited kid going to his first ball game.

At the motor pool, I stop in front of a Ford van. It is kind of pathetic—weathered, faded blue in color, cracked side window, dent in one fender, and the double side doors hanging ajar. On the positive side, it is 4-wheel drive, essential here in snow country. Buzz is no longer babbling.

Trying to be positive he says, "A coat of paint might help. And maybe new tires and…oh my lord," as he looks inside. "Bob, it's a mess. Have we got the money to fix it up?"

I try to sound positive. "Yes, we do. I have been promised by the sheriff that we can have it brought up to snuff. I'm just not sure what his definition of *snuff* is."

Buzz looks at the inside of the van shaking his head. "You said blank canvas, but I'm not sure the canvas is even here." Geeks have humor also.

He starts a list of items he would like for the interior and I do the same for the rest of the heap.

Back at the office, I call my wife, coincidently, a former realtor. I need information on the dentist's Elko house. Is he selling it? Is he still living there? She will find out and call me.

What a partner I got in this deal—wife, lover, best friend, talented artist, and someone who knows the ins and outs of the real estate business.

In a short while she calls me back. The house is going on the market soon. He is only there part-time while he sets up his Las Vegas dental practice.

First, she did some on-line checking. Finding no information, she called the dentist's Elko office. She told the person who answered the phone that she had always liked the dentist's home and wondered if it was going to be available. The clever little devil did not reveal her identity, only said she had been in the house at a function. It turns out the person on the other end of the phone was the *office manager*, herself. She was only too happy to give my wife all the information on what the dentist (and she) were planning. She even gave P.K. the name of the realtor who will be handling the sale.

"How's that, Lieutenant?" P.K. teased. "Once again, I come to your aid. What would you do without me?"

I can feel her radiant smile through the line. "You know, my love, if you get tired of the ocularist business, I can always use another investigator."

"No way, sweetheart. I've seen you in action. You're tough on your poor guys." She laughs. "Gotta go, eyes to make. See you tonight. Love you."

My next stop is the office of Undersheriff George. I give him the name of the realtor and ask if he knows her. He does. However, the city fire captain knows her better. It's his wife.

Gotta love small towns…everyone knows everyone else.

I am not a big fireman fan. Like most cops, I have tormented and harassed my share in the past, but I have stayed out of trouble for years. Maybe my reputation didn't follow me to Elko. I can only hope. I don't know if George can read my concerns, but he offers to talk with the fire captain. He will ask to have the wife inform us as to the dentist's plans.

I thank George and as I'm leaving, he looks up at me and states, gently but firmly, "We have a good relationship with the *fire laddies* out here. We want to keep it that way." Then he looks back down at his desk.

Crap, he does know. Of course, Charlie. Blabber mouth.

Chapter Fifteen

It took a lot of begging, pleading, and a couple cases of beer, but I managed to get the county motor pool supervisor to expedite the renovation of the van. It's now presentable, after some bodywork, a cheap white paint job, four tires, and a full tune-up. The guys in the shop got in the spirit of the assignment and found two swivel seats for the back and even insulated the walls and roof area. Temperatures get extreme here in northeastern Nevada.

Buzz built racks for the equipment and wired the van for electricity and computer cables. He's getting into this project. *His Project*. I hope I haven't created a monster. However, since he's the only one who knows what he's doing, we need the monster.

Joseph scavenged curtains for the back windows and a set to go behind the front seats to close off the front from the back. With no one in the driver's area and the curtains drawn, it looks like no one is home. Now we need a name to paint on the side, some commercial type of business that no one will call. Gary suggests:

Amalgamated Enterprises Inc.
Locally Owned
All Work Guaranteed

"Brilliant, Gary," I say. "No hint of what the company does or how to get hold of them."

"But all work is guaranteed," Gary announces in a smug voice.

George refers us to a retired sign painter who recommends using fancy Old English script. "Done right, no one will be able to read it anyway," he assures us. He is correct.

We are almost ready for the dentist, or any other criminal who might need an *eye* kept on them. Buzz is hastily assembling what electronics he can beg, borrow or steal—-well, borrow hopefully. The mischievous sprite has even managed to place a video camera into a cooling vent on the roof. It can be controlled from inside and rotates 360 degrees. The *MacGyver* in Buzz is coming out. Remember MacGyver? He could apply scientific knowledge to everyday objects like duct tape or chewing gum and save the world.

****

George promises me the fire captain's wife will contact us as soon as she knows about the dentist's moving plans. I express my concern about the confidentiality of our plan, especially with a firefighter's spouse.

He sighs. "Bob, relax. She thinks the dentist is an egotistical ass. Her words. She will call us as soon as he tells her to list the house."

"But isn't she worried about her commission?"

"She'll get her commission when the house sells… You aren't going to tear it apart, are you?"

"No. No, of course not." I decide to quit while I'm behind.

The next few days go by without a call from Mrs. Fire Captain.

Buzz phones and proudly announces the van is

ready for testing. And I know just the place to test it. He pulls up to the office, and I must say, it is impressive. Miraculous even, if you had seen it just a couple of weeks ago. The interior looks more like the Batmobile than a rolling stakeout van. The crew is wide-eyed.

"Buzz, this is incredible, better than on TV or the movies." Gary is awestruck. He is crawling all over the inside. "Radios, computers, Wi-Fi, even a printer. Where did you get all this?"

"Don't ask," I admonish. "I think this is a case of—the less we know the better."

"No, it's all legit. I promise," Buzz protests.

"Buzz." Joseph speaks up. "I have known you for some time now. I have never heard you say *legit*. You don't talk like that. Is that what the guy you got this stuff from told you?" He taps the top of several pieces of equipment.

Buzz starts to stammer. "No, no, nothing was stolen or anything like that. Honestly, it's mostly excess county parts and damaged equipment I've kept. Never know when it will come in handy. There is not a lot of IT work to do around here. I just kept collecting all the left-over equipment in my back room, and I've been tinkering with this stuff all along. I guess I was hoping I could be a real Buzz." He smiles. "And now I am!"

"Yes, you are, *Buzz*," I say. "Now let's get this Elko County vehicle on the road and see how all this fancy equipment works."

We all pile in and take off with Buzz driving, and he's grinning ear to ear. Yes, geeks can have fun too. We drive past the dentist's house and observe a shiny red Cadillac in the driveway. It has a paper license plate which means the car is new. We turn around and park a few houses away, on the other side of the street. All of us clambered into the back, and Buzz pulls the curtain. There are only two seats in the back. Buzz takes the main position in front of the equipment and I sit in the other. Gary and Joseph just hunker down as best they can.

Buzz is in his glory, turning on each apparatus and adjusting every button and knob. Soon the various screens light the interior with a soft green glow. This *is* neat. He focuses on the front of the dentist's house. Clear as a bell.

The sparkly new car's paper license plate shows only the date of expiration for the temporary permit. Being the good cop that I am, as we drove past, I noted the dealer's name on the license plate frame, as well as the expiration date of the paper plate. The date shows this car is only three days old. If the Caddy had a regular plate, Buzz, using the computer in the van, could have run it through DMV and obtained the registered owner's name.

After a few minutes, a well-dressed woman in her late thirties comes out the front door, locks it, gets in the Cadillac, and drives off. If she locked the door then no one else is home, we hope. I slip into the front and drive the Batmobile after her, keeping a safe distance of course. Joseph struggles into the passenger seat. "Too cramped for my big ass back there."

The woman leads us right to the dentist's office. She parks and goes in the employee entrance. After she is in the building, Gary slips out of the van and saunters by the Cadillac. Taped to the front window is the dealer's report of sale with the registered owner's name visible. Gary notes it and comes back to the van.

Surprise, it's the office manager, Jeanie Martin. She just got a new car. We will follow up on that information.

The shakedown of the van was a success. Back at the office we tell Buzz the pizza and beer are on us tonight. We may not use it often but when we need this rolling cyber center, it will be invaluable.

Now, back to our regular work. This case will have to wait until we hear from the realtor. We still need the crime lab results on the capsule I found in the pocket of the victim's pants. But luck is with me when I call the technician and he informs me the capsule was the same brand as the bottle we found at the park. In addition to the manufacturer's ingredients, there was the addition of *arsenic. This confirms we are on the right track.* Only smudges of fingerprints. No help there.

Having already obtained information on any vehicles registered to Dr. Morrissey, I would like to obtain a search warrant for his house, vehicles, office, and have the wife's body exhumed. I call D.A. Bates and ask for a meeting. She says in thirty minutes. Good. I gather my file and notes and get ready to go to her office. My phone rings and it's the fire captain's wife, the realtor.

"He's already left for Las Vegas and wants it on the market as soon as movers are done and house is cleaned. Movers are scheduled for day after tomorrow. I am to schedule house cleaners when the movers are done. I will pick up keys from his Elko office. Does this help, Lieutenant?" she asks.

"Yes, ma'am, it does. Could you pick up the keys today?" Anxiously tapping my fingers on the desktop.

"I'm on my way. Anything to help. George told me

what's going on. I never did like Dr. Morrissey, but murder his own wife. Disgusting, revolting. You bet I'll go right now."

The nice fire captain's wife is going to bring the keys to our office. Just because she married a fireman doesn't mean she's not okay.

Gary will wait for her while I go to the D.A.'s. I'm getting enthusiastic now, the thrill of the hunt, that kind of stuff.

I enter D.A. Bates' office and we exchange pleasant greetings. Placing the material I have accumulated out in front of her, I go over the information. Based on the facts, the D.A. has no problem agreeing to request a search warrant for the house, garage, any outbuildings, and any vehicles that may be present. She agrees, reluctantly, to include computers. Since poisoning is involved, an internet search for information on that topic may still show.

Lowering her eyes to the desk, the D.A. quietly says, "I may not like the man, but I need to be extremely careful not to overstep any legal questions that could taint evidence you acquire. I'll try to sell it all to the judge, for the complete warrant." She is doing her job but I'm getting the feeling there is more here than meets the eye.

My feelings. Usually correct.

I return to the office to find the fire captain's wife still here. She tells us Dr. Morrissey's office is open, but with the new dentist, who bought the practice. The office manager, Jeanie Martin, gave her the house keys, and is driving to Vegas tomorrow. Apparently, the good dentist has been in Las Vegas since the first of the week. Must have left right after the funeral. I give the realtor kudos. She also has the address and phone numbers of the new office in Las Vegas, as well as for the house the dentist is renting. I will never say a harsh word about firemen again.

Oh, you know I can't keep that promise.

Chapter Sixteen

D.A. Bates hasn't called yet, and it's getting close to the end of the day. I'm anxious to know if she was able to obtain the search warrant. Experience tells me she knows which judge she wants to ask. Some are more lenient than others. That may not be the correct terminology, but you get the picture.

I go home to my bride. She throws open the front door as I arrive and announces *our* new home is going to be move-in ready in a month. P.K. went to the building site today. She informs me our new abode is looking gorgeous. The extras have been installed, and the landscaping will be done after the house is finished. I reach into my pocket and pull out my cell phone. I poke some buttons and show her some photos.

"You rat. You've been there. When?" She gives my shoulder a playful punch. "Were you going to tell me?"

"Easy, baby. I went to the D.A.'s office then stopped by the site. I was going to surprise you, but the salesperson said you'd already been there. We're on the same wavelength, aren't we?"

"Always have been, my love."

Later, relaxing with some wine, I fill her in on Dr. Morrissey's case and she tells me about her current patients. That is part of what makes our relationship so strong. We can sit, talk, and discuss anything. No one puts the other down for his or her ideas or thoughts. I cherish our *together* time.

The next morning D.A. Bates calls and informs me she has obtained a warrant for the complete search of Dr. Morrissey's property and computers. I thank her and promise to let her know what we find.

"Please find something," she implores me.

There is a story here; I feel it more than ever. I may never know what it is, but I hope it doesn't come back to hurt the case. If she has knowledge concerning this person she isn't sharing, then we could have problems with a defense attorney's motion of concealed evidence, or bias, or who knows what. If she knows something damaging, she should step out of the case, now.

My team and I start our plan of action. Buzz gets the van, while Joseph and Gary meet up with the crime lab technicians.

We all descend on the house. Buzz will videotape the search. At the curb are two trash cans, stuffed to the brim. We mark them as evidence. I have the keys and after knocking and receiving no answer, we enter. No one is home. We put on gloves and booties, so we will not contaminate any possible evidence.

The house is huge. High ceilings, well furnished, some art on the walls, but it has a *cold* feeling. Too sterile.

Nothing is packed. The house looks as if Dr. Morrissey just walked out the door. There is even food in the fridge. The victim's clothes are gone. Some of Dr. Morrissey's clothes remain, but there are gaps in the closet. He had to take something with him to wear. He must expect the movers to pack up everything. He was in a hurry. Maybe the funeral interrupted his plans.

First, we poke through all the drawers and closets in every room. In the master bath are double sinks. All the cabinets are empty. On one side, there is the lingering scent of a feminine presence—perfume, powder, delicate aromas. I ask the lab to test all surfaces for any residues, especially in the drawers. They will dust for fingerprints and do DNA checks. This will be their procedure throughout the house. In the master bedroom, there are no personal items. Already removed.

In one room, which had obviously been Mrs. Morrissey's office, there are photos, trophies, and ribbons from the various marathons she had entered. A lot of blue ribbons. This lady was good.

Standing alone in the room, I feel frustration, confusion, and a little fear. It's not coming from me. It is the room. In the past, I have felt emotions from people when I was at a crime scene. This time it is emanating from the room.

A computer sits on her desk. *Well, little fellow, what secrets do you hold?* Buzz will remove it and see if he can find anything interesting.

All the other bedrooms are apparently for guests; they had no children. More reasons her running was so important to her, *I suspect*. We check the attic and crawl spaces for anything of interest, with negative results. Nothing suspicious in the house. The garage is empty of vehicles. He has two cars in his name. Where is the second car? One would have been the wife's. The office manager has a very nice *new* car—umm—do you think? Sure, he traded his wife's car in on the Caddy. We will be checking on that. Apparently, he does not believe in a long mourning period.

We search the front, back, and side yards for any sign of recent digging. Everything is neat and orderly; probably a gardener maintains it. No sign of pets, for that matter, no sign anyone else lived in the house.

Leaving Joseph to oversee the lab crew, Gary and I start canvasing the neighborhood to inquire about the Morrisseys. Neighbors usually love to gossip, unless they are close friends. This is an upscale neighborhood. Two-story homes with lots of brick and rock facades. The houses are set back from the curb with sprawling, well-manicured lawns. Lots of space between houses. It's becoming apparent there was not a lot of close interaction between neighbors.

We are able to talk with three women who knew the Morrisseys. It's evident they did not care for the dentist. All liked the victim.

One of the neighbors, a Mrs. Howell, is eager to talk about Diane. She is in her seventies, I would guess; medium build, appears to take good care of herself, with permed, blue tinted gray hair and fresh make-up applied to a kind, wrinkled face. Widowed and living alone, the lady tells us she and Diane Morrissey had been good friends. Mrs. Howell is outspoken about the dentist. This woman feels the victim was throwing herself into civic affairs and endurance running because of an unhappy marriage. She tells us that Diane Morrissey had been depressed and pushed herself into the running as an escape, worked out for hours almost every day. She had been concerned about Diane's' declining health and tried to get her to go to *a real doctor,* not the *health nut* she was seeing.

"I thought she was being attended to by a real doctor. There was an attending physician's name on the coroner's report."

"Oh, he's a licensed M.D. I thought he was too busy to pay attention to his patients. He would walk in, poke at you, and spew some mantra—lose weight, eat right—and then he would go on to the next patient. I went to him for a short time. I had enough of his lectures on my weight and eating habits. He was so obsessed about weight and eating that he did not care about my family history, how I was trying to lose weight, or that I was starving myself. No interest at all. No excuses, just do it. That was his motto."

"He must have been pleased with Diane," I interject. "She didn't seem to have any extra fat."

"Oh, he kept after her too. Kept pushing the supplements on her. Take this one; take that one. Your body needs this mineral, and that herb." The lady starts to cry. "I'm sorry. She was my friend, and I saw her waste away and could do nothing to help her. Lord knows I tried."

I must ask. "Did her husband have any concern about her health?"

"*No*, he was encouraging her to *keep running*. Diane was talking about quitting for a while, to get her health back on track. He told her not to be a wuss. Said it would pay off in the end. Told her he bragged about her marathon running to his dentist buddies. That did it. She wanted his approval, so she kept killing herself." Suddenly she stops talking and looks at me.

"Why are the police here?" I could see in her eyes that she was now thinking the worst—did he kill her?

I look at her with that face we cops can use, when needed, and say, "Ma'am, we are just investigating the whole matter and have no indication that anyone—"

She cuts me off. "Don't give me that official line. You're here for a reason. I know you cannot say, but if he did—I'll kill the son-of-a-bitch myself." With tears streaming, she clenches her fists. "Diane was my friend."

I place my fingers over my ears. "I didn't hear a thing you just said. Please be assured that we will get to the truth in this matter."

She calms down somewhat as I give her my card, in case she thinks of anything that might be of use. Then, using the Colombo line, "One more thing, if you don't mind. How did Mrs. Morrissey feel about the move to Las Vegas?"

"Actually, she was happy about the move. Diane was tired of the winters here and was ready for warmer weather. I think she was hoping it might put some spark back in their marriage."

Must not have known about the *office manager* if she was looking forward to the move.

The lab staff have finished their work and after a final check of the house, we leave. I tell my crew what I just learned from the neighbor.

Joseph says, "That dentist bastard killed her. I know it. Let's get to those trash cans and check them with a fine-tooth comb."

"Fine *tooth*. Was a pun intended?" Gary asks.

"Shut up," says the dignified Native American.

Chapter Seventeen

Buzz is diligently downloading the victim's computer, while the rest of us are sifting through the trash from the dentist's house. Adorned with masks and gloves we judiciously look at each item.

"Phew," gags Joseph. "This stinks. How long has this been here?"

"In view of the condition of the food in the refrigerator, I don't think Dr. Morrissey has been home for several days. Who put these cans out, the office manager? That may be why she was at the house yesterday." I speculate.

Of interest to us are two empty bottles of supplements. The same brand Mrs. Morrissey had been taking. We will have the lab check for prints and residue.

Buzz has found more than a few items of interest in the computer. It has two user accounts, each with a different password. One for each of the Morrisseys, we presume. One account, likely hers, had multiple searches for marathons, schedules, and hotel information covering the dates of the marathons. She had also looked at vitamins, herbal remedies, and other similar subjects. In the most recent inquiries, she had been searching for reasons for her deteriorating health. She provided her symptoms and looked for answers. Ironically, one of the results showed, among other causes, arsenic poisoning. Buzz says Diane Morrissey went back to that site several times in the days preceding her death.

"She was apparently intrigued by that information," Buzz adds. "She then went to some other websites looking for specific information about arsenic poisoning. Her husband's account was not used much. The *good doctor* probably has a laptop and keeps it with him. That would be typical. However, he did have some old e-mails from several months ago that seem to be between him and a female. Looks as if she had been a patient and the relationship developed into something more."

"Buzz, are you suggesting that the *good doctor* was having an affair?" asks Gary.

"Yes, I am, and he cut it off rather rudely, by e-mail. No class."

"Buzz I'm surprised at you. I didn't know geeks had such thoughtful dating ethics," laughs Gary.

Joseph pipes up with, "I remember a former Long Beach resident who would 'love 'em and leave 'em' without *any* notice."

Gary glares at the big guy. "Yeah, well I've changed since then. You made your rounds too."

"All right, you two, back to the case. Buzz, can you ID the dentist's girlfriend from her e-mails?"

"I can do better than that. She has a Facebook account, gave her info to the dentist. Give me a minute and we'll see who she is." He taps the keyboard and then up comes a Facebook account for the lady— *complete with photo*.

We all look at her picture and collectively gasp. It looks almost like our District Attorney. It is not, but it could be her sister. Well it turns out after perusing the Facebook page, it is the D.A.'s younger sister. She took the break-up very hard according to her page. Does not identify the man involved but she was apparently quite distraught. There are no more entries in her page afterwards.

My concerns about the D.A. being involved in this case have proven to be correct. She was not the one who had the affair, but I'm betting little sister told her about it. I call and ask the District Attorney if I may have a few minutes of her time to discuss the Morrissey case. She seems cautious but tells me to come over to her office.

"What do you have, Lieutenant?" she asks as I enter her office. I close the door. She looks a little *deer in the headlights,* but keeps up the front. "Turn up anything we can use?"

I tell her straight out, no beating around the bush. "You sister had an affair with Dr. Morrissey, isn't that right?"

She closes her eyes and softly says, "Damn, you're as good an investigator as they say. How in the hell did you find out?"

I tell her about the computer and her sister's Facebook page.

"Of course, no secrets these days. I warned her about social networking. She came to me after the louse broke up with her. I had no idea she was seeing a married man. She knew better than to tell me."

"Is she okay now? Her last Facebook page was not pretty."

"After drug rehab in California. Yes, she is a lot better." Then looking straight at me asks, "Do you want me to recuse myself from this case?"

"No, I'm comfortable with your professionalism. I do not have a problem with you handling it, but it's your choice."

"I want to see it through. If you think I'm out of line along the way just tell me. Deal?"

"Deal."

I fill her in on what we found at the house and the computer.

"Mrs. Morrissey was getting concerned about arsenic poisoning, just before she died. That's huge, but nothing we can use." She is back to being a District Attorney now. "I don't think I can justify an exhumation at this point in time. We need something more."

"On the way over here, I was trying to sort out everything we have. I seem to remember there were some hairs on the clothing she was wearing when she died."

She perks up. "Where is that clothing now?"

"In *my* evidence locker."

"Presence of arsenic in the body is contained in the hair, right?"

"Yes, ma'am."

"Get it analyzed."

"On my way." I get up and start to leave.

She stands and comes over to me, then touches my arm. "Thank you, Lieutenant."

I nod and leave.

Chapter Eighteen

Back at the office, Buzz is buzzing. "Lieutenant, I think the doctor looked at his wife's computer history the day before she died. He signed into his account on the home computer and then in a few minutes, her account was accessed. Unless she was right there in the room, that does not seem right. Her search history was checked. In the last couple of days, she only looked at the sites about arsenic. If we knew her schedule, maybe we could tell if she was home or not."

"If it was the dentist, he saw his wife was worried about being poisoned," Joseph adds. "How can we find out where she was that day?"

A bell rings in my head. "I know where she was the day before she died. She was with my wife and George's wife. They were at the art gallery then went to lunch together. Buzz, what time was her computer accessed?"

Quickly clicking keys, he states, "Twelve fourteen p.m. Sounds like lunch time to me."

I grab a phone and call my *unofficial partner.* Thankfully, she cannot seem to stay out of my cases. I have never had a witness this close to me.

"Hi, my love, hope you aren't busy with a patient. I have a quick question."

"Oh no, it's all right. I've been working hard all morning, but I always have time for you."

"From the background noise you must have a room full of patients, huh?" I hear the unmistakable din of a busy restaurant.

She laughs. "Can't fool a cop. Yes, Elaine and I are at lunch. What can I do for you officer?"

I get serious. "What time were you with Diane Morrissey the day you met her?"

"Oh, gosh, from like, ten in the morning at the gallery and the board meeting. Right after the meeting, we all had lunch. We were probably at the restaurant until after two in the afternoon.'

"She was definitely with you at twelve, twelve fifteen?

"Oh yes, she didn't leave until we finished lunch. I won't ask you anything. I know better."

"Thank you, see you tonight."

I look at the guys. "The dentist had to be the one who accessed his wife's computer. Mrs. Morrissey was with P.K. and George's wife at noon. He knew she was getting on to him. I bet he upped her dose for the next day and told her he'd pick her up at the park. He put acid on her phone, so she couldn't call for help. I'll stake my pay on it."

Buzz jumps up. "The phone, I haven't tried to download it yet. Give me a few minutes."

"I thought it was dead?" Gary questions.

"Not necessarily," Buzz says, heading to his lab. "The acid only ate the contacts to the battery. The memory should be intact."

Joseph, ever the logical one, frowns. "You know, even with all the evidence we have found, we only have a thin circumstantial case against the asshole. If that."

"I agree, Joseph. But we are not done yet.

Remember how long it took me to catch Weaton? We'll get this guy. Perseverance pays off."

"I don't want this jerk to get away with it," Gary adds. "It's a little personal, you know, with Katie and all. She was smart enough to protect herself, but how many women weren't?"

"It's personal for others, too," I add without explanation.

I have Gary take the victim's clothing to the crime lab and request the technicians to test any hair discovered on the clothing for traces of arsenic. Later that afternoon, Buzz returns with a printout from the internal memory of Diane Morrissey's cell phone. 3:43 p.m., the day before she died, Diane texted her husband's cell number.

—*My car won't start. I'm at the gym.*—

Immediate response

—*I'll pick you up in a few minutes, after I call a tow truck.*—

Buzz informs us, "The next day, the day she died, she called her husband's cell at 12:46 p.m. using the preprogrammed button on her cell. This would have been after the fire department's training exercise. The number was entered into the phone but did not transmit. The battery was disabled, but the internal memory remained intact. She pushed the button several times then tried to use the keypad. Of course, none of her attempts worked."

This must have been when she dropped the phone on the picnic table at the park and began to struggle toward the county maintenance garage, desperate for help. It was 1:35 p.m. when we found her. The coroner said the time of death was approximately thirty minutes prior.

How long would her body have lain out there, if we hadn't decided to go shooting? Then there were the vultures Joseph saw. I do not want to think about it.

We got to her before they did.

Chapter Nineteen

Trying to tie up the loose ends, I go to the local Cadillac dealership. I ask for the sales manager. The salesmen swarm me, trying their best to tell me they can make just as good a deal as he can. Finally, I flash my badge and *again* ask for the manager. They fall all over themselves to find him. Almost immediately, a worried sales manager comes trotting up to me. He's in his fifties, overweight, red-faced, dressed in typical car salesman clothing—*tacky*.

"Is everything all right, officer? I was told you wanted to see me," he meekly asks.

"Let's go to your office," I suggest.

He leads me to the messy hovel he calls an office. It reeks of stale cigarette smoke. Jeeze, it's a Cadillac dealership, but since they also sell GMC trucks, maybe they're his real forte. Elko is more pick-up and SUV country.

Nervously, he sits down behind the desk, which is covered in papers, post-it notes, and an overflowing ashtray. From his breath, he probably has a bottle of whiskey in his desk drawer.

"Please have a seat." He gestures toward a cracked leather side chair.

"I'll stand," I reply. "Did you happen to sell a new model Cadillac to Dr. Morrissey lately or take a trade-in from him?"

I have his full attention now. His eyes dart around the room looking for help or possibly an escape route. He stammers some crap about having to check. He isn't sure of 'what all they sell', that kind of bullshit.

Using my best *officer presence voice,* I lean toward him and say quietly, "I am asking a couple of simple questions. If I do not get an immediate answer, I will call the District Attorney and request a subpoena for the dealership's financial records, for the entire year. And I will post a marked sheriff's car at your entrance until I get the records. Do I make myself clear?"

He starts talking so fast he sounds like a teen-age girl on her cell phone, "Yes, the doctor had a car towed in several days ago. He told the service manager it wouldn't start. The service manager checked under the hood and found some damaged wires. He said it looked like intentional destruction, not from any mechanical problem. When the doctor was called and told the car was ready, he said he wanted it to be a trade-in for a car for his office manager."

Of course, no questions were asked. The doctor paid for the transaction, and the car was registered in the lady's name. He reminds me the doctor is a 'good customer'.

I ask to see the trade-in. Unfortunately, it has been cleaned and detailed already. Why couldn't they have dragged their heels? I talk with the staff who cleaned the car. They say it was spotless, not much work to detail it. The sales manager claims the doctor removed everything from the old car when he bought the new one.

That's all I can do here. I look at the still quaking sales manager, hand him my card, and tell him if he thinks of anything else about the doctor or the cars, he needs to call me.

I never liked car salesmen.

Chapter Twenty

When I arrive home, I fill my wife in on the reason I called and questioned her. After I'm done bringing her up to date on what we know, she is so mad she wants to go to Las Vegas and get him.

"I only met Diane once, but I liked her immediately. He didn't have to kill her. Couldn't he just divorce her? It has to be about money, has to be."

"I agree, that seems to be the logical conclusion, and maybe there is a large insurance policy. She would have undoubtedly gotten half of the business if they divorced. We will be checking it all out."

"*She* put him through dental school. She said so at lunch. That ungrateful son-of-a-bitch. He needs to go down, Robert." There goes the '*Robert*' again.

****

The next afternoon, the crime lab informs me there are heavy traces of arsenic in Diane Morrissey's hair samples. I phone the D.A. She says it still doesn't point to the dentist. I agree and ask if we can exhume the body for further testing.

"Why? What's the point?" she retorts. "We know there is arsenic present, and it will still be in the body for years to come. When we get some hard evidence, then we can exhume."

"Yeah, I know. Just the same, I don't have any idea where to go next with this case. I can't prove he damaged her car, put acid on her cell phone, or put arsenic in her pills. It's all purely circumstantial. I'm damn frustrated. I'll mull it over for a while and then do what I always do, start from the beginning and go over everything again. Charlie's rules."

"Who's Charlie?"

"Nevermind. I'll let you know if I come up with anything else."

I hang up and close my office door, gather all the facts, documents and anything related to the case. I lay them all out in front of me for a *start from the beginning* review.

It keeps going through my mind, the dentist got worried after he read his wife's search history. He realized she suspected he might be poisoning her, then he did *something* to end it quickly. I still want to exhume her body. Three or four hours after she arrived at the park, she was dead. Her cell phone was intentionally disabled, so she could not call for help. Her death was premeditated, without a doubt. *Proving* it, is my job.

The crime lab hasn't completed their report on all the evidence they collected at the house. The house. There must be something we're missing. What the hell could it be? My mind goes back to our search. The bedroom and master bath were cleared of any of the wife's personal effects. The kitchen still had food left in the fridge and cabinets. Mrs. Morrissey was only eating healthy stuff apparently. There were unopened organic products in the cabinets, and the refrigerator was packed with fresh vegetables. Typical items on the kitchen counters—coffee maker, toaster, and blender...wait a minute, the blender. She would probably have made one of those blended goopy, green shakes full of God-knows what. I call the crime lab supervisor and ask about the blender. Were there any prints or any residue inside? I vaguely recall it appeared to be clean, but I didn't handle it. I left that for the lab.

The supervisor states, "Both the husband and the wife's fingerprints were on the blender. We haven't gotten to the inside of it yet." I detect an unspoken *oops.* I think *we* may have *overlooked* that. The supervisor assures me it will be checked immediately. In all fairness to them, there was a lot of work in that house. I asked for just about everything to be printed, tested, scraped, and on top of it all, checked for DNA.

I'm continuing to review my case when my friend, Preston, from Las Vegas Metro PD calls. "I keep checking for your wayward boy, but so far no results. Just wanted you to know I hadn't forgotten."

"I wasn't worried. How are you guys doing?"

"Marie is just fine and I'm busy as hell. The crazy people down here are killing each other left and right. The Homicide Unit doesn't have to worry about running out of customers. How's business up there?"

I tell him I have my own homicide and the suspect is now in Vegas.

"Oh great, can't you keep them up there? We don't need to import murderers. I would rather export them. And how is your lovely wife? Still happy with Elko? You know I could use experienced help down here. Just saying."

"We are doing great here, just bought a new house and should move in by the end of the month."

"Sounds like a housewarming is in order. Count on Marie and me. I *will* take the time off."

"You're on," I reply.

Of course, when I tell P.K. about Preston's phone call, she is thrilled.

"Yes, there will be a grand housewarming. Come one and come all." She is shouting into a pretend megaphone.

"It's not *that* big a house, my dear, but it will be fun. I don't suppose you had thoughts about a house-warming before now, had you?"

She smiles shyly. "Well, maybe Elaine and I discussed it a little."

"Uh huh. Just maybe." I love my little imp.

Chapter Twenty-One

The following afternoon the crime lab manager calls and tells me there was residue discovered under the blades of the blender. It appears to be a combination of substances. The lab is trying to identify individual materials, but the sample is so small, it's difficult. He will keep me advised on any progress.

I'm not turning up any new ideas for follow up, so it is time to get on with my *regula*r work. I've received a couple of e-mails from the training director of the Human Resources Department. Good a time as any to see what *required* training we've missed, because *we were doing our job*. I realize these matters are important, but they usually come at an inopportune time, like during normal working hours.

My unit is behind in our firing range qualifying. Reason: we found a body. Nevertheless, we still must qualify, or they will take our weapons away. How can we play *cops and robbers* without guns?

The next item, in which we are deficient, is CPR training. The firing range matter I can schedule. The CPR requires me to call the training director and fit us into a scheduled class. Unfortunately, our world does not work on a schedule. You never know when some dastardly deed will be perpetrated on the good citizens of Elko County and we will have to respond to save the world…or at least Elko County.

Luck is with us. The regular classes are already completed. The training director tells me she will contact one of the instructors to arrange a mutually agreeable time for us.

"How about you give me the instructor's number and I can work out a time directly with that person?" Third party negotiations are time consuming.

She gives me the name and number of the instructor. Wouldn't you know it, the instructor is a *fireman*. Fine, it couldn't be a plumber or a carpenter or even a nurse. It turns out to be the fire captain I met at the park, when we found Mrs. Morrissey's body. I can deal with him. In fact, I wanted to talk with him more anyway. His wife has been extremely helpful to us.

A quick phone call and the class is scheduled. It will be the end of next week before the fire captain can fit us in his busy schedule of days off, hunting, fishing, and oh yes, work.

All right, I'll behave myself.

The class will include all four of us. Buzz is now my responsibility, so the *techie* gets to share in the fun. In fact, when I inform everyone of the class, Buzz is the only one who is enthusiastic. "We get to use the portable defibrillators now; I'd like to find out how they work."

An evil grin crosses Joseph's face. "I'll be happy to demonstrate on you."

"I'll wait for the instructor, thank you." Buzz gives him a peevish look.

"I'd think twice about that." Gary points a warning finger at him. "After all, he is a fireman."

Buzz throws his hands up. "What is it with you guys and the firemen? Aren't you all here to protect the public?"

"*We are*," Gary declares. "They're here to save cats from trees."

Chapter Twenty-Two

We eventually get the crime lab results. Nothing to shout about. Dr. and Mrs. Morrissey's fingerprints are all over the house, along with a horde of other people's prints. Apparently, they were big on entertaining. There is one set of fresh fingerprints, which we presume to be the office manager's, since we did see her come out of the house. It appears she touched doors, windows and a few other places, consistent with making sure the house was secure before she left for Vegas. She did handle the trash cans, but there is no evidence she touched any of the items inside. The blender is no help. No known poisonous residue is found on the blades but, as the lab guy said, the sample was too small to properly analyze.

So, no *smoking gun,* or for that matter, no gun. The *smoke* is the arsenic, but who put it there is up for grabs. My only suspect so far is, of course, the dentist. To be completely fair and unbiased, I do need to explore all possibilities. Someone else might have wanted to murder Diane. Just because he was having an affair, or affairs, does not mean he is a murderer. The acid on the cell phone battery contacts and the vandalized car do point toward him. If we are going to successfully prosecute this case, then we need to eliminate all possible suspects.

Meanwhile, the long-awaited CPR class is now upon us. Bright eyed and whatever, we assemble in the county's training room. Who knew we had a *training room*? I must get my shit together with this administrative stuff. I came here to solve crimes. Oh yeah, there is the *Lieutenant* title plus being the *Department Head for the Investigations Unit.*

We all enter the training room together. The fire captain is happily playing with the dollies and other equipment he has brought.

I'm just being a jerk.

Brent is a good guy and couldn't be better toward us. He is an amazing instructor, who manages to make the driest of classes more interesting.

We're doing well with the practice manikins, learning how to do chest compressions properly, assess the airway, all of that. We've all taken this class before, but techniques do change and it's essential to be current. Mouth to mouth resuscitation is no longer emphasized. Good quality chest compressions have been medically deemed more beneficial. Under certain circumstances, the use of a portable defibrillator is encouraged. Most public buildings and a lot of shopping malls now have them.

Being an electronics nut, Buzz wants to learn all about the device. We get to that part of the class and the instructor goes over the protocol. Basically, when it's deemed time to *defib* the patient, the person handling the device is to say loudly, "CLEAR!"

This will tell the other rescuers they better back off the patient or they, too, will receive an electrical shock.

It is Buzz's turn to handle the paddles and administer the defibrillation charge. He properly checks the device, gets it up to speed and then yells, "RE-BOOT!"

That breaks us all up, including the instructor. Only Buzz would do that.

"What? We are re-booting the heart. Right? This is serious stuff. I don't understand you guys."

We all pass the course and are allowed to go on saving lives or *re-booting* if necessary.

After class, I talk with Captain Brent about Diane Morrissey.

"I don't actually know much about her," Brent tells me. "I know her husband is a dentist, and she participated in our training exercises. My wife knows her better. They're both on the board of directors for the art gallery. In fact, my wife was quite impressed with your wife's paintings. She said P.K. will make a fine addition to the gallery's artisans. You've met my wife, Jane. She's the realtor for the dentist's house."

Oh great! Will it never end? Fireman's wife likes P.K.'s work, fireman's wife is the agent for the dentist's house, and a fireman teaches our CPR class. I smile, nod, and tell him how proud I am of my wife. Which of course I am. This is not cowboy and Indian country; it is fireman and Indian country. I have yet to meet a cowboy here.

Ignore all the above ranting, please. I feel better now.

Brent has been great. I ask if I could talk with his wife sometime and he says, "Sure, why don't you and your wife come over to our place, maybe tonight? We'll have drinks and you can talk with her. I know she liked your wife and wanted to meet her again. To be honest, she suggested it when I told her you would be in the class today."

I am doomed. Here I am, stuck in the barren,

frozen north-east of Nevada and socializing with a fireman. I bet it's a set up. He knows about my history. I bet my picture is posted on the Fireman's Union web page. The entire fire department will be lurking inside Brent's house, waiting to pounce on me.

P.K. is delighted with the invitation. We arrive at the enemy camp…it's a large two-story home in a prominent neighborhood. What else would you expect from a realtor and a fire captain? Of course, the interior is stylishly furnished. The captain's wife is still dressed like *Jane the Realtor*, business suit and all. But Brent is in a sweatshirt and jeans. He acts like a real person. Not at all like a fireman. Not quite a cop, but close. I guess the rule is—there is an exception to every rule.

After a cocktail and some polite conversation, I ask Jane about Diane Morrissey's friends. She tells me Diane had a close friend named Louise Davis. They were both married to dentists and both competed in marathons.

She nods at my bride. "In fact, she mentioned it at lunch, the day we met you, P.K. She said Louise was beginning to take the competitions too seriously and she wasn't much fun anymore. Then Diane announced she would be moving to Las Vegas, because her husband was going to start a new practice there. Louise said she would miss Diane, but was happy for her friend, finally getting her wish and moving out of the cold weather. Everything changed when Louise found out her husband would be joining Dr. Morrissey in the Vegas dental practice. That's when Louise began to get *different*. Diane believed Louise was happy when she thought her competition was leaving. Louise had been the *leader of the pack* for the area's runners, before

Diane started to compete.

"You know," Jane continues, "it's odd, now that I think of it. Diane was in much better health at first. She was working out, doing marathons, as well as her charity work. That's when I first heard Louise's name mentioned. They became friends and started training together. Diane always joked about how frustrated Louise would become when she lost a race. Then Diane began to win *all the time*. But later, Diane's health began to decline. I know she went to a doctor Louise recommended and began to take all kinds of supplements."

I interrupt. "Her health declined *after* seeing the new doctor?"

Suddenly placing her hand over her mouth, her eyes widen. "I—I never even thought about that." She stutters, "I—I mean she was fine before the new doctor. My God. Do you think, I mean, no, that's just not right, or is it?"

"That is something we have to look at. Did Diane keep competing?"

"Oh, yes. She was so gutsy she would still win a lot of the time. Not like she used to, but she certainly had the spirit. She was struggling though. Diane told me Louise would even make special energy shakes for her before they had a big race."

All at once everyone turns and looks at *me*. I look behind me…was something there?

"What? Oh, is this the *Elementary, my dear Watson, part*?"

"Yes, dear," says my lovely wife. "Even though I still think the husband is a rat, maybe he didn't kill her. This Louise Davis, and maybe the helpful doctor, sure look worth checking out, don't you think?"

I do the professional *sigh*. "I am here, to inform the public, we in the sheriff's office will leave no stone unturned in our quest for the truth."

Everyone starts spewing out their theories, ideas. and whatever's. I let them talk without making any comments. I can't reveal all I know. My wife knows all, but she's a cop's wife and knows to watch what she says. I can't corrupt the case by revealing facts which are not public knowledge—the affairs, the car being tampered with, and the damaged cell phone. Especially to a *fireman. He would probably put it on their web page.*

All right, I better reveal why I am the way I am about firemen. It is nothing personal, well maybe it was at one time, but it's just a thing of nature, you know like, cats and dogs. Firemen are always the *heroes*, saving cats from trees, running into burning buildings, that kind of stuff.

We, on the other hand, are perceived as the bad guys. Encounters with us are usually negative.

Writing tickets: "I was only going fifteen over, can't you give me a break?"

Arresting Uncle Joe for DUI: "He wasn't *that* drunk. He didn't mean to drive over the lady."

Domestic violence, with the wife who called for help jumping on your back while you are trying get the husband under control: "I love him; don't hurt him. He's sorry he hit me."

Putting our lives on the line the whole time we're on shift as opposed to *them,* sitting around waiting for the call, to go be a *hero*.

Okay, now having said that, *both professions*

provide vital functions in our society, which protect the public. We will be there to support and protect each other.

But like cats and dogs, we will taunt each other.

Chapter Twenty-Three

It's now time for the nuts and bolts of investigations—following up on leads. I need to speak with the doctor who had been treating Mrs. Morrissey and then speak with Louise. I make an appointment with the doctor.

Dr. Andresen's office is downstairs in an older two-story building. A bank takes up most of the first floor. On one side is a small office tucked into the corner, with a street entrance. Yep, that's Andresen's. He has been in town over five years. One would think he'd want a fancier location. The practice is either not doing well or he's just cheap. My wife's office is in a newer area, with most of the top local physicians. I'm not bragging, just observing.

Entering a dimly lit waiting room, I'm met by gentle flute music. How very Zen. Then a wisp of incense burns down my throat. Lurking against the wall around the small reception area are several shabby vinyl chairs, awaiting their next victims. It's a mystery to me why doctors don't have comfortable chairs, unless they are chiropractors. Some kind of artwork hangs on the walls, but it's too dark to identify them. Perhaps abstract art.

A twenty-something receptionist peers over the top of her frameless glasses, her stringy blonde hair hanging limply on either side of her narrow face. Bet her grandmother was a hippie from the sixties. The young woman is waif-thin. Bastard probably doesn't pay her a living wage. I feel like buying her a cheeseburger.

"Lieutenant Carson, I presume?" she murmurs softly, before I can show my badge.

She has enough strength to inform the doctor of my presence and shows me into his office.

The sparsely furnished office is also faintly lit. A lone lamp glows on his desk with what can't be more than a 5-watt bulb. Apparently, he has excellent night vision. The doctor is scary. He appears to be in his thirties. Hard to tell, as he is tall, thin, and pasty. I show my badge and we exchange pleasantries. He offers up a limp handshake. Likely fearful I'm carrying some sort of transmissible disease. He could be married to the receptionist, same gaunt look. Cancel her cheeseburger.

As my eyes adjust to the semi-darkness, I can see what appears to be diplomas on one wall, along with a class photo. I have verified with all the appropriate state agencies that his licenses and credentials are legal and up to date. No negative actions have been brought against him. I wish I had a flashlight, so I could read the damn things.

Doctor Andresen gestures toward a dark corner. "Please have a seat. How can I assist you?"

I am unable to discern a chair. Could be a vat of acid for all I know. "Thanks, but I've been sitting all day. I'll stand. Dr. Andresen, I know you were treating Mrs. Morrissey. What was her medical condition?"

"Normally I couldn't discuss a patient's medical history, HIPPA and all that, but since Mrs. Morrissey has passed, I will be glad to offer my opinion, as her physician. I will tell you, Mrs. Morrissey simply would not listen to me. I kept telling her she needed to stop going to those social affairs with her husband. All those rich foods, alcohol, sugar, and smoky atmospheres. So unhealthy." Throwing his hands into the air and shaking his head, he looks like a disgusted parent. "She would eat the wrong food and then take the supplements. They were fighting each other. I am sorry she died, but that was how it was going to end. I told her so."

"You still haven't explained her condition, doctor." I cock my head toward him. "What were the supplements you prescribed for her?"

"They were commercial herbs and vitamins to help build up her resistance. She was killing herself with the marathon running and the social life. I was trying to help her get a grip on her health.

"Did you advise her to stop the marathons?"

"She was adamant about them. Just as she was about the parties. Such a decadent lifestyle. If a person won't help themselves, what can I do?" He's looking toward the ceiling, raising his hands upward, as if praying to Hippocrates.

He must have forgotten the part—First Do No Harm.

Moving toward the light on his desk, I'm trying to look into his intense blue eyes, seeking any emotion. I see arrogance. "Thank you for your time, doctor. I will be contacting you if I have any further questions"

Conceited, unfeeling bastard. He does not see a person as anything but a machine that must be maintained. No concern about the human being inside. Sad commentary on the medical profession.

After interviewing him, I immediately go eat six

glazed chocolate donuts.

Since his cousin is in the dental profession, so to speak, I had asked Joseph to find out what she knew about Louise Davis. I know gossip abounds in medical circles.

The cousin reported Louise and her husband, Dr. Davis, have been in Elko for around six years. He was just out of dental school when a long time Elko dentist hired him. According to Joseph's cousin, the younger dentists hope to outlast the old geezers, and then have their own practices. It is apparently a natural progression. In this case, the *old geezer* is the picture of health and not planning to retire anytime soon. Therefore, when Dr. Morrissey offered Dr. Davis a chance to join him in a dental practice in Las Vegas, Davis jumped at it. They were already golfing buddies.

Dr. Morrissey, becoming romantically involved with his office manager, also isn't unheard of in the business. I am informed when Jeanie becomes the *new wife,* she will stay on as the office manager. She will be watching the money and her husband. Fascinating... The original wife put the slob through college and then he repays her by cheating.

There was no real gossip about Louise Davis. It was known she was a marathon runner, but not much else. The wives did not hang around the husbands' offices much. They probably weren't encouraged to.

I debate whether to interview Louise now. The Davises haven't left for Vegas yet. I need to talk with Dr. Morrissey soon. He is still looking very much like a suspect.

I have more digging to do. Who vandalized Mrs. Morrissey's car? It apparently occurred while she was working out at a gym. I need to find out which gym. Luckily, there are not too many in the Greater Elko Area.

On a hunch, I decide to re-visit the neighbor lady I spoke with the day we searched the Morrissey house. She seemed to be a close friend and might save me some time.

Mrs. Howell is as congenial as she was the first time we met. She is dressed in a gray jacket with matching slacks, sensible shoes, and reeking of a flowery perfume. I ask if she is going out, as I don't want to detain her.

"No. I don't go out much these days. My husband died three years ago, and now that Diane is gone, I have no real friends."

She invites me in and offers to make coffee, so I accept. It might relax her as we chat. However, after the six donuts, I'm going to be wired as hell. While she is getting our beverages, I scan the living room and any adjoining rooms I can observe without being too obvious. Since P.K. and I will soon move into our new home, I'm looking for furniture and decorating ideas. (Moreover, a cop is a natural snoop. It's in our training, and I suspect, in our DNA.)

When Mrs. Howell returns with the coffee, I mention her dining room set. I kind of like it. She eagerly shows it to me. Solid, heavy wood, just my style. Large, but a table that size would fit in our new home nicely. Mrs. Howell then invites me to tour her house, since I had mentioned my wife and I were looking at furniture. The home is well-furnished and everything looks expensive. Somewhat above a lieutenant's budget, even with a successful ocularist for a partner.

Mrs. Howell then shows me her office. It is also quite impressive, with a massive dark wood desk and two identical, ornate bookcases. I notice the many photos on the shelves are all of Diane Morrissey. The pictures are personalized to Mrs. Howell. They're photos of Diane winning medals. Hmm.

"Is that Mrs. Morrissey?" I ask innocently.

"Uh, oh yes. She would give me pictures when she won an event. I think she liked having a fan." I detect a hint of something…embarrassment, maybe nervousness.

I ask her about the gym Diane frequented and Mrs. Howell gives me the name of the place and where it is located.

"Did you go with her?"

"I did a lot of the time, except when she was working out with *Louise.*"

Ohhh. I detect some emotion.

Playing dumb, which I can be good at, according to my wife (usually when I forget to do something) I ask, "Who is Louise?"

"A jealous *bitch* who tried to take over Diane's life." She spits out the words, her eyes flaming. Then Mrs. Howell catches herself. "I'm sorry, but Louise was always monopolizing Diane's time and trying to control her. You know, the constant training and going to all the marathons." Her eyes soften, and she tears up.

Well, well, this case is taking on its own twists and turns, isn't it?

I know I need to pursue her reaction, so I inquire more about Louise.

She is another dentist's wife, I am told. When I ask

about the jealousy part, she tells me she meant Louise was becoming irritated. Diane was winning more races than she was. That matches up with what I've already learned, but the intensity of emotion in Mrs. Howell intrigues me. The photos on the shelves are like a shrine or hero worship, like teenagers have for a pop star.

"I imagine Diane was pleased you thought enough of her accomplishments to display her victories?"

Mrs. Howell casts her eyes down. "No, she was quite modest about winning. I just put these out after, after she died." She sits down and begins to cry, wring her hands. "I just get so worked up about this whole matter." Boy is she…!

"So, you two were close friends?"

"Yes. We used to spend a lot of time together. That was before *Louise.*"

Ouch. Hit a nerve again. Gently, I continue, "You knew Diane was going to move to Las Vegas with her husband."

"Yes, and it broke my heart. I would miss her. She said I could come down and spend time with her there. I was okay, until I learned *Louise* was also moving to Las Vegas."

The tone of her voice is controlled but her eyes give away her fury. What the hell am I into with this case? Chasing murdering truckers was simpler. No sub-plots.

I decide to steer the conversation away from Louise for now.

"You mentioned you would workout at the gym with Diane. Did you also do marathons?"

"No. I enjoyed working out for my health and to be honest, to spend time with Diane. I supported her and was her training partner, at first. I would try to keep her eating right and even made her special drinks for her runs. Not the crap that *doctor* was pushing on her. I made healthy, natural foods." Her eyes flash again.

I nudge her a bit more. "When I talked with her doctor, he told me Diane was not eating properly. He complained she ate rich foods at social gatherings and drank alcohol."

"She would go to some of the parties the medical people held. She did eat and drink at those get-togethers, but I do not think a couple times a month would kill her. She was not a big party person. They had gatherings all the time, but she watched herself. I have been to her house for numerous functions, and I have never seen her intoxicated. Diane was into the running. The day after a party, she was hell-bent for the gym. We used to laugh about it during a party. 'You know where we're going in the morning,' she would say to me. And to the gym we would go, until that *woman* came along!"

Truckers were a lot easier. Less complicated.

Chapter Twenty-Four

Well, Mrs. Howell was a trip. I don't think she killed Mrs. Morrissey. She obviously had a deep affection for the woman, and she was losing her; I don't know what to think.

I could see her trying to kill Louise. But as far as I know, Louise is still alive. Hope so. I don't need any more bodies. I have a growing list of suspects, but just one body. The gym is my next stop. But that will be tomorrow. Right now, I'm going home, to the woman who got me into this case in the first place.

After I relate my conversation with Mrs. Howell, my wife looks at me with those beautiful eyes and says, "I'm sorry, baby. I pushed you into this. No. No, I'm not. You're the best, and Diane deserves the truth to be brought out. You'll do it. I know you will." She reaches over and gives me a big kiss. Like that makes it all right. Well for the moment it does. And it always will.

We have the walk-though inspection for our new home, scheduled in three days. We are both excited, yes even me. We spend the rest of the evening just babbling about where this or that will go and what we need to get for this or that room. This is fun. I didn't think we could be any closer, but the excitement and planning melds us into one.

The next morning, I'm at the gym talking with the manager and some of the staff. They all thought highly of Mrs. Morrissey. It's obvious. They mentioned her declining well-being. Both the manager and one of the female staff had tried to get her to slow down and not push so hard.

"She was more determined than ever to win the next race. I don't know why? She had won so many already," the manager says, leaning back on a weight machine.

"Because she wanted to leave Elko a winner, that's why," says the lady trainer. "Diane wanted to beat Louise one more time, before she went to Vegas."

"But Louise was also going to Las Vegas," I interject.

"Yes, she was, but Diane was going to stop doing marathons after she moved."

"This is the first I've heard," says the manager.

"Diane told me in confidence. She thought she could maybe save her deteriorating marriage and start over in Las Vegas. She knew her husband had affairs, but he told her things would be different in the future."

More muddying of the waters. Was he or was he not having an affair with the office manager? Or, was Diane's death how *things would be different* in the future?

As I'm talking with the staff, another trainer comes over to us. The word has gotten around, the *Heat* is in the room.

He is a huge, buff guy in his early thirties, I would say. He looks at me, leans down, and asks in a soft voice, "Can I talk with you, privately?"

"Sure," I say and look at the manager.

"Use my office." He points to a doorway.

We go in and the large, muscular man gently closes

the door.

"Is this about Mrs. Morrissey's car?"

"What do you know about that?"

"I did it."

"Why?"

"My girlfriend works for Dr. Morrissey. She's a dental assistant."

"Okay. But why did you mess with her car?"

"I overheard Mrs. Morrissey and Mrs. Davis laughing, about the *spit suckers* their husbands hire. That's a derogatory term dentists use when talking about their assistants. It upsets my girlfriend when she hears the term. It's disrespectful. Hearing them talk, out loud, it just rubbed me the wrong way. I wanted to get back at them. Mrs. Davis left soon after. I went outside, and Mrs. Morrissey's car was off to one side of the lot. I went over and was going to slash her tires, but then I saw she had left the window down. I reached in and popped the hood. I grabbed some wires and yanked them, so she would end up stranded somewhere. I didn't mean any harm. Just wanted to stick it to the rich, who use and abuse their workers."

"That's it?" I ask.

"Yeah, when I heard she died, I felt horrible. Then when I heard a cop was here, I had to tell you. It didn't have anything to do with her dying, did it?"

"No, I don't think it did, but I would like to speak with your girlfriend, away from the office. You can be there. I want to hear from someone on the *inside* of the office just what goes on there. What is your name?"

"Joel. Why would you want to talk with my girl? She doesn't even know about what I did."

"Joel, if I can speak to her, I will forget about what

you did. This is much more serious than malicious mischief. That is all I can say for now. Deal?"

"Sure, uh, when do you want to talk with her?"

I look Joel straight in the eyes and firmly say, "The sooner the better."

"I'm meeting her for lunch at noon. Is that okay?"

Joel will be having lunch with his girlfriend at a nearby deli. I tell him not to say anything to her beforehand.

"You need to explain to your boss why you asked to talk to me, Joel."

"Oh, yeah, he'll fire me if he knows what I did."

"And he should," I add. "But why don't you just say you got a ticket the other night for speeding and wanted to ask me about it. Do as I ask, and I'll forget about the car."

At noon, I am in the deli when Joel and his lady come in. They order, and he brings her over to my table.

"Patty I want you to meet—uh, I don't even know your name."

Joel, I gave you my card, remember? It had my name and number if you needed to call me.

He's a jock, all muscle and not a lot of, well you know.

"Hi Patty, I'm Lieutenant Carson from the sheriff's department, I would like to ask you a few questions about Dr. Morrissey's office, if you don't mind. This is not about you or Joel. I just happened to run into him at the gym this morning. He mentioned you worked there."

"Sure, what do you want to know? Dr. Morrissey is an okay dentist. I've worked for worse."

I inquire about the office, how it runs, how the staff gets along with the doctor and of course the office manager. Pretty average for the profession she says, stabbing at her salad. The dental assistants hate the hygienists, who think they are above everyone else, including the dentist. The dentist is condescending to the staff, about normal, she says. As we talk more, Patty indicates she is not aware of any indiscretions, but says Dr. Morrissey is not above flirting with some of the female patients. I steer the conversation around to the office manager again. I ask how she and Doctor Morrissey get along.

Patty looks at her salad, pauses, and then says, "I don't know, but they, Jeanie and the doctor, spend a lot of time alone in his office. Usually at the end of the day, while we're cleaning up. They're typically still there when we leave. I don't mean to imply anything, but we can't help but speculate, you know?"

"Did Mrs. Morrissey ever come into the office?" Natural follow up question. Visualize my raised eyebrow as I await her answer.

"Not too often." Then Patty giggles. "One afternoon she came in at the end of the day. Doctor and Jeanie were in his office, with the door closed, as usual. We all looked at each other and I thought…*wow, this is not going to be pretty.*"

I'm all ears now.

"What happened?"

Patty lets out a sigh of disgust. "The kiss-ass hygienist, who talks down the doctor all the time, calls out in an extra loud voice, 'Hi Mrs. Morrissey, how are you today?' Of course, doctor comes out of his office, alone, and is all lovey-dove to his wife."

"What about Jeanie?"

"The doctor's office has a side door to the hallway, so I guess she slipped out. We were all disappointed Mrs. Morrissey didn't catch them together."

I can't help myself. I'm laughing.

"When did this happen?"

"Oh, about two months ago. It was good for us because the next payday we all got a raise."

"How about Jeanie and the doctor?" Investigative minds want to know.

"The next day when we got to work, they were in his office and you could hear her yelling at him. After that, anytime she went into his office the door was kept open. They sure cooled it, at least in front of the staff."

"Jeanie went to Las Vegas with him, you know that?"

"Yeah, we all think something is still going on. She just got a brand-new car, a Cadillac. Sure a lot better ride than she used to have."

I talk with Patty a little more, but that seems to be all the gossip she has. The new dentist is keeping all the current personnel, so she's happy.

Jeanie is definitely still on my list of suspects; at least I did not add to the total.

Chapter Twenty-Five

I get the crew together for a brainstorming session. It always helps to discuss cases out loud. Sometimes I will pick up on a clue just by verbalizing the facts. Joseph and Gary are a great help. They are always playing the devil's advocates by trying to knock down my theories and to offer their own. We do this ritual whenever any of us has a complicated case. It is also a bonding exercise for the team.

Joseph takes a long drink of his coffee and expounds, "Dr. Morrissey, good for it, no doubt. Louise Davis, also a candidate. Mrs. Howell is still in the running, as I see it. Now we have Jeanie the office manager. Definitely a solid suspect. How about the doctor Diane Morrissey went to? He might feel she was making him look bad, since she was not listening to his guidance."

Gary looks at his partner. "Whoa, dude, you're on a roll. I hadn't thought about her doctor. There have been less bizarre motives for murders, so yes, I agree, he should be on the list."

Joseph suddenly straightens in his chair. His head turns toward Gary. "You agree with me? I've made a mistake somewhere; you never agree with me."

"How would her doctor kill her?" I ask. "Unless he was the one who supplied the *supplements* she was taking."

"She had been declining over a period of time. Arsenic in her supplements would slowly cause her health to decline," comments the wise shaman.

"Just how much do you know about this poisoning stuff? And who made these cookies you brought in this morning?" Gary says as he holds up a chocolate-chip cookie he had just grabbed.

"I don't know. I got them from the drug house we busted yesterday," Joseph casually offers. "They were all over the place. Didn't want them to go to waste."

Gary just stares at the big guy. He knows he's being messed with, but he still puts the cookie down.

I continue to munch on my cookie and wash it down with coffee.

"Let's get back to the case. What's next? I think it is time to talk with the good dentist, and then Jeanie, the office manager. They are both in Las Vegas now. We know Louise is still in Elko, so she can wait a bit. Any thought, guys?"

"Since you are ready to move into your new house, I volunteer to make the sacrifice and travel to Vegas," Gary offers.

"Your generosity is noted, kind sir, but 'tis I who must make the journey. It is my responsibility," I respond nobly.

"I got to get out of here; the B.S. is rising rapidly," declares Joseph, heading for the door.

Meeting over, I call Preston, my buddy with the Las Vegas Metropolitan Police Department. It's known as Metro.

After bringing him up to date on my case, Preston says, "Hey, come on down. Only condition is, you must bring your wife along, or mine won't forgive you."

"Deal. I'll call back when I have a firm schedule."

"You will be staying with us, you know. Marie would have it no other way."

Nothing left to do but run it past Undersheriff George and, oh yes, tell my wife. Yeah, good idea, *Robert*.

Fortunately, for my sake, P.K. has a couple of open days in her schedule so we can do this.

Whew! Could have been ugly.

Chapter Twenty-Six

Las Vegas here we come.

Preston's offer to stay with them is greatly appreciated, as I must pay for my wife's airfare. The County is good to me, but not *that* good. Hotels in Vegas are pricy. When we land, I pick up our rental car, and we head off to Preston and Marie's house. I drop P.K. at their place, with Marie, and leave to interview Dr. Morrissey and Jeanie. Preston has located the dentist's office for me and even offered to meet me there. Actually, I believe Metro doesn't want an out of town cop running around unchecked in Las Vegas.

Pulling up to the location, I see the *new* Caddy, which the nice doctor bought for his office manager. It's in the employee's parking area. It is next to another Cadillac sedan, which has the same Elko dealer's license plate frame. Yep, we are in the right place.

Preston will loiter in the office and observe, while I do the interviews.

We hit the office just at lunch time. Planned it that way. The unmistakable stench of *dental office* hits you as soon as you open the door. There's a typical reception area—vinyl chairs, outdated magazines, and a kids' play area in one corner. Probably with hardened toys, on which the future customers can potentially chip their teeth. The receptionist is not at her station as we enter the waiting room.

We open the door to the main office. Looks like a normal dentist's office. Several patient stations on the right side of the area and offices on the left side. I spot Dr. Morrissey walking out of the patient area. Jeanie is in one of the side offices. The doctor is walking toward Jeanie's office when we confront him. I identify myself.

"Elko Sheriff's office? Why are you here to see me?" Eyes wide open. He's stunned.

"I need to talk with you about your late wife, doctor. It is quite important I assure you."

As I'm ushered into his private office, I nod toward Jeanie and quietly say to Preston, "Keep an eye on her."

His office is expensively furnished for just opening the practice. I close the door. He doesn't appear nervous, just confused. I get him to sit down, and I do the same, settling myself into a soft, quality leather chair. He goes to a large leather executive chair behind his desk.

"Nice furniture, doctor. This desk is beautiful," I say sincerely.

"It came with the practice. The dentist I bought it from just left everything. Yes, it is quite nice, thank you. But what can I do for you? Why are you here?"

"Before we go any further, I need to read you your rights."

"But, why? I don't understand, what is this about?" If he is acting, he should go professional. I am used to people lying and hedging, but I'm buying his reaction.

I read him his Miranda rights, and he acknowledges that he understands them, but he is still, "Why, what is this about?"

"Doctor Morrissey we have reason to believe your wife, Diane, was murdered."

I let that set in.

He slumps back in his chair. The color drains from his face. For a minute, I think he is going to be sick.

"But, who, why? She was the nicest person I've ever known. Who would want to kill her? That can't be. You must be mistaken. Where did this come from? Who is saying this horrible thing?"

"She was poisoned with arsenic. We found it in the hair samples from her clothing. Before you ask, yes, the DNA matched."

Dr. Morrissey is just babbling. "No, it can't be. Who would want to hurt her? Arsenic, my God! No wonder she was sick. Who? No, not Diane. Why?"

Sitting up in my chair I look hard at him and say, "If she was the nicest person you have ever known, then why did you have affairs, with patients and apparently even with your office manager." I cast a glance toward the door.

He just crumbles in front of me. Tears start to flow, and he begins sobbing. "Yes, yes, I did all that, but I loved her, I did. I guess like Clinton, I did it because I could. We had wonderful times together, before I ruined it. I know I did. I promised her when we moved down here it would be different. I meant it." He looks toward the door. "Diane almost caught us one day. I realized what a fool I was, risking her for a fling. Well, several flings. Jeanie, my office manager, told me I had to make up my mind. I told her I had, and I was staying with my wife."

"But you brought Jeanie down here, didn't you?"

"She is the best business person I have ever seen. Keeps an eye on all the operation. Keeps me in line, financially at least. She still wanted to come, and after I got up and running, she was to find another dentist to work with. We had cooled it, we had. Then, when Diane…" He stops, wipes his eyes. "When she died, I was lost. Yes, Jeanie was there for me. It wasn't supposed to be that way. I wanted to get back the life I had with Diane."

My senses tell me he is being truthful. I can't let him off yet.

"Doctor, at lunch time, the day before your wife died, where were you?"

He just stares at me. "The day before?" He reaches into his desk drawer. I immediately place my hand on the weapon under my coat.

His hand comes up with an appointment book. I relax.

"I'm old fashioned; I still have to write everything down." He leafs through the book and then shows me a page.

"I was having lunch with my golfing buddies at the Basque restaurant downtown. Why do you ask about that time?"

"Because someone accessed your wife's home computer. We know she wasn't there. Who would that have been, doctor?"

"No one. No one should have been there. Well, I don't know, but…"

"But what doctor?"

"That crazy neighbor across the street, Mrs. Howell. Diane did give her a key. She was always hovering around Diane, helping her plan for her runs, keeping schedules, her biggest fan in the marathons. The woman drove me batty. Diane felt sorry for her. Her husband had died, and she was lonely. Wacko, I thought! She was fixated on Diane. She wouldn't kill Diane. Probably kill everyone else, if she thought it would help Diane."

"Would she have access to your wife's computer?"

"Who knows? Diane pretty much let her follow her around the house, like a puppy." He stops and looks at me. "I didn't mean to infer Mrs. Howell would kill anyone; she is a sweet old lady, just a bit eccentric."

I am wrapping up with Dr. Morrissey when there is a loud commotion in the outer office.

Then I hear Preston yell, "Drop the gun, drop the gun!"

Chapter Twenty-Seven

Motioning the doctor to get down, I stand, pull my weapon out, and ease the door open a crack. I see a white male in his twenties standing just inside the door from the waiting room. He is disheveled and dirty, like he lives on the streets. He is waving a semi-automatic pistol in his shaking hand.

Preston keeps telling him to drop his gun. I cannot see Preston, but from the location of his voice, he must be near the office manager's area, to my right.

The intruder starts to scream, "Give me some drugs, give me some drugs!" Eyes bulging, he is waving the gun toward the ceiling and around the empty office. Then he seems to focus in on the sound of Preston's voice. He turns toward Preston, putting the gun to his own head. Preston is saying, "Don't do it, man. We can talk this out."

The man then lowers the gun toward the floor. "I gotta have drugs—coke, meth, morphine, anything—I'm hurting so fucking bad." He begins sobbing like a child.

Preston is talking calmly. "We can help, just put the gun down."

The man jerks, like he just woke up, swings his weapon up, and points it toward Preston.

I can't wait; pulling the door open, I fire two quick shots at the man's chest. I hear two more shots. My heart skips a beat; I hope to God those shots are from Preston's gun. The man slumps down to the floor. The gun drops from his hand.

"Preston, you okay?"

"Yeah, I'm fine, I'm fine. It's all clear now. The guy was alone. I owe you, Bob. That wasn't going to be pretty. I thought we came here for an interview, not a damn shootout!"

"Tell me again why I should move to Vegas," I mutter as I motion to the doctor to stay put. I step into the main office area and see Preston moving toward the man on the floor. Jeanie is still in her office. I cover the man. He's not moving. Preston secures the gun from the floor and then checks the man.

"He's still alive." He uses his radio, calls for an ambulance, and advises dispatch of what occurred.

I examine the would-be thief crumpled on the floor. He is unconscious, but his heart is beating, his breathing is shallow. Two shots hit him in the chest. Looks like one above and one below the heart. I make sure his airway is clear. Can't do much else. Not a lot of external bleeding.

I call out to the doctor, "Can't you help?"

"I'm a dentist not a medical doctor, I—I wouldn't know what to do," he stammers.

"Fine, then just sit in your office and write a statement of what you saw."

Preston tells Jeanie to do the same. No need to contaminate the scene.

Preston kneels next to me. He drapes an arm around my shoulders, hugs me. "That was close."

"Too damn close," I agree. What just happened is closing in on me, too. The threat is over, and the adrenaline is subsiding. That's how it is. Training kicks in, you react, then it's over and you realize how close it was.

There are sirens surrounding us now. Officers are piling into the office. Preston is now standing in the reception area, to keep them from messing anything up. Paramedics arrive and tend to the man.

Finally, a Metro lieutenant arrives and takes over the crime scene. The lab and shooting teams also arrive. Preston and I are now just sitting and writing our statements of what occurred.

I look at him. "Just what did happen?"

"I was chatting with the office manager to keep her occupied when the door burst open and this wild looking guy comes charging in, gun in hand. I was standing in the doorway of her office and told her to get down as I drew my weapon and ordered him to drop his gun. I was sure hoping you heard the noise. When he pointed the gun down, I thought maybe I had a chance to get him to give it up. I took a step toward him and was trying to talk calmly when he pointed the gun right at me. You fired just then. Man, I was never so glad to hear gunshots in my life. I did fire two rounds just after you. If you hadn't been there, if he fired first, I might not be here. Look at my hands. I'm shaking. Thank God you were here, Bob. That's all I can say. I've been doing this a lot of years, but that was the closest I've ever come to being shot."

"I'm just grateful it worked out right. If you had been hit, I would have felt I didn't my job." I put a hand on his arm. I see my hand is trembling as I extend it.

"This guy has two holes in him. We each fired twice. Damn it, where are the other two? They must be mine because he was already dropping as I fired. Man, you were quick," Preston states.

"You were trying to talk him down. I was just keeping him in my sights. As soon as he raised his gun toward you, I fired." I look at the wall behind where the man was standing. Yep, two holes, about chest high, in the wall. I point to them.

Preston calls to the Metro lieutenant and points to the holes.

"What is behind there?" Preston asks anxiously.

"Relax," says the officer. "You only slightly wounded a file cabinet."

We look at each other and smile. We are starting to come down from it all. The gunman is on his way to the hospital. He will probably live, but the extent of his injuries is unknown.

We do our interviews with the shooting team and are informed we will be allowed to leave soon.

"Actually, I'm not done with my interviews," I tell the lieutenant. "I am not finished with the doctor and have yet to speak to the lady in the other office, if that's all right with you."

He looks at me, then at Preston. "Uh, yeah sure, why not. We have their statements. Go ahead. Just stay out of this area." He sweeps his hand around the center of the office.

I go back into his office with the dentist. Preston goes with Jeanie into hers. Dr. Morrissey is a mess. This is a slice of life he has never seen. I chat with him a bit to try and settle him down.

"How can you be so calm?" he asks me.

"Believe me, doctor, when something like that is happening, it's like slow motion. All is clear as a bell. I know what I'm doing and what is going on around me. It's afterwards, after everything is over, we're a hyped-up mess."

"I'll stay with dentistry."

I go over some of the information I acquired from him previously and then get to the matter of the damaged cell phone. Buzz said it was an *old-style* dumb phone, not a more modern *smartphone*. You can't reach the battery in a smartphone. It is meant to be non-replaceable, so you must *replace* your entire phone. The older dumb phones have a removable battery. There was damage to the battery contacts in Diane Morrissey's phone. Some acid type of solution had melted the plastic and the contacts under the battery.

"We found your wife's phone at the park. She only had an older cell phone, not a smartphone?" I ask.

"Yes, that's right. Diane hated the new ones. She hung onto her old one. It was simple, and it was all she wanted. Phone calls and text messages were all she used it for."

"Did you know it was not working that afternoon?"

"She had problems with the battery all the time. I wanted her to get a new phone, but she liked her old one. In fact, I cleaned up the battery contacts the night before she went to the park. It was working when I finished. She was happy and told me I had saved it *one more time*. What do you mean it wasn't working?'

"Just how did you clean up the battery contacts?"

"I tried to wipe them with a rag and Windex, and then when they still weren't clean, I took some of her nail polish remover and saturated the contacts. That seemed to do the job. The contacts were clean when I finished. Then I put some more remover on the contacts to protect them and closed it up. It worked fine then."

Showing my feminine side, I ask if he knows the difference between acetone and non-acetone polish remover. He did not.

"Doctor, if you saturated the phone with acetone polish remover, it could have melted the plastic and the soldered connections to the battery. The phone would then go dead over a period of time. I'm not saying that's what happened, but it is a possibility."

"God, oh God, oh God. I could have killed her. No wonder she never called me, because she couldn't."

He is a sobbing wreck now. I change places with Preston and have him sit with the dentist.

"What did you do to him?" Preston quietly whispers with a puzzled expression.

"I'll fill you in later."

Chapter Twenty-Eight

I now go to Jeanie. She is still shaken up after what she just witnessed. Preston has done his best to calm her.

"Why did I think Las Vegas would be so good? What just happened was horrible. Things like this don't happen in Elko."

"Well, yes they do. Just not as often. Larger population like Vegas, bad things happen more often."

I talk to her in general a little bit to get her more relaxed. Now it's time to get to the reason I'm here.

"Jeanie, when was the last time you saw Diane Morrissey?"

"The day before she died, in the afternoon. She texted Donald, Dr. Morrissey, that her car wouldn't start. He was busy with patients and asked me to go pick her up and to have her car towed to the dealership. I did and took her to her house."

"Where did you pick her up?" I ask like I don't already know the answer.

"At her gym. She had been working out. She had a marathon run coming up."

"How did she seem to you?"

"She was grateful to be picked up. She knew Donald was probably tied up with patients."

"How was she health wise, you know, physically?"

"She was very tired. Dr. Morrissey had mentioned

she was getting more and more run down with all the marathons. She wouldn't quit. She wanted to do one more marathon before the move to Las Vegas. Maybe if she had quit, she would still be alive."

"How did you get along with Diane?" I ask, looking right at Jeanie.

"We got along fine. I didn't see her very much. She didn't come to the office often. There were some social gatherings we were at together. That was about it." She is getting a little fidgety.

"I take it she didn't know about you and *Donald*?"

That did it.

"You know about that. I'm so embarrassed. It shouldn't have happened. I know better than to get involved with an employer. It just happened. Too many long hours, planning the Las Vegas office, just everything. Diane almost caught us together one day in his office. I told him the next day he had to make a choice. He said he wanted to save his marriage. I respected his decision. He still wanted me to come here and help him get this office running. Then he would give me a recommendation to another dentist. And before you ask, yes, he bought me the red Cadillac out there. You probably already know about it."

I nod in the affirmative.

"While you were taking Diane home, did she say anything about what she was going to do the next day?"

"I think she was going to do something at the park outside of town. Something with the fire department. She was always involved in some activity. I asked her how she would get there if her car wasn't running. She said she had already called another woman who would take her. She made the arrangement while she was waiting for me to pick her up at the gym. Diane didn't know how she was going to get home yet, because she wanted to do some running on the exercise path at the park afterwards. I told her since Donald was playing golf in the morning, he always played on Wednesdays, I bet he could pick her up. They would be done around the same time. She was happy with that."

"He was to pick her up?" I ask.

"Yes. When I went back to the office, I told Donald he should offer to pick her up and maybe go to lunch. I'm not a bad person. I know we were wrong."

She looks at me. "Why are you here? You're from Elko, right? The other officer was nice, but he wouldn't tell me why you're here. Said he didn't know. He was just sent to show you around town."

"Diane Morrissey was murdered."

Jeanie's mouth drops open; she tries to talk but nothing comes out. Then, "*Murdered*? Why would anyone want to murder her? She was a very nice lady. Always nice to me. I guess she never knew about us. I felt guilty when she was around after it started. Murdered? How? Who would want to do that to her?"

"At this point of the investigation, I don't know. Her body does have traces of arsenic in it." I throw that information out to see where it falls.

"Arsenic! Someone gave her arsenic?" Jeanie shudders. You can see her mind whirling, trying to make sense of what she just heard. "Arsenic," she repeats.

I ask Jeanie if she has completed her move to Vegas yet. She says no, not quite. She still has her condo back in Elko. Her plan was to sell it after she settled here.

"After this, I'm not so sure about moving here permanently."

I inquire about Dr. Davis, Morrissey's partner in the Vegas office.

"He's going to start next week. His wife is still in Elko trying to sell their house."

"You know her too, I imagine?" Letting out a little more line.

"Louise. She's a piece of work. I think she's the reason he's coming down here. I think he wants to get away from her. He keeps telling her not to worry about moving, until the house sells. What a pushy, controlling bitch. Chuck is such a kind, gentle man."

Well now, maybe if *Donald* isn't interested anymore, there may be a shot at *Chuck*. Stop it, Robert. Not professional, but something to think about. This dental world is as good as any soap opera.

I talk with her more, but I'm satisfied for the moment with her responses.

I tell her and Dr. Morrissey, *Donald*, I'm done for the time being. The Vegas investigators are also finishing up and tell them they may leave. The doctor's office staff came back from lunch and were sent home, over the doctor's objections. He was allowed to post a notice on the door for patients to call and reschedule. After all, it's still a crime scene, *doctor*.

Preston and I are again informed we can leave soon. The investigators have taken our weapons for testing. We will get them back in the morning, maybe. Preston will be on administrative leave until the report is finished. I am free if I don't leave Vegas. Preston speaks up for me.

"You know he's a cop; he is supposed to fly back

to Elko tomorrow. I know how these things work, guys, come on. I've been on shooting teams too, you know."

The Metro lieutenant takes us both aside. "You can go home tomorrow. We will do the ballistics on your weapon later today and get it back to you. I've got some new members on the team, and I need to show them the *right way*. We have done everything *by the book* already. I will get the report signed off at HQ tomorrow. I could give the dentist his office back now, but he's such a *dick,* I'm just going to make him wait. If that's okay with you." He smiles.

"You can keep it as long as you want, as far as I'm concerned. You know, if you get him out of here, I wouldn't mind looking around his office." Worth a try.

The lieutenant grins. "His office isn't part of the crime scene. Knock yourself out. I'll send him packing."

I look at Preston. He is now shaking his head and laughing.

"You sure you don't want to come work here. I like your style."

Then he says, "We better call the wives and tell them we'll be late for dinner."

"Do we have to tell them why?" Here I am playing *cops and robbers* again.

"Hopefully not." Replies the also married man.

As the words come out of his mouth, both of our cell phones begin ringing.

Mine is my beautiful, supportive wife.

"Are you all right?"

"Of course, why do you ask?"

"Oh, just because *Dr. Morrissey's office* is on the television's *breaking news story* right now! Robert, what happened there?"

"I'm fine, and so is Preston, honey."

Preston is doing the same fast-talking.

"Marie, I'm fine, yes Bob is too. No problem. We were lucky to be here at the right time and prevented what could have been a terrible incident." Boy he's good.

"P.K., we are fine, we were fortunate to have been able to stop what could have been a horrible crime. Just luck of the draw. We did not start this, honest." Better quit while I'm behind. I'm not as good as Preston.

We are both told, in no uncertain terms, to get our asses home-ASAP.

"They still love us," laughs Preston as we both hang up.

Preston and I check out the doctor's office. Nothing of interest there.

"Well, why not Jeanie's office as long as we are here," I casually suggest.

"As I said, I like your style," he answers.

We don't find much here either. She appears to be well organized. The computers are off, so we can't snoop. There is a list of patients on her desk. It seems to be a going practice. The doctor told me he was able to buy it at a good price from an older established practitioner, who was having health problems.

There is a *to-do* list also on her desktop. The items seem to be work related for the most part:

Schedule for hygienist

Check with Payroll Company

Confirm when Chuck will arrive, check on apartment

Only interesting item was a note to: *Check with*

Anna Re: $

The entry jumped out at me. Like it was trying to get my attention. I will eventually need to find out who *Anna* is.

I have learned over the years to pay attention to something that seems to stand out. I almost see this line blinking at me.

Nothing else of interest here, so we thank the lieutenant and head to Preston's home and *our fate*.

Chapter Twenty-Nine

After being greeted with hugs and kisses, the *third degree* begins. Boy, these two are a team.

"Who got shot?"

"Which one of you did the shooting?"

"Did you think we wouldn't find out?"

"You both have cell phones."

"The TV news here is faster than the two of you."

Preston and I just stand there. I look at him. "We haven't even been read our rights. I wouldn't say anything if I were you."

"Do we need an attorney?"

"All right, that's enough." Marie laughs. "Come on in the family room and have some wine and tell us your side." We do, and they are finally convinced we did not initiate the incident.

They both are stunned. "Honey, you could have been shot," cries Marie as she throws her arms around Preston. "Bob, thank you for being there. And for being a good shot. We didn't know what happened. We just saw the dentist's office building on TV and Metro was all over the place because of a shooting. We didn't think you two were involved."

Then my sweet little wife announces, "But, Robert has been known to race at breakneck speed *out* of his jurisdiction just to get in on some action. I had a feeling you were somehow involved, *dear*." She is holding me tightly.

We have more wine and then our wives go to check on the dinner they have somehow found time to prepare, along with all their TV watching. Later in the evening, the doorbell rings. It is a uniformed Las Vegas Metro Police sergeant.

"Hi, Preston. Seems like you had some action today. I have your weapon and that of a Lieutenant Carson. The lab is finished and said to bring them to you here."

Preston invites the officer in. He has known him for many years. Marie pours him coffee and we all chat a bit. He of course wants to know what went down at the dentist's office. It was all over when he came on shift. We tell him the details.

"What are the odds you two were there when that druggie came in? It could have been ugly. It was fate; you were meant to be there."

Preston and I look at our wives, smile, and nod agreement.

"Fate or not, my husband could have been killed," Marie suddenly sobs. She has been tough so far but now it is coming out. Preston holds her close.

The sergeant looks uncomfortable. "I better go. Thanks for the coffee." I show him to the door.

"I feel horrible," he says.

"Don't. She had to let it out eventually. Better now than keeping it bottled up."

"Yeah, I guess. This is a rough life for the spouses. Probably why I have two ex-wives."

We all settle back down.

Marie says she is fine now. "I know the risks. I've lived with them for years, but since he became a detective, I began to not worry as much."

P.K. says, "Becoming a detective hasn't seemed to calm Robert down much. Unless he hasn't told me what happened before I met him." She gives me one of *her* looks.

"All right, anyone for dinner?" Marie jumps up and P.K. goes off with her.

Preston looks at me. "More than once I have offered to quit. Bless her, she always says, 'It is your career, you are good at it, and I can't ask you to stop. I won't.' I love that lady!"

"I know and I agree. We have special ladies," I say.

Dinner and the rest of the evening goes all too quickly. As we get comfortable in our room, my wife snuggles close to me. "If I hadn't cajoled you into taking this case and Preston had been killed, I would never have forgiven myself, or if you had been the target. *Don't listen to me anymore.*"

"No, you were right to question the case. It is a homicide. Justice will prevail, I promise you. I'll always listen to you and value your insight and intuition."

"Now that we have found each other, I can't imagine being without you. I know you're not crazy, but damn it, the world is. I want my husband with me, forever."

"Honey, I have always felt I am watched over by angels or eagles or somebody. Crazy as that may seem. I have come through some wild things without a scratch. No excuse for being foolhardy, but I believe I was meant to stay around *for you.*"

"Could your angels watch over me too?"

"They have been, since the moment I met you."

Chapter Thirty

The next morning P.K. and I say our good-byes and head to the airport for the return flight to Reno and eventually, Elko. What a trip. Much more than I had planned. I still haven't narrowed my suspect list—only widened it. At least we had a good visit with Marie and Preston. Well sort of. It was good, but the shooting incident was hanging over all of us.

Those moments remind us we are mortal.

Back in Elko, all is well. My crew has been solving crimes and the new home is ready for us. My crew is now *my moving company*. They all offered on their own, no coercion. George has also offered to help. We will have several pick-ups at our disposal. The west is truck country.

We are scheduled for this Saturday. George comes in and says the move will have to be Friday. "George, that is a work day. We can't do it then. Everyone would have to take a day of leave. It is planned for Saturday."

"It will be Friday and that's final." He smiles at me.

"But, George, I can't ask my men to take the day off. What's with you?"

"Okay, it is supposed to be a surprise, but Charlie called, and he has arranged for a real moving company to come and do the job. His wedding present, since he hasn't given you one yet. Let P.K. and Elaine handle the movers. You can drop in and out. Your wife already knows; Elaine told her this morning. See? No problem. Welcome to Elko. I told you we would take care of you if you moved here."

I'm overwhelmed. Charlie, you son-of-a-gun. If I know him, he probably used this as an excuse to sell his motorhome, so he wouldn't have to travel anymore. He hates that thing. Bless his crotchety heart.

It's not yet Friday, and I still have a murder to solve. After the Vegas trip, I'm beginning to think whenever I leave Elko for a case, *I shoot someone.* I hope I can resolve this case right here. Drawing down on someone occurs frequently in law enforcement, but it does not often get to the…pulling the trigger part.

Louise Davis must be interviewed before she makes the move to Las Vegas. I would also like a warrant to search the office of the *health nut* doctor, who was giving Diane Morrissey her pills.

I contact District Attorney Bates and inform her Mrs. Morrissey was apparently getting her *supplement pills* from her M.D., and just maybe he was slipping her the arsenic.

"Why would he?" she asks. "He's a doctor. He is supposed to save lives, not take them. Besides, why would he lose a paying customer?"

"Maybe because he's a whack job and takes it personally Diane would not follow his exact instructions. We know the capsules had arsenic in them. We found no trace in the Morrissey house. To eliminate suspects, I think a search of the creep's office is in order."

"Why do I get the impression you don't like this guy?"

"You go visit him, then tell me he's not weird."

"There are a lot of weird people, Lieutenant, but it doesn't mean they're all murderers."

"Just go see him. Make up your own mind."

Sighing, she picks up a pen. "What's his name and office address? I'll call the judge."

Apparently, she has decided *not* to visit him first.

Now for Louise Davis. With any luck, her hubby will still be in town and I can chat with him too. A phone call to the dental office of Dr. Davis tells me he is still in Elko, but not taking any new patients, as he will be moving his practice soon. All I needed to know.

I grab Gary and we head over to the Davis residence. We will just *knock and talk*, no advance warning. This technique works best in these situations. Takes the suspect off balance. She does not know she is a suspect. Why give her time to think she might be, by setting up an appointment?

Gary and I arrive at a fine house in a good neighborhood, almost as upscale as Dr. Morrissey's. A woman answers the door. She is wearing exercise clothes. Looks like she just finished a workout, hair loosely pulled into a ponytail. I'm betting this is Louise.

"Hi. Mrs. Davis?" I show my badge. "I'm Lieutenant Carson of the Elko Sheriff's Department, this is Detective Horton. May we have a word with you?"

"Of course. What is this about? Want to come in?"

We enter, and she shows us to the adjacent living room, adorned with trophies, ribbons, and certificates. I play dumb. I seem to use this technique a lot.

"Impressive. What are all these awards, if I may ask? Yours?"

"Yes." She pauses. "They are some of my winnings. I run marathons. You will have to excuse my appearance. I just finished working out." She reaches to her hair with both hands and does that whipping around of the hair and repositioning the rubber band thing that women can do. Satisfied for the moment, she looks at me.

"What do you want to talk about? Has there been a problem or another burglary in the neighborhood?"

"No, ma'am, I would like to ask you about Diane Morrissey."

Louise turns stone faced. I think she stopped breathing for a moment.

"Diane? Why would the police want to know about Diane? She was a friend of mine. Well, you must know, or you wouldn't be here. Please sit down." I have her attention now.

"When was the last time you saw her or talked to her?"

Louise puts a hand to her eyes as if to hold back tears and takes a breath. "The day she died. I was with her in the morning at the Fire Department's training exercise. In fact, I drove her there, because her car had some sort of mechanical problem. We liked to do the training thing. It was fun, playing the injured. We volunteered for it all the time. I had to leave when it was over. We, my husband and I, are moving to Las Vegas. He is going into partnership with Diane's husband. I had to meet with the realtor about the house." She looks off into space. "If I had stayed maybe I could have gotten her help in time to save her life. I feel so guilty. It's always on my mind."

While she is composing herself, I give Gary a *look*.

I cast my eyes around the room. He gets the hint. He stands up and holds his back like it's stiff. He begins to walk around the room. He scans the trophies and sort of wanders around. Louise doesn't seem to notice him. Good boy. He's scanning whatever he can get a look at.

"I know Mrs. Morrissey also ran, so I guess you two ran together, like a team or something?"

Louise visibly stiffens. "NO. No, we each competed individually." She catches herself. "We were competitors, but we were friends first." Interesting reaction, I note.

"Do you know the doctor Diane was seeing?" I ask innocently.

"Oh yes, Dr. Andresen. I go to him also. In fact, I told Diane she should go to Henri. (She pronounces it An-ree.) Uh, Dr. Andresen. He was quite helpful to me with my endurance running. He is a wizard with the natural and herbal supplements our bodies need."

"Does he do his own compounding?"

"No, but he deals with only the best of the suppliers," she proudly states. "You know, the purest, organically grown, safest products."

I ask Louise about the brand of supplements Diane used. She tells me it was the same brand she uses.

"Sometimes we would take turns picking up each other's orders. Dr. Andresen would have them packaged separately for each of us with our names and the dosage instructions. He is just such a dear man."

"Anree?" I ask phonetically, mimicking her words.

"Henri, H-e-n-r-i, it is French. Henri Andresen. A-n-d-r-e-s-e-n." She spells for me.

I can't even pronounce my own doctor's name and she can spell hers. This the same weirdo I met?

Hummm? I glance at my watch and say, "Oh, I'm sorry, I forgot I was supposed to be at a meeting. I want to keep talking with you, but please excuse me for a moment while I call and reschedule. Detective Horton will chat with you." I get up immediately and go out the front door. I can feel Gary's eyes giving me the *WTF* look.

Outside I call Joseph. *Please be in the office.* He is.

"What's up, boss?" Joseph asks in his usual unruffled manner.

"Has the D.A. called regarding the search warrant for the doctor?" I'm not so unruffled.

"Yeah, a little while ago."

"Joseph, I want you to grab the warrant and have a marked unit meet you at the doctor's office. Start the search; you know what we are looking for. Gary and I will be there as soon as we can. I am with Mrs. Davis and I don't want to leave her until you are at the doctor's office. As soon as you're inside the office text me, okay?"

"Yes, sir. You think she and the doctor are in cahoots?"

"I'll tell you later. Get moving!"

I go back into the house. Gary and Louise are discussing the finer points of marathon competition. The boy is good. Took the ball and ran with it. I knew he could think on his feet.

Rather than interrupt, I join in the conversation. I'm trying to kill time, so Joseph can get to *Henri's* office. Louise is into talking about herself, so she has lost sight of why we are here, for the moment. After a bit, she takes a breath and, unfortunately, gets back to the crux of our visit.

"You never said why you're here. Why the questions about Diane? I thought the matter was all settled. That's what my husband told me."

"Mrs. Davis, unfortunately there are a few unanswered questions surrounding her untimely demise, and we have been tasked with finding the answers. We want to close this tragic situation as quickly as possible. We certainly appreciate your assistance and insight into her life."

I swear I can *hear* Gary's eyes rolling at the line of B.S. I just spewed.

Then my cell phone *dings.* I give it a quick glance.

Joseph texts, *I'm in.*

I thank Louise for her time and give her my card with the usual—*if you should think of anything that might help please call—blah, blah, blah.*

Back outside, Gary yells, "Just what the hell was all that? A heads up would have helped. You left me with that crazy woman. Thank goodness for those damn trophies. I don't know what I would have thought of to keep her busy."

"I wasn't worried. You are one of the best bullshitters I know."

"After that load of crap you just handed her, you're the best, boss. I was impressed. Work of a master." We both laugh and then I fill him in on the search warrant.

"I didn't want to leave her until Joseph was at the doctor's office."

"Yeah, good thinking. She seemed too enthralled with *Henri.*"

Chapter Thirty-One

Gary and I swiftly arrive at Dr. Andresen's office. Joseph has two marked sheriff's patrol cars with him and an Elko PD unit. The Elko PD just wanted to see what the action was.

Walking into the office, we see one deputy and the Elko officer are entertaining the doctor and his receptionist. The physician is livid. The deputy tells us Joseph is executing the search warrant, along with the other deputy.

The doctor looks at me. "What is the meaning of this outrage? Why a search warrant?"

Looking at the doctor, I say in a calm, quiet voice, "Gary, will you please read him his rights? And then come join us in the search."

Nodding at the uniformed officers, I say, "Thank you, gentlemen, and please keep him with you until we return."

"Rights? Why read me my rights? I haven't done anything. I demand an explanation."

I keep walking into his office and hear Gary say, "You have the right…"

I find Joseph in the doctor's private office.

"Hi, Bob, take a look at this." With a gloved hand, he holds up a bottle like an old apothecary jar, glass stopper and all. Inside is a white powder. The bottle has a label that says, *AS3O2.* "You know what that is?"

"No, but the AS part doesn't sound good."

"It is arsenic trioxide. A byproduct of gold mining. Something that is done a lot around this area." Joseph articulates as if lecturing a class.

Having finished giving Dr. Andresen his Miranda rights, Gary walks in and hears his partner.

"Yeah, arsenic is all over this area. The tailings from the gold mines contain it. The mines have to keep the tailings out of the ground water. It's a huge environmental issue."

"I stand in awe of both of you. Yes, I know about arsenic in the gold mines being a problem, but what is this version?"

"Some of the mines would separate out the arsenic and sell it to pharmaceutical and manufacturing companies. They make rat poison and treat wood products. It is also used to treat some forms of leukemia." Professor Joseph instructs. "Not by an M.D. like him." Joseph cocks his head toward the outer office. "But by oncologists. You know, cancer specialists."

"What else have you found?" I ask the lecturer.

"Man, you want it all, never happy." He feigns a pout. "Well, Diane Morrissey's medical information is in the file cabinet. I haven't looked at it yet. It is in the room over there." He points to a door off the doctor's office. "There is a supply of the same brand of supplements Mrs. Morrissey had been taking. Looks like he buys the stuff by the case. Some of them are in plastic baggies with patient's name and dosage written on them. That's as far as I've gotten."

"Great job, Joseph, great job."

We begin to look at the files of all the patients. One

thing is immediately odd. Most of the files are in the top drawer of the cabinet. Louise Davis is there. Diane Morrissey and half a dozen other patients are filed in the second drawer. This was where Joseph found the bottle of arsenic.

We each take one of the second drawer files and peruse them. It becomes clear these are the *problem* patients. There are notes about excessive alcohol consumption, poor diets, lack of exercise, and strongly worded comments on the patients' *disregard for the doctor's instructions*.

Looking at the top-drawer files, these folks are seemingly behaving themselves, per the doctor's notes. A couple of them appear to be heading toward the *naughty* drawer. There are critical notes on their lack of following the doctor's guidance. His notes are readable, odd for a doctor. Usually they scrawl so badly I wonder if they can read their own words.

Gary sums up our thoughts. "This guy's a phony. If I can read his writing, he's got to be a fake."

We compare the marked bags of supplements with the *naughty and nice* lists. We open one of the *errant* patient's bags and look inside the bottle. The capsules have the same-appearing white residue on them, as did Mrs. Morrissey's capsules. These people will have to be notified immediately. The capsules from a bottle for a *good* patient are free of any residue.

I then call the D.A. She answers immediately.

"Have you found anything? I pushed this warrant on the judge. He will have my hide if it's a bust."

"It's a bust." I pause. "But by that I mean, we are going to bust the doctor."

"Damn you. I about died when you said that."

"I'm sorry, I can't help myself sometimes." Then I quickly fill her in on what we found.

"Bring him in. This is huge, Lieutenant; sorry for being nervous, but this is an election year, you know."

"We'll be here for a while longer, then take him back and interrogate him, at least until he *lawyers up*. And before you ask, we did read him his rights and he acknowledged he understood."

The doctor is sitting and fuming, in the typically uncomfortable waiting room chairs he expects his patients to sit in.

Justice I say.

We finish with the office and then *bag and tag* everything of interest for evidence. I then walk out to the waiting room and with great ceremony tape a sign on the front door of his office—*Crime Scene, Do Not Enter.*

I formally place Doctor Henri Andresen under arrest for suspicion of homicide. His bluster fades and he goes limp in the chair. I knew if you sat too long in those damn things, it was fatal. He is speechless, then sits up and begins to pontificate about how we are violating his rights and demands to know why he is under arrest. I interrupt and ask him about the arsenic trioxide and the bags of specially prepared supplements for the *naughty* patients. Before I can finish, he starts to rant. "I just wanted them to pay attention to me. I am a doctor, they are stupid, especially Diane Morrissey. I did not want her to die. I just wanted her to pay attention. If she started to behave and listen to my advice, then I would have backed off on the arsenic. She would slowly have gotten her health back. I didn't give her enough to kill her, I swear!"

Looking at the uniformed officers, I say the classic words, "Get him out of here. Book him, murder in the first degree."

Chapter Thirty-Two

District Attorney Bates is waiting for us upon our arrival at the sheriff's office. She gets a quick rundown from me and goes off to see how many charges she can file on the doctor.

"I'll expect your complete report in the morning," she calls over her shoulder as she exits our office. Then stops, turns around and adds, "Great job, guys."

I look at Joseph. He lets out a sigh. "I know, I was there the whole time. I'll write the report."

After Dr. Andresen is booked, Gary and I go over to the jail. He still has not asked for an attorney. I want to know just where, and how, he acquired the arsenic trioxide. Possession is legal. However, lacing people's diet with it, is not.

A deflated Henri begins, "My brother worked in the lab of one of the gold mines here. He showed me the bottle. It was very old, and I liked it. He gave it to me. He said to be careful of the arsenic. It could kill someone. I knew that, I am a doctor after all."

"So, *doctor after all*, why did you give it to your patients?" Gary leans in toward him. "At what point did you think repeated doses would be safe?"

"I was so angry with those people; they didn't care about their health. I wanted to frighten them into listening to me. I was trying to save them."

"You were affronted those *stupid* people would not

follow your every word. You wanted to teach them a lesson." I snarl at him. I'd like to smash this guy's face into the table.

We leave before one of us gets out of line. He needs an attorney. More to the point, he needs to be put away. He is not right. But, that's the D.A.'s concern.

****

Unfortunately, following a meeting with the coroner and the D.A., it becomes apparent the doctor did not kill Diane Morrissey. The coroner states she would not have died that quickly, from the amount of arsenic he had been giving her. Something she ingested, the morning of her death, killed her very quickly. Brent, the fire captain, said she seemed to be her normal self when he left her. Yet within an hour, she was dead.

Now I need to finish interviewing Louise. Gary and I head straight to her house. She answers the door. "Why are you back? I told my husband about your visit. He couldn't understand why you were talking with me about Diane. What is going on?"

"Mrs. Davis," I say slowly. "Diane Morrissey was murdered."

She clasps a hand to her mouth. "No, oh no. Who would want to kill her? How, why?" She stops. "Why are you talking with me? You don't think I did it. Do you?" Louise steps back, looks past us toward the street. "Come in. You can't just stand there. People will start to wonder. Come inside."

We do, and she closes the door with a hard shove. I have her sit down and explain to her, "This is a homicide investigation and I must advise you of your Miranda rights."

"Do I *need* an attorney?" she asks.

"Only you know the answer to that question, ma'am. I would like to ask you a few more questions. If at any point you feel the need for legal representations, I will stop."

Louise blinks and says, "I did *not* kill her. Go ahead ask what you want."

"Tell me about the morning of her death. When you picked her up, what happened? Tell me anything she may have said."

"I got to her house about eight-thirty or so. Her nosy neighbor, that Howell woman was there. She was always at Diane's. I think she was a *groupie* for Diane. We had to be at the park by nine, for the fire department thing, so we left. We got to the park just before nine."

"Did she have anything on her mind, say anything out of the ordinary?" I probe.

"No, Diane seemed fine. She had not been feeling well for some time, but she was up for the drill at the park. It was a thing we enjoyed together. The firemen would scold us for giggling about our injuries. They would be stern 'This is serious ladies.' We didn't care. They needed victims, and so we were happy to be their victims."

"How was Mrs. Morrissey by the end of the drill?"

"She seemed pretty good. I wanted to take her home, but she said she was going to run the park's exercise course and then call Donald to take her to lunch."

"Did Mrs. Howell stay at the Morrissey's house when you two left?"

"No. She went back across the street to her place. She is such the pest. I don't know why, but she is just downright nasty to me. I never did anything to her."

"Louise, do you have a key to the Morrissey's house?" Gary steps in.

"No. Why would I?"

"Mrs. Davis, where were you at noon the day before the fire drill?"

'Oh, jeeze, I don't know. Wait, no, I was home. Diane had to be at the art gallery. She was on the board there. Why? What does that have to do with any of this? Before you ask, I was alone at home."

"Last question, and this is important. You told us you left the park to go meet a realtor about selling your house."

"Yes, I did." She looks puzzled.

"It is important we confirm the time you met the realtor and how long you were together."

Louise reels off the name of the fire captain's wife and tells us they were together for over an hour. The realtor took photos of the inside of the residence for the listing. That's why it took so long. I give Gary a look and he excuses himself. He will be calling the fire captain's wife. Is she the only realtor in this berg?

After Gary goes outside, I enlighten Louise with the news that Dr. Andresen has been arrested and explain to her exactly what he has been doing to his patients. It will be all over town by morning, so no problem in telling her. At first, she is in denial over her beloved Henri being involved in something so dastardly, but she settles down and then gets frightened.

"Did he poison me too?"

I tell her about the two files.

"He told me he would get Diane's attention about her lifestyle, but I didn't take it as a threat. He would have poisoned me too. Me, who brought him so many patients. He is a monster. Did he kill Diane?"

"No, we don't think so. He made her sick but not enough to kill her."

Gary comes back in the house and confirms with a subtle nod Louise was with the realtor for the time specified. We leave the now befuddled Mrs. Davis. She is not alone; we are befuddled also. Nevertheless, she is not out of the woods yet.

"Should you have told her not to leave town without notifying you or something like that?" Gary asks. "Not that I'm questioning your judgment or…"

I cut him off. "No, that's okay. Never hesitate to question me. I just don't feel she did it. Besides, we know where she will be in Vegas."

"Yeah, I sort of agree with you. She didn't react as if she had anything to hide. None of the suspects did, did they?"

"No, damn it, they didn't."

Chapter Thirty-Three

In the evening, my wife and I unwind from our day. She had a good day and was even able to work on her paintings, in between patients. I can't get any time between suspects, too many of them.

"What's next, my love?" she asks. "Everyone except Dr. Morrissey has holes in their stories somewhere. I thought he was the *sure* thing at first. But you do have a real homicide."

"You got me into this so help me figure it out, Pumpkin." I smile at her and take a sip of wine.

"I like Louise for it, personally. She's not out of it yet, right?" asks my wife.

"No, she's not. She picked up Diane that morning and left her at the park. It is still possible she had access to the Morrissey's computer the day before. She has no one to verify her whereabouts that afternoon. She says she was 'home alone'. The fire captain was possibly the last person to see Diane alive, but I ruled him out. He wouldn't want to lose a good *victim* for his disaster drills."

"Stop it! That's not funny," she scolds.

"Hey, I'm just trying to work through the players here. You know I like Brent. In fact, why don't we invite them over soon? I enjoyed talking with him. You liked her. Probably any evening will work, since we know firemen are almost always off duty."

"You can't fool me, Robert; you want to ask him more questions about that morning, don't you?" Damn…can't fool her.

"Well, if he's here, enjoying my liquid refreshment, why not?"

"You are incorrigible. Part of your charm," says my biggest fan.

Since 'Captain Brent' was the last to see Diane alive, he just may have some tidbit of information to offer. Happens a lot in cases. A person thinks something isn't important or just doesn't remember it, until their memory is jarred by the investigator. Besides, now I am at a loss as to my next step. I have checked and double-checked all my facts. I want to exhume Diane's body and have a complete autopsy done. I think the D.A. will go along with it now. Probably Dr. Morrissey will also. Working on getting the exhumation order will be tomorrow morning's priority.

Tonight, I am going to try to put it all aside and cuddle up with my ladylove. Later, after dinner, we sit outside and enjoy what will be our next to last night in this house. It has been a special place for us, our first home together, the beginning of our lives together. Good memories here. One more day and we move. There is nothing left to do. My personal planner has everything all packed, labeled, and ready for the movers.

Then my cell phone rings.

"No, not now. Give me one quiet night." I beseech the heavens.

P.K. looks at the caller ID. "It's Joseph, honey."

"Joseph, this had better be good," I snarl.

"It is boss. Remember Harold, the grandfather of Mathew, you know the kid who ran off to Vegas?"

"Yes, I sure do. What happened? You sound happy. Did he come home?"

The big guy is as excited as I have ever heard him.

"No, much better. Mathew has sent a letter to the family with pictures. He is a lead dancer in one of the shows in Las Vegas. He even sent tickets and backstage passes for the family to come and see him. I guess he is a big deal. He said he wanted to be in a major show before he told the family. To prove he had made something of his life. You should hear the shouting around the Rez. Everybody is coming over to the family and sharing their happiness. It's cool, Bob. You two ought to come out. Grandpa wants to thank you."

"For what, Joseph. I didn't actually *do* anything."

"Yes, you did. Grandpa says you gave him hope. Hope Mathew would be all right. I told him you called your friend down there in Las Vegas and he said he would check on the kid. Grandpa says that made the difference. He knew Mathew would be all right. He said to me, 'You are an old soul who also was once a shaman. He felt you to be powerful and Mathew would be okay.' Honestly, that's what Grandpa told me."

I cannot answer. I have no response. I have thought about Mathew, a lot, but that was it.

"Let's go," says my bat-eared wife, who hears everything. "For Grandpa."

We go to the reservation and it is pandemonium. Old, young, and in-between are all at Grandpa's house. There is barely room to move. The old man hugs both of us. He is one happy senior citizen. Ten years have dropped from his face since the last time I saw him. He has tears of joy in his ancient eyes.

"Joseph tells me you do not believe you did this. My son, listen to me. You are wiser than you are aware; your soul has centuries of elders guiding you.

"The Great Spirit sent you to Elko and to Joseph. He will be your warrior and your student. He will carry on when you leave. Do not look worried." He places a weathered hand on me and one on P.K. "I do not mean anytime soon. However, you will move on to even greater things in this world. But first, you two must come to Las Vegas and share in this joy with our family."

With tears in her eyes, my wife says, "Of course. We would be honored."

I am trying to absorb all the things he just told me.

Joseph shoves a glass into my hand. "Here, you need this."

Chapter Thirty-Four

The next morning, I stop off at the district attorney's, on my way to my office. As I walk in, she looks up and says, "Yes, I agree it is time for an autopsy."

"Thank you, but how do you know that's why I'm here?"

She smiles. "After reviewing the facts on Doctor Andresen's case, it is apparent he didn't kill Mrs. Morrissey. He helped maybe, by weakening her, but he did not administer enough arsenic to kill her as quickly as she died."

I just look at her. I spread out both hands as if to say, *And you came to this conclusion because...?*

"Okay," she blurts out. "I called a toxicologist. I went to college with her, and we've kept in contact. She agrees with you. Something else had to have caused such a rapid death."

"I'll be in Las Vegas next week, and I can tell Dr. Morrissey what we've found out. He is probably ready to agree to the exhumation."

"That would be easier. Getting a court order, against his will, would take time."

My, my, that was easy.

When I arrive at my office, I see Joseph has already placed his leave request on my desk for Thursday and Friday of next week. This is when the family will be going to see Mathew. I will ask the undersheriff for time off, but I will also be working at least one day. The day I approach Dr. Morrissey concerning the exhumation.

"I want to go, too," whines Gary.

"Sorry, bud, you're on call all next week."

"Not fair."

"Yeah, yeah, life never is." I am such an understanding boss.

Next, I see Undersheriff George and fill him in.

"I think you should go see Dr. Morrissey right away. I know you're moving tomorrow. So why don't you and your wife take the next week off and go to Vegas on Monday. Get the doctor to agree to the exhumation, have him sign the papers, and fax them to the D.A. Then enjoy the time off. You've been sweating bullets over this case. With any luck, the lab may have some answers by the time you're back. Can't do anything else until then."

I look at George, and for once, do not say anything but, "thank you."

I take stock: Move into a new house on Friday. Saturday and Sunday to settle in, and Monday, head to Vegas for a week off (except for obtaining the exhumation order). See a show where I know one of the entertainers. Backstage passes, as I remember. Hanging around with everyone backstage will be different.

I better call my wife and tell her now. Waiting until tonight will not do.

"Are you serious? Move tomorrow and then leave on Monday for a week. The house will still be in turmoil. Oh hell, why not? I scheduled the time off for the move anyway. The turmoil will still be here when we get back. I'll get some clothes set out now, so we won't have to look for them on Sunday. See you tonight, my love. Don't forget, Jane and Brent are coming over."

"Tonight?" I forgot, and I was the one who pushed it. I wanted to talk to Brent again.

"Yes, dear, tonight."

Things are moving quickly. Sometimes, when trying to solve a case it's a good sign, if nothing gets lost in the flurry of activity.

After we have dinner, my little marvel actually cooked dinner on the night before we move, Brent and I settle in the packed-up living room, adult beverage in hand, to talk. The dutiful cop's wife keeps Jane occupied elsewhere. What an asset P.K. is. She knows what I want to do and covers me.

I get Brent around to the morning of Diane Morrissey's death. He's no fool. He knows I am still looking for some clue as to exactly what happened that morning.

"Bob, I can't think of anything more than I have already told you. She was fine when I left. She even had a couple of containers of drinks. She said she would be just fine."

"What containers?" I'm sitting bolt upright now, leaning toward Brent. "There weren't any around the table where she left her phone."

"*I don't know.*" Brent stammers, "I saw she had two plastic cups with lids. Looked like she was ready to do her exercises. I didn't see anything wrong." He is pushing back in his chair as if to distance himself from me.

"What did the cups look like? Starbucks or

something like that?"

I settle back, I don't want him to get paranoid. These cups are news to me. This is what I was hoping he would come up with, something not yet recalled. Therefore, you need to keep talking with witnesses; they will eventually mention things not important to them at first.

"No, Tupperware kind of large plastic cups, with lids. I'm sorry I didn't even think of them. Are they important?"

"If I can find them. And I just may already have them. Thank you, Brent. I apologize for snapping, but this is the kind of information I've been looking for."

"No problem. You say you may have them?"

"I have a bag of trash from the park. It is in our evidence locker, but not sorted yet. With any luck they will be in the bag."

"Wow, Bob, you're not thinking poison, are you?"

"Between you and me, yes, but it is only a theory at this point. So..."

"Yeah, I know, you said *nothing*. Poison? Who? Oh yeah, you can't say, I know."

Chapter Thirty-Five

The movers are at the house the next morning before I leave for the office.

Thank you, Charlie.

P.K. seems to have it all organized. George's wife, Elaine, has come over to keep her company. I walk outside and run into Charlie and his wife walking up the driveway.

"What are you doing here?" I say as I give them hugs. "Thanks again for the movers. Much appreciated."

"It was the only way to keep you fighting crime. Otherwise, you'd be wasting your time doing manual labor. I know how much you hate that." Laughing, he slaps my back.

I look in front of the moving van and see Charlie's motorhome.

"You still got that? You hate it. Or maybe you don't now?"

"I got sort of used to driving it and you know, it's not too awful. Parking is a bitch but aside from that I'm having fun," he sheepishly admits.

Mrs. Charlie says, "Honest, it was his decision. The deal was we would sell it after the tour of the country. *He* has decided to keep it. Now I have two houses to clean." She grumbles good-naturedly.

"You toddle on and go serve the citizens of the

county; we'll make sure all is properly handled on this end," orders Charlie.

This is going to be a show, P. K., Elaine, and Mr. and Mrs. Charlie. The poor movers won't get a break. I gladly go to work.

Once there, I get the bag of trash from the evidence locker. I commandeer the conference room and get my troops assembled.

"I wondered when we would get to this crap," says Joseph. "What brought this on?"

I tell them what the fire captain said, about the two cups Mrs. Morrissey had at the park. We spread a plastic sheet onto the table and start to take out the contents of the bag. Of course, we are wearing gloves while pawing through the trash. Buzz is videotaping it all.

There *are* two plastic drink cups with snap-on lids. One is near the top of the bag and the other is farther down. In between are a lot of bloody looking bandages, tape, and other paraphernalia from the fire exercise, we are presuming. Brent told me they had *victims* spread all over the park area. So not all the waste materials went into the dumpster. Some of the participants took them off wherever they were and placed the mess into the trashcans near them.

For all the bloody wrappings in here, I hope the firemen were able to save some of their victims.

I take the two cups and place each of them into evidence bags. The one from the lower part of the bag had a *'D'* written on the lid with what looked like a sharpie pen. The other cup, from near the top, had no markings. Both contained some dried green residue. There is nothing else of immediate interest in the bag of trash, just some coffee cups, water bottles, and more bandages. I have Gary take the plastic cups to the lab to see what they can find—any fingerprints and hopefully determine what the green stuff is. Joseph and I put everything else back into the big evidence bag and return it to the evidence locker.

The wily Indian looks at me and slyly says, "You know, boss, we should all go over and check out your new house. Make sure the movers are doing it right." I think my man is looking to get out of working, after the fun of pawing through the trash.

"Good idea," I say. "Wait for Gary to get back and we'll go."

Buzz shouts, "Let's take the Batmobile." He loves that van.

Why not. It's a *big sky* type of day. Huge white puffy clouds and the sun's rays are warming up the land. Who wants to work indoors?

As we pull up to the new house, the moving van is already unloading. There are three men, typical husky, hands on, workers. Elaine and my wife are inside.

"I knew you couldn't keep away," declares my happy girl. She is so excited with the house.

The guys start checking out the place. "Where are Mr. and Mrs. Charlie?"

"This is just the first load, so they are waiting at the old house," P.K. answers.

As two of the movers are bringing in a piece of furniture, Gary is just walking into the living room. I notice his head jerk imperceptibly. He causally eases up and pulls me to one side.

"What, do you need a bathroom? It's okay take your pick, the water is turned on."

In a subdued voice, he says, "No, that guy, the one with the sunglasses on his head, he has a warrant outstanding."

"Oh, Gary, for the love of…not now. What's it for? Traffic ticket?"

"No. Assault with a deadly weapon. He beat the hell out of his ex-wife. I got the case when you were in Vegas. We couldn't locate him. That's him. I recognize him from his driver's license photo."

"You are sure?"

"Positive."

"Get Joseph. I'll get the girls out of the way."

The two movers are heading outside for more furniture. The third one is already outside. I gather up P.K. and Elaine.

"Ladies, I will ask you two to go to the master bedroom and lock the door. I will tell you when you can come out. Now, please."

Being good cop's wives, they do as requested, no questions. I manage not to see the…*I do not believe you are doing this on our moving day,* look from P.K.

Yeah, I know, that is how I feel too. Our big day, our new house, and I can't get away from work. That's the life of a cop, always on duty.

Well, I did say it was too nice a day to work indoors, so we will work outdoors, at my new house.

Gary and Joseph are at the front door. I tell Buzz to stay inside. Gary will arrest the man, Joseph will back him up, and I will keep the other movers at bay. The three of us walk up to the movers as they are carrying a sofa. The one we want is carrying the back. Gary tells them to stop and put the sofa down. As the man complies Gary says, "Put your hands behind your back.

We have a warrant for your arrest."

The man tries to move but Joseph puts his huge hand on the guy's shoulder. "Don't move, asshole, or you are going to the ground."

Gary snaps the cuffs on the fugitive.

The other movers appear to be in shock. They just stand there, not sure what to do next. The driver is the supervisor. "We just hired him as a casual laborer today. He's not a regular. I'll call the boss and we will get more help to finish. We don't know him."

I radio for one of our patrol cars to come and take the arrestee to booking. I go back in the house and call to the ladies. They come out.

"So, which one did you bust?" asks Elaine. "The one with the beady eyes, I'll bet. I didn't like him from the start."

P.K. looks out the front window as the arrestee is placed into a patrol car. "They all had beady eyes but his were the beadiest."

"The beadiest? Indeed. Where did you get that from?" I laugh.

P.K. gently puts her arms around me. I look down into her beautiful eyes; there is a hint of a tear. I kiss it away. She gives me a firm hug, then straightens up and says, "Officer, would you go back to work before you arrest the whole moving crew. I'd like to get this done today."

Cop's wives, gotta love 'em. Anyone else would be in a panic by now. Not these gals. Take it in stride. Well, not actually.

They say a silent prayer every time we walk out our door—that we will walk back in—when our shift is over.

Chapter Thirty-Six

Having made this part of town safer, we head back to the office. Gary will follow up with his arrest report and Joseph and I will get on with our cases. I check with the lab on the cups. There's some clear fingerprints, and the techs are comparing them to prints we have on file. Nothing on the green substance yet.

The district attorney has filed numerous charges against Dr. Andresen. I guess he is on the verge of a nervous breakdown thinking he may have killed someone. *Maybe he needs a good doctor*.

I decide to investigate the office manager, Jeanie, and check out her local history. She does have a condo in town, still in her name. I head over to the area. Very nice place. Attractively landscaped, clubhouse with a swimming pool, *very nice place*. Her name is on the mailbox. The manager's office is open, so I stop in and casually ask about her.

"I understand Jeanie has moved to Las Vegas. Will her place be up for sale?" I am so clever.

"No, I doubt it. Her partner is still living there," the woman informs me. "Anna tells me Jeanie will be back before long. The Vegas job is just to get the dentist set up. She and Anna are too close to be separated for long."

I thank the woman for her time and start to leave.

"We do have another unit that will be available

soon, if you're interested."

Thinking quickly, I say, "Where is it located in relation to the pool?"

"Oh, it's on the far side of the complex. Give me your number and I'll call you if something closer comes up."

"That's all right. I'll check back." I then beat a hasty retreat.

Well, well. Jeanie has a *partner* and she is screwing the dentist. Anna! That was the name on Jeanie's desk with the note—*check with Anna Re: $*

Jeanie, you have moved yourself up the *suspect* list. I was just considering you as an opportunist but now…Hmmm? We *will* chat more next week.

The lab manager calls and tells me they have identified Diane Morrissey's fingerprints, on both cups. There are other prints, but they haven't been able to identify them yet. All prints appear to be that of women, he says. They are analyzing the green residue.

Now it is getting interesting. How much interaction was there between all these people? I'm looking forward to a weekend of getting the house in shape and not worrying about the damned case. I hope.

I come home to the new house after work, and it is all neat and tidy. That's my wife. Well, with help from Elaine and Mrs. Charlie. I can't imagine Charlie was anything but a pain.

Charlie greets me from my favorite chair.

"About time you got here. I've been cracking the whip on these women to get everything in order, so we can all go to dinner. Here, sit down and have a couple fingers of Crown Royal."

My chair. My Crown. The nerve. Well, since he

did pay for the movers, I guess I can give him some slack. "Hang on, Charlie, I'll be right back." I go looking for my wife.

I find her with the other ladies putting the finishing touches on our guest room. P.K. comes over and gives me a big kiss. "I just love this place. Come let me give you a tour."

"Can we start in the master bedroom?" I ask with a grin.

"Stop it, we have company. Everyone has been wonderful. This was just the best day, with them being here to help."

I glance toward the family room. "Even Charlie?"

"Even Charlie. He has actually been a big help."

"By planting his ass in my chair and staying out of the way?"

"No, smarty, he was a help."

The two of us take a tour of the now fully furnished house. It looks just great. It is a Wow. There is nothing left to do. Even the pictures are hung on the walls. I thought that was going to be my job for the weekend. I point at one of the large paintings my personal artist had done.

"It looks great there. How did you guys get it up there?"

"Charlie hung it."

"Charlie, not that Charlie?" I say as I cock my head toward the family room.

"I can hear you, smart ass. Yes, that Charlie."

"Thank you, Charlie."

Chapter Thirty-Seven

The weekend goes well. Charlie and wife leave on Saturday, and my wife and I just *settle* into the new home. We have scheduled a housecleaner for the old place, so we are done with it. We will miss it; we made some great memories there.

Monday we are on a plane to Las Vegas, via good old Reno. (P.K. and I made some great memories in Reno, too.) We were able to make connections, so we arrive in Vegas late in the afternoon. We get our rental car, buckle our seat belts tight, and head into the wild and often bizarre commuter traffic of Las Vegas. I am always thankful for my defensive diving skills when we're here. We are on our way to Preston and Marie's house; they want to take us to dinner at one of their favorite places. Enjoyable way to start the week. *Assuming we don't all die in this traffic.*

Tomorrow, it will be back to work. I need to re-interview Dr. Morrissey and Jeanie. Maybe even talk to Dr. what's his name, Louise's husband. Yeah, I want to poke at him and see what I get. I call and make an appointment to see Dr. Morrissey tomorrow.

****

I park in the good doctor's parking lot. I trip up the stairs and as I open the door to the reception area, that nauseating odor of the dental world fills my senses again. God, how do they stand to work here? Even a smoky, beer-soaked bar room smells better.

The doctor is not much better mentally than he was the last time we met. He has no problem agreeing to the autopsy and signs the necessary paper work for the exhumation.

"Please tell me what you find. I just cannot get over this. Who would want to kill Diane?"

I tell him I will keep him up to date on the investigation.

Next on my list is Jeanie. Her emotional show was good the last time I was here, but now she is all business. I also observe she hasn't taken a lot of time with her hair and make-up. She has apparently decided it wasn't worth the effort.

"What can I do for you, Lieutenant?" she asks as if I were a customer.

"Does Anna know you are planning to sell your condo?" I ask casually.

Jeanie turns white. She just looks at me blankly.

"What, why, how did you?" She is flustered. "What are you talking about?"

"You told me you were going to sell the condo and move to Vegas," I calmly say.

"How do you know Anna?" she demands.

"Actually, I don't. We've never met."

"Why would you ask about her? Why are you asking about the condo? It's mine. I make the payments on time."

Boy did I hit a nerve. *Love it when that happens.*

"This is a murder investigation, remember? We check into everyone who knew Mrs. Morrissey. Why would you be distressed I know about the condominium? You told me yourself about it."

Her mind is racing. Good. Let's see where this goes.

"So how long have you and Anna been together?"

"What difference does that make? What I do in my private life is my business," she states indignantly.

"What was the deal with hitting on Donald? You were already in a relationship. Or are you just a social butterfly?" I am treading on shaky ground here, but I sense the need to push onward.

"Donald, Dr. Morrissey, just happened. It meant nothing. He just needed some female companionship. It's over. I told you that."

"So, are you planning on moving to Las Vegas or was that just a story to keep your job for now?"

Jeanie takes a deep breath, sits back, and says, "It's a good job. I had planned to stay in Elko with Anna. When Donald announced he wanted to move the practice to Las Vegas, I didn't know what to do. Yes, I need the job. He pays better than the other jerk dentists I've worked for. I thought I could stick it out for a while and get Anna to move here, too." She pauses. "Okay, the truth is I thought he might want to dump his wife and maybe I could take over the whole thing. Be his wife, but still have Anna. It was a crazy idea, but it looked doable at first. When Diane almost caught us, Donald said it was over. He wanted *her*. I didn't know what to do. I still don't."

"Maybe there is still a chance with him, now." I am certainly teetering on the edge.

"No. He said no more. He's in mourning. He thinks he killed her somehow. I don't know, it's crazy."

Leaving Jeanie to mull over her life choices, I find Louise's husband, Dr. Davis. He is between patients and is more than willing to give me a few minutes of his time. Outgoing and congenial, he is the opposite of Dr. Morrissey. He is tall, medium build with a handsome face. Louise has done well. Clear blue eyes that maintain contact when speaking to you. I like him already.

"Donald has told me about what happened to Diane. He is devastated to think he may have kept her from calling for help by trying to fix her phone. Is that true, he actually ruined her phone?"

"He didn't do it any good. But, if having a working cell phone would have made a difference in saving her life, we don't know yet," I say in my best *professional* tone. I can conjure up a damn good *professional* tone when needed.

"Well, doctor, how is the move sitting with you? Have you become a Vegas-ite yet?" I ask. Now I am being *friendly chatty*.

"It's different, that's for sure. When Donald first approached me, I was dubious. Still, I am getting used to this area. The shows, fancy dining and all, are fun. That will settle down after a while I'm sure. I am looking forward to the partnership being a good financial move. I majored in business administration in college before I went into dentistry."

"Business administration. That seems to be a good field. Why did you change, if you don't mind asking?"

Dr. Davis sighs. "My family. My dad and grandfather were dentists. I had to carry on the tradition. I was an only child and my folks were paying for college. Talk about pressure, the old guilt trip you know?"

"I'm sorry to hear that, doctor. Maybe you can put your business background to good use here, keeping an eye on the finances of the practice. I understand Dr. Morrissey isn't into the business side of the practice."

Think, doctor, I am giving you a hint here. I still remember Jeanie's notation-*check with Anna Re: $*

"Yeah, I've noticed. Jeanie certainly seems to be on the ball, but in business school, I was taught the old adage—Trust No One. *That's* still good advice."

"Sounds like good advice to me. How about you, doctor? Did you have much contact with Mrs. Morrissey?" I inquire.

"No. I'd met Diane, of course, but the four of us didn't hang out together. My wife, Louise, was good friends with her. They were into the marathons, you know. An occasional social function was about it for me. Are you sure she was murdered? It seems so senseless. I mean, Diane was one of the nicest ladies in our group. I hate to admit it, but the wives of the doctors are usually a snotty bunch. Honestly, most of the doctors are too. We tend to think too highly of ourselves."

"Well, doctor, your candor is refreshing I must say." I like this guy. Where did he come from?

I chat with him a little longer, and then I let him get on with his patients. I can't find anything of concern with him. If I lived in Vegas, he would be my dentist. I fax the exhumation papers to the D.A. and that is the end of my work for this week.

Back at Preston's house, I find the girls happily planning our week in *Sin City*. Between all the dinners and shows, we'll be getting the royal treatment. Friday night will be the casino showroom performance with

Mathew. It's one of the newest extravaganzas on the Las Vegas *Strip*, and receiving rave reviews. The Elko family and friends will be coming in on Thursday. Look out, Vegas, this is a wild bunch.

Sometimes things do turn out right.

Friday night Joseph calls and asks us to meet him in the lobby of the casino; he has our tickets. We arrive to find Joseph, along with all the family and friends, already in the lobby.

"Have you seen Mathew?" I ask.

"Yeah, he looks great. Kid's built muscles from all the workouts he does for the dancing. His head is screwed on right, too. Wait till you meet him, you'll see."

Soon an usher comes to escort our group into the enormous theater. We have seats down front, on one side of the stage. A little too close for my liking, but hey, I need to quit bitching. I am not in charge here. The kid is proud of his accomplishments and wants his family to share in the moment. That is what is important. The theatre quickly fills up; this is obviously a popular venue. The curtain rises, the music surrounds us, and the dancers converge on the stage.

"There he is, there he is!" shouts the excited Grandpa. The whole group starts to chant, "Mathew, Mathew."

It is a joy to watch them.

"He's amazing," shouts Marie. "Did he dance before, professionally?"

"As far as I know, just at pow-wows, but he is a talent. That's apparent," I say.

Joseph leans over and adds, "He was always kind of flashy at pow-wows. The elders got after him for not being *traditional*, but he was a show unto himself. I got a kick out of his moves. So did the younger ones."

Mathew is the featured dancer in several glitzy numbers. He is putting his all into it, you can tell from the sweat coming down his beaming face. Yeah, Grandpa, you can be proud. Who'd ah thunk? A troubled kid from an Elko reservation comes to Las Vegas, and not only stays out of trouble, but also gets into show business. He defied the odds. Joseph is correct, as usual. The kid is a good person at heart.

After the show, Mathew comes out, hugs and greets everyone. He tells us we can go backstage and meet the rest of the cast. Preston comments that the producers must truly like Mathew to allow this. Usually the *backstage thing* is restricted.

As we are meeting the other performers, the producer comes up to Grandpa. "I must tell you how hard your grandson has worked for this. He was in some small shows around town when I first saw him. He has a light about him. He almost shines when he dances. I had to hire him. I worked his butt off, I'll tell you that. He wanted to excel."

Grandpa is crying now and just holding the man's hand and shaking it.

"Thank you for saving him. I knew he was a good boy. He just needed a chance."

"Mathew kept saying he wanted to make his Grandpa proud. Sir, I can tell you that he has made me proud, too. He's a good example for the other youngsters in the cast. No drugs, just an occasional drink. I tell the other performers, *follow his example, he's going places.*"

Emotions go downhill from there, not a dry eye in

the house. We all join in a toast and a sip of pricy champagne, which the producer has graciously provided for the occasion. There is something appealing about this Vegas lifestyle.

The four of us say our congratulations and leave the partyers to their own devices. P.K. and Marie are still misty-eyed as we leave. Well, to be honest, Preston and I are too. Being a part of this heartwarming evening was special.

Chapter Thirty-Eight

What a terrific week. Always a great time with Marie and Preston, but Mathew's performance was the highlight. We catch up with some of the family at the airport. Grandpa is still beaming. He comes up to me, squeezes my shoulder, and just smiles. His kind old eyes say it all.

Back home in their new house, Mr. and Mrs. Carson slow down and relax. A busy but fun filled week behind them, they are ready to enjoy the rest of the weekend together, before it is back to the workweek. This is the best part of our life, *our time*, we savor it.

Monday comes too soon. The crime lab has left me a phone message and so has the district attorney. I call the lab first. The test results on the sippy cups are quite interesting.

Truly scary.

The cup with the *D* marked on it showed protein, and various vitamins and minerals in the residue. The unmarked cup had some of the above but, more important, was the potassium cyanide and ethylene glycol found in high concentrations. The lab supervisor said based on what he knew of Diane Morrissey's health and body weight, if she drank even part of this mixture, she would have died within an hour, maybe even less.

Terrifying. We are dealing with a serious killer here. This is not...*I want to make you sick.* This is...*I want you dead.*

"We were able to determine from the fingerprints we obtained, at least two other people handled the cups. Mrs. Morrissey's prints are the only ones we can identify."

"How about trying to find a match with the various prints we found in the Morrissey's house?" I ask.

"I was afraid you were going to go there. Do you know how many people were in that house? Yes, of course you do. I was hoping you had some suspects by now, so we wouldn't have to run *all* those prints."

I say nothing.

The lab person utters something unintelligible and then says, "Okay, Lieutenant, we'll get started right away."

"The County of Elko thanks you for your assistance," I say as I hang up.

Next, I call the D.A. The body has been exhumed and the coroner is conducting an autopsy. She tells me it will be several days before we have an initial report and longer before the final report is completed. I relay the lab findings on the cups to her.

I can hear her sharp intake of breath over the phone. "That had to be a horrible death. Poor lady. Where are you as far as narrowing down the suspects?"

I tell her I will get Louise's prints and go from there.

"How about the office manager, Jeanie, I think? She also seems to be a likely suspect."

"I don't think so. Don't get me wrong, I'm no fan of Jeanie's, but I don't get the right vibe off her.

Nevertheless, we'll add her fingerprints to our list and see what shows. She may surface later in another way." I do not elaborate further, purposely. Just to be a shit, that's all. Occasionally I do that. Too often, according to my wife.

I tell the D.A. I must go and hang up before she can pursue the matter further. I call Louise and ask her if she would mind coming to the office for a few minutes. She is somewhat taken aback but says she will come later in the day. I do not offer any reason for my request.

I tell the guys, "Inside, I don't feel Louise is the one. I can't explain why." Joseph and I have talked about this *feeling*s thing. Since I have been in Elko, I have been getting more *feelings* than ever before.

Joseph states, "You have this *feeling* because I'm a good influence." Then he laughs. "You're just maturing your instincts, boss."

"But you're younger than I am. What took me longer?"

"Slow learner." He smirks and walks away.

Gary is snickering. "You asked for that one, boss."

"Yeah, I did."

Then to break the good mood, in walks Louise. I tell her in order to complete our investigation I need to get the fingerprints of everyone associated with the case.

"Fingerprints? Why? What would my fingerprints have to do with this?" She seems baffled and confused, but not apprehensive. I have Gary take her prints and thank her for coming in. Still confused, she leaves. I take Louise's prints over to the lab straightaway.

"This might help reduce your work load," I say,

knowing better.

"And I suppose this person's prints were also in the house?" The supervisor asks cynically.

"Yeah, but I'm betting they're on the cups also."

"Thank you, Lieutenant. We'll be in touch."

Back at the office the D.A. calls and she sounds decidedly excited. "We have the preliminary results from Mrs. Morrissey's stomach content. Exactly what the lab found in the cup: cyanide and ethylene glycol. One of those cups was an instrument of murder. The one without the *D* marking, correct? The one you found near the top of the trash can?"

"Correct. Any other findings?"

"Only the presence of arsenic in her hair. That, we already knew. They're continuing the autopsy, but I think we have enough. There is no doubt she was murdered. This was in no way accidental."

I inform the D.A. I have Louise's fingerprints for comparison to the ones on the sippy cups.

"If hers are present, then there is still one other unidentified set, right? Any ideas who that might be?"

"No. Louise picked Diane up that morning and drove her to the park. These were not store-bought drinks. Someone made them. The cups are identical. What I can't figure out is the one with *D,* obviously for Diane, contained no poison and yet the unmarked one, did. Was there a lot of contents in her stomach, you know enough for two cups of the goop?"

"The coroner told me after Diane ingested the poisonous liquid it caused her to vomit. She aspirated on her own emesis while struggling to breathe. How horrible. All alone and choking to death." I can hear the emotion in the D.A.'s voice.

"That would explain why she had been crawling when we found her. As she was getting weaker, she was desperately trying to get to help. With what we know now, I guess there would have been no way to save her, even if we had arrived earlier. At least we got to her before the vultures."

I hear a soft gagging sound on the phone and the D.A. says, "I've got to go." She hangs up.

I don't feel so good either.

The guys stick their heads in my office. "Lunch time, Bob. How about chili from Juan's Café. You know you like it," Joseph teases.

Now I swallow hard. "No, uh, not now guys. I've got work to do."

They look at each other and then at me. Gary is about to say something when Joseph elbows him and says, "If you need anything gives us a call." He pushes Gary out and they leave.

Thanks Joseph, for noticing. I have no appetite right now.

I start to go over the scenario in my mind again. Who else is left that would want Diane to die so violently?

The phone rings. I jump. I was lost in thought.

"Carson," I snap, not meaning to.

"Lieutenant, this is Henry from the lab. Bad time?"

"No, no Henry. I'm sorry, I didn't mean to growl like that. I was lost in thought. What do you have?"

"The prints you brought in belonging to Louise Davis? They're a match to one of the sets on both cups. We are still working on the other set from the many at the Morrissey's house."

"Thank you, Henry. Appreciate the quick work."

I must talk with Louise, now. I call her home, no answer. I don't leave a voice message. She was going somewhere when she came in for her fingerprinting. Said she was going out anyway and decided to, *get it over with,* as she so politely put it. I call Gary at lunch.

"Yes, boss, want us to bring you back a bowl of chili?"

"No. Listen, did Mrs. Davis happen to mention where she was going while you were printing her?"

"Yes, she was going to have lunch at the *club* with friends." Gary draws out the club word. "Snotty bitch. I'm having gut wrenching chili and she's lunching at the *club*."

"I'm going to the *club* to see her. You guys stay on the air, in case I need you."

I drive over to the country club where the dentists and the rest of the elite of Elko congregate.

Chapter Thirty-Nine

On the terrace overlooking the golf course, I locate Louise at a table with four other women. I walk around the edge, so I am looking at her but from across the room. She sees me. I motion to her. She gets it and excuses herself from the table. I step out onto the cart path and out of sight of the women.

"Lieutenant, what are you doing? You could have met my friends."

"I didn't want to cause you any embarrassment, Mrs. Davis. I need to ask you an important question and time is of the essence right now. Remember, I have read you your rights. Did you and Diane have energy drinks on the morning you took her to the park?"

"She did. I didn't. She was going to run after the drill, I already told you. I had to go to the realtors. You checked on that, too. Why are you asking about the drinks?"

"Two identical plastic cups were found at the scene, Mrs. Davis. One of them had a D marked on it and the other had no markings. Your fingerprints are on both cups."

"Sure, I carried them to the car and held them while Diane got belted in. Then she held them while I drove to the park."

"Who made the drinks?" I am looking intently at her, trying to search her eyes for any reaction.

"That nosy neighbor, Mrs. Howell. She made one for each of us. The old witch. I knew she hated me for barging in on her friendship with Diane. I wouldn't drink mine. Heaven only knows what she would have put in *mine*. I just left it with Diane when I went to the realtors." Louise gets a horrified look on her face.

"No! Is that what killed poor Diane? Was it meant for *me*?" Louise turns pale and almost faints. I help her to a chair.

"At this point in the investigation, I do not have the answers to those questions. I will keep you advised." I leave her with her friends who have suddenly appeared and swarmed over her.

Back at my car, I call the guys. "Meet me at Mrs. Howell's house, now."

I come flying out of the golf club entrance and both are waiting.

"I didn't say to follow me here, but good job. Let's go code-three until we are within a block or so."

"We couldn't let you go to the *club* without back-up," drawls Gary.

We quickly make our way to Howell's neighborhood. Cutting our sirens, we ease onto her street and pull up to the front of her house. We all bail out, and I motion to Gary to cover the rear. As Joseph and I approach the front door, we hear a gunshot. It came from inside the house.

Gary is on the radio. "You guys all right? That came from the rear of the house."

"We're good. Keep the back covered," I answer.

The front door is locked. I look at Joseph. He steps back and kicks the door. It gives a little. On the second kick, it pops open. We enter, weapons drawn, senses on high alert.

"Mrs. Howell! Sheriff's office! Are you all right?"

As we start to move inside, I hear crying coming from the rear of the house. I move in that direction. Joseph is behind me. We carefully enter the living room. "Clear," I whisper. Then into the dining room. "Clear." I still hear the crying. It is getting louder. I bet I know where it is coming from. We ease into the hallway. The sound is coming from a room down the hall on the right side. It is the *Diane Morrissey trophy room*.

As I quietly approach the open doorway, I see Mrs. Howell, standing looking up at the ceiling. In the ceiling above her is a fresh hole. She is now sobbing uncontrollably. In her right hand is an old .32 caliber automatic pistol. She is pointing it upwards near her head.

With a soft voice I say, "Mrs. Howell, it's going to be all right. Put down the gun. No one needs to get hurt." Startled by my voice, she doesn't move.

I keep talking to her. I step in a little. Joseph passes around me.

Still crying Mrs. Howell wails, "I can't do anything right. I killed my best friend, not the evil one I wanted to kill, and then, I can't even kill myself."

I keep talking in a soft tone while Joseph slips up and grabs her hand holding the gun. He easily takes it away. She is ready to collapse now. We pull a chair up and ease her into it. I radio Gary and tell him to have the lab come out. I read Mrs. Howell her rights. She just nods her head that she understands. I ask her why she was going to shoot herself.

She takes a deep breath, wipes her eyes, and looks

at the hole in her ceiling. "Louise called me. She asked if I put anything in the drink, I made for her. She knew. How did she know? She said Diane drank it. I didn't know. The mixture was for Louise, not for Diane. Why did she drink it? She wasn't supposed to; it was for that monster *Louise.*" She spits out the word.

"Louise called you, when?"

"Just now, before you got here. When I realized what I'd done, I got my husband's old gun. I was going to kill myself. I pointed it at my head and missed. How could I miss my own head?" She starts to bawl like a baby.

We talk to her a while more, mainly just to let her calm down, before we take her to jail.

"You were in Diane's house a lot I guess?"

"Oh yes, she gave me a key. I would go over and straighten up before she got home so her husband would think she was keeping up the house. Diane was not a good housekeeper."

"Did you have access to her computer?"

She lowers her eyes, as a child caught doing something wrong.

"Yes, Diane would use it in front of me and I knew her passwords."

"You knew about her husband's affair?" I push.

"Yes, it was in the past and I hoped there would be no more."

"You saw Diane was searching arsenic poisoning?"

"Yes, she was worried why she was not getting any better and was always looking at the medical sites for answers."

"What did you think when you saw the arsenic searches?"

"I thought that Louise was somehow poisoning her. To keep Diane from upstaging her in the marathons. *That* is why I wanted to poison Louise!" She starts to sob again.

"Mrs. Howell, where did you get the cyanide and glycol you put in the drink you made for Louise?"

"The potassium cyanide was my husband's. He worked for the gold mines. He had all sort of chemicals around the garage. I added the antifreeze because I read it tasted sweet and then maybe Louise would drink all of it. I did my own web searches, you know."

"Mrs. Howell, you are under arrest for the murder of Diane Morrissey."

A patrol car arrives to take her off to booking.

I call the district attorney. "I did not see that coming," she says. "The last one I would have suspected. You said she loved Diane. She was not trying to kill Diane, yet she did. How tragic. Wonder how Louise feels?"

"Probably still shaking."

Mrs. Howell does not have to worry about cooking dinner tonight. The county will provide it. We secure the house after the crime lab finishes their work. The garage contained a plethora of toxic chemicals. The gold mine employees seem to have all brought home some bad stuff for unknown reasons. The environmental people will have to spend some time cleaning this place before anyone else comes in.

Mrs. Howell gives us the names of some relatives to notify. The District Attorney will take care of that duty, thankfully. How would you like to make that call? "Hi, your mother has just been arrested for murder."

It is quitting time. I go home to share my day's

adventure. "She had a gun and you just walked in and took it from her? She had already shot it. Did you have your vest on?"

"Actually, Joseph eased up on her from behind and grabbed her gun hand. She was so emotional, it was easy." Weak attempt on my part to defuse the forthcoming storm. Best I could come up with on short notice.

"Robert, Robert, Robert! Don't do these things. You know I am scared to death of something happening to you."

"Okay, honey, next time I'll just shoot the old lady and be done with it."

P.K. throws her arms around me, tightly. "All right, smartass. You handled it the best way. But you can't blame me for being upset."

Then we settle down and I fill her in on the rest of the day. "Wow, how did Louise react when she realized *she* was the target? She dodged a real bullet."

"I think she is going to join a convent," I joke. "Actually, I don't know how she is going to handle it. She will be making her own smoothie from now on, that's for sure."

A serious look crosses my wife's beautiful face. "So, the husband, Dr. Morrissey is innocent, except for being a louse. The office manager is clear, and Louise didn't do it. I never saw Mrs. Howell as *the one*. I knew the dentist was a slime ball, so I'm vindicated on that one. I kind of thought the office manager was good for some of it."

"Actually, my love, I think Jeanie will surface in the near future."

"How, why? What did she do?"

"Let's wait and see. Say a month or so." I just smile and take another sip.

"You're not going to tell me, are you?" She jumps on me and begins to tickle. That is my weakness. I am ticklish. Sadly, she is not. I fight her off.

"Truce, peace, come on, you know it's not fair. Just give me a month."

"Then I can tickle?" says the impish blonde, her hazel eyes glittering.

Later, after we go to bed and P.K. is fast asleep, my mind will not settle. I do this a lot during a heavy case, but usually when the case is finished, I can easily doze off.

Why not now? The case is over, damn it. I have gone over the details repeatedly in my head. Nothing missing, no other suspects, so what is wrong? Poor old, lonely Mrs. Howell did put the poisonous substances into the fatal beverage. Admits it. She wanted Louise out of the way, but Diane drank the potion. Tragic, but that finishes the matter. So why can't I accept this is the end? The 'i's' are dotted and the 't's' are crossed. Eventually I fall asleep, but waking up before the alarm, my brain is again thumping on me.

Leave me be! This is the end, what else could occur?

Chapter Forty

By morning, the news is all over town. I immediately call Dr. Morrissey in Las Vegas and tell him. Jerk or not he deserves to know the truth. He is grateful for the call; he had not heard yet. I refer the calls from the media to the D.A. I have a report to write.

My crew jumps in to help me with the mounds of paperwork that have accumulated in this case. We are all trying to sort it out in our minds.

"Mrs. Howell is probably going to be pled as *mentally incompetent,*" Gary offers. "Doctor Andresen will get *involuntary manslaughter* I bet."

"As well as lose his license, I hope," spouts Joseph. "I don't know if Louise has any religion, but she would do well to embrace one," he adds.

"You know the case was getting to all of us. Twists and turns, this suspect looked good, and then the next one pops up," Gary offers. "I'm glad to be done with it. Time to move on to normal stuff."

"Gary, somehow I don't feel we have seen the end of this case," I delicately say.

"I agree, boss," Joseph says. "I feel it is not over yet. I did not want to say anything, but since you already have, I will. It kept nagging me all night. I even got out of bed and went outside. Owl came and landed on a tree in the yard. I looked at him for answers. He just looked back and shook his head. Then he flew off. 'Big help you are,' I yelled at him."

"You guys and your *feelings.* Come on, no one is left. The murder is solved even if it wasn't a murder; it's over. There isn't anything left to solve," says an exasperated Gary.

Joseph and I just stare at each other, looking for answers.

The mood is broken when Undersheriff George calls and informs me the sheriff wants to see both of us, in his office. Great, now what? Did some other high-profile case pop up in the *city's* jurisdiction and we were volunteered to handle it, again?

The sheriff is all congratulations, handshakes, and smiles. He motions us to sit down. He goes to his desk. I take the seat closest to the door. I don't trust his smiles and happy talk. This cannot be good.

"Bob, I don't have to tell you how grateful I am George convinced you to join us."

Here it comes. I can make the door before George can stop me. Depending on what *it* is, he may fight me for the door. George looks clueless too.

"Lieutenant, I have worked on the budget and we can authorize you another detective position. The County Manager also agrees."

I look at George. He looks at the sheriff. The silence is deafening.

With raised eyebrows, the sheriff looks at me. "You *would* like another detective, wouldn't you, Lieutenant?"

No, sir, I would prefer to work nights, weekends, and all those long hours I have worked since I came here. I simply wouldn't know what to do with all that free time.

"Lieutenant?" The sheriff has a quizzical tone to his voice.

"Oh, yes, sir." I sure would. I am in shock. Usually you need to fight for paper and pens around here, "Yes, sir! I'm sorry; you just took me off guard."

The sheriff is laughing his ass off now. George too. I can tell he didn't know about it either.

The mood becomes relaxed, and we sit and talk for some time. The sheriff wants to know all about the Morrissey case. Finally, he hands me the authorization to hire a new detective and says personnel will post the position right away.

As we are walking away from the sheriff's office, George is muttering, "I used to beg on my knees for help, and he has already given you two detectives since you started."

"He likes me better. What can I say?"

George slugs me in the arm and goes to his office. I continue to mine.

I tell my crew we can add to our staff and ask if they have any suggestions for likely candidates.

"I think it's going to be the same old story. The old timers are happy with their shifts and free time." Joseph pauses and gets a far-away look in his eyes. "Free time. Gary, do you remember what that was like? I can't." Then he laughs. "Sorry, boss, I couldn't resist."

"He's probably right about the old timers not wanting to take this duty on, but I do know some of the newer guys who just might be interested," Gary says.

"No one from Long Beach. One of you is enough," I add.

"There aren't any. That's unfair, boss, I've been

good."

"For what?" offers his partner.

I continue to work on the Diane Morrissey case report. I can finish without interruption, for once.

Time to go home to the woman who worships the ground I walk on.

"You again? Weren't you here last night too? I could get used to this. You are kind of cute. Can I get you some wine?" I can always count on my wife to lighten the day.

"You know, lady, I wouldn't mind spending more time here. Maybe I will hire another detective, so I can come over here more often."

"Listen to you. Always full of it. You know what a lady wants to hear, but don't make promises you can't keep." She giggles and then makes *tickle* fingers.

I back away from the fingers. We embrace, deep kisses and hugs, no tickling.

"Seriously, the sheriff offered me the opportunity to hire another detective, immediately."

"You jumped on it, didn't you?"

"Absolutely I did. The position will be posted tomorrow."

"You mean I may actually wake up with someone next to me in the morning?"

"It hasn't been that bad. I do come home to change my underwear, sometimes."

"One of the few times I get to see you naked." She bats her eyes demurely.

I grab for her.

Chapter Forty-One

The ensuing days are full of meetings with the District Attorney, court appearances, and all the dull but necessary procedural stuff that goes with the prosecution of a case. In this case, it is two cases—Dr. Andresen and Mrs. Howell.

They both need to be in a secure mental facility as far as I'm concerned. She tried to kill someone she disliked and ended up killing her best friend. He thinks he is here to save the world by making his patients sick, in order to teach them a lesson. Sad.

The personnel department has completed the posting for the position of Detective I, for my unit. There is a seven-day filing period. Now it is wait, let personnel take their time sorting the applications, and then schedule the oral exams. The opening is not for their department, so why should they *hurry.*

Is my sarcasm showing? Sorry, but I have been in public service too long to expect anything else.

I'm getting anxious. It's now the seventh day of the posting. I call the personnel director to see how many, or if *any*, applications were received.

"I'm sorry, Lieutenant, but by personnel regulations we must wait until close of business today for all applications to be received. Tomorrow we will process whatever we have received. We will advise you of the results when we have completed the process."

I hate personnel people. They are so pompous.

By the *close of business today...* I want to grab him by his scrawny neck and...you get the picture. *Picture.* I could put his picture on one of our silhouette targets at the range. No. Just wait. Don't bring bad karma down on yourself. Bad Lieutenant! Bad Lieutenant!

We are finally having our *Housewarming Party* this weekend. The preparations help take my mind off this crap. P.K., Elaine, and to a begrudging extent, George and I have been getting things ready. Joseph and Gary's ladies have also jumped in and offered their help. That makes me feel good. We are a family.

I must admit, it will be fun. P.K.'s big brother and family are going to stay with us. Charlie and wife are coming. Preston and Marie will make it to the frozen north, as he calls Elko. Mike Harper from Reno P.D. and his still fiancée (a record for him) will also be here. Everyone we know from Elko, except persons I have arrested and the personnel director, are invited. The invitations were simple and explicit—No Gifts. Come and share in our happiness.

Beverage contributions will however be accepted. I know this group.

My personal party-planner is keeping my off-duty hours so busy I don't have time to brood and plot what sort of horrible grief and misery I want to cast upon the personnel director.

The following day after lunch, the aforementioned personnel director calls my office. Cautiously, I answer. I am expecting 'guess what, Lieutenant, we had a water leak in the office last night, and all the applications are ruined. Sorry.'

"Carson," I answer in my usual snarly professional

tone.

"Hi, Lieutenant. We finished with the applications for Detective I and we have five qualified candidates. I'm ready to schedule interviews. What would be your preference on a date?"

I poke myself in the eye. Yes, I am awake and not dreaming.

"That's great. As soon as possible, please."

Then I invite him to the housewarming.

Once my new best friend, the personnel director, contacts the candidates, he will set the appointments for some time next week. Works for me. My crew wants to know who is on the list. Several interested deputies have contacted them.

"That information cannot be made available at the present time, gentlemen. You know we have regulations regarding personnel matters," I say in my best *pretentious ass* voice.

"Don't give us that shit, Bob. Who is on the list?" Joseph pushes.

"Actually, I can't say. But incidentally, the e-mail from personnel is up on my computer, so don't look while I get another cup of coffee."

When I get back with my coffee, Gary and Joseph are discussing their choices, *if* they knew who was on the list, which of course they don't, since I can't tell them.

"Not a word, you guys. I mean it. No one, not even your significant others."

"About what, boss?" This smart remark comes from Gary.

"Could we have input if we had any preferences, in case some people we know might just be on the list?"

inquires the innocent-acting Joseph.

"Close the door," I order. They do so, and both sit down. I look out the window and then up at the ceiling, as if I am not paying any attention. They discuss their opinions of deputies they know, who *might* be on the list. When they are finished, I turn around and say, "What are you guys doing in here? Don't you have cases to work?"

They leave.

I ponder what I have not overheard. Two candidates meet both of their approval. One of the candidates seems not to please either of them, and they don't know much about the remaining two deputies. They are newer officers with whom my guys have had little interaction. Good information. I store it away.

The RSVPs for the housewarming are becoming scary. I'm glad I mentioned the beverage bringing to anyone who asked. I hope no one calls the cops on us. Oh yeah, they will be there too. At least some of them.

Someone needs to protect, while we *serve*. (What a terrible pun.)

We are ready for the party. If half of the people who responded come, we will exceed the occupancy limit of the premises. Fortunately, there is a large back yard and plenty of street in front. Yes, we did invite what neighbors we have. Always a wise move when planning a big, loud party.

Buzz knocks on my door. "Come in Buzz. You don't have to knock if it's open."

"Uh, excuse me, Bob, but I was wondering if…"

"Oh for Pete's sake, Buzz, out with it."

'I was wondering if I could bring a guest. You know, a woman."

"Buzz. Of course, you can. A lady friend? Certainly. Do we know her?"

"No. Becky works IT for one of the gold mines. We've been dating for a few weeks."

"P.K. and I look forward to meeting her."

Blushing, Buzz backs out of the office.

****

It's a great time of the year in Elko, warm, not stifling hot, but clear and sunny. At the appointed hour, the guests begin to arrive. A fun-filled afternoon goes well into the evening. Considering the number of adult beverages consumed, we are a well-behaved group. Patrol cars come and go but that's for food and coffee only. I purposely avoid looking at nametags in case one of the *candidates* comes by. Must be very proper about this.

Buzz arrives with his Becky. Everyone has been dying to see her. Not me. I'm just glad he has someone. Well, okay, to be honest, I'm curious too.

Gary is first to see them come into the house. "Wow." Gary is never a man of few words.

We all look up. Joseph says quietly, "The boy done good." Joseph *is* a man of few words. P.K. and I go to greet the couple. Buzz introduces us, nervously. Becky is obviously scared to death to meet all these people. (What right-thinking person wouldn't be nervous in a room full of cops?)

My wife, with her usual charm, takes over by giving Becky a hug and then introduces her to the rest of the guests. Everyone is in good humor, so Becky is relaxing.

She is an attractive woman, five-foot six or so, slim build, shoulder length black hair, and well dressed in tan sweater and dark brown tailored slacks. Cannot be a geek. No, something's wrong here. Don't they all have thick glasses and dress in rumpled wash and wear clothes and aren't particularly concerned about their appearance? Then we all start to chat and oh yeah, she is a geek. But a very charming one. I agree with Joseph; the boy done good.

Buzz, bless his digital heart, videotapes the event. He manages to do it with a beer in one hand and never spills a drop.

Everyone leaves by late evening and we are back to family. "This is a great house, you guys. You did well. I didn't think Elko had come this far," says P.K.'s brother.

"Hey, listen, Elko is great. Don't make fun of my town, brother dear." My wife is standing up for her new home. Wow, she does like it here. It's all in good humor. Finally, the ladies call it quits and go to bed. Bro and I sit up for a little longer.

"Bob, I know I've said it before, but I am so glad you and my sister got together. You two are so close, so in touch, I guess so *in love,* is the best description. When she went into the eye-making business, I had no idea it would change her life. Well, the future was you two finding each other. Here's to you *two*." He raises his glass.

"Yeah, who would have thought a bloody prosthetic eyeball would lead to romance." I raise my glass. "I am so blessed to have found her; she is everything I could have ever wanted in a partner for life."

Chapter Forty-Two

Wild weekend…it was great to see everyone in a relaxed atmosphere. Now back to work. The interviews for the Detective I position are set for tomorrow. I must say the good old personnel director made it happen. I wouldn't doubt the sheriff had some influence, but I will give the *director* his due.

Tuesday is here, and I am ready. I clear my mind of the opinions of my crew. I will consider them, after I meet the candidates. We have three scheduled interviews this morning and the remaining two after lunch. I have been in their shoes so many times in the past. I understand what they are going through and now I know what management also goes through. We must choose the best available person from five qualified candidates. A wrong decision can have dire consequences.

The personnel director will sit on the oral board, as will I, and I have asked an Elko City Police sergeant to join us. I've worked alongside him in the past. I like his style. He will have good input.

The victims—*candidates*—come and go for their scheduled interviews. Victim is how you feel when you are the person everyone on the board is scrutinizing. Every breath, every word is weighed and noted. You can't wait to get out of there. Then you think of all the different ways you should have answered the questions.

It's hell. But we do it and survive.

So did the five deputies. In fact, they all did a good job. Some were strong in one area while others did better with a different subject.

The personnel director looks at us as the final candidate leaves the room. "All look good to me. Gentlemen, I don't envy you. I will leave you to your deliberations. See me when you are done. I'll be waiting in my office." With that he leaves his notes on the table and exits the room.

The sergeant looks puzzled. "Our personnel guy stays with us to make sure we aren't pulling any funny stuff. Is he for real or what?"

"Would you believe a week ago I could have choked him out? He is leaving this basically up to me, with your approval of course. What's your opinion of the candidates?"

"One and three are my gut feelings. They seem to be the sincerest about becoming investigators, not just wanting to jump up the ladder. You know like some fire departments, where guys will take a bunch of courses and exams, then wind up the youngest battalion chief to never have so much as pissed on a real fire."

"Whoa, dude. Nice to know I'm not the only one who talks like that. I knew you were smart when we first met. I bet your picture is on their website along with mine."

"Mine was there first," he jokes.

"Down to business. One and three would be my choices, too." I look up toward the ceiling. "In fact, I think my crew would also approve of either one."

The sergeant looks at the ceiling. Not seeing anything he chuckles knowingly.

"Okay, which one will it be?"

We discuss the two men at length. We do have their applications and personnel files available. I think that's legal. Must be—or the personnel director would not have left them on the desk. We look through the files. No problems in either one's past. One is married and has small kids. The other is single, with the law enforcement curse of a divorce with alimony payments. No children. The divorce caused no problems with the department, such as complaints from the ex about non-payment or worse. So far, both look good.

The married guy has less time with the department than the other, but he served in the Army in Iraq. Had two tours over there. He has received top reviews from his supervisors: "even tempered", "doesn't over react", "always goes the extra mile", "thinks like a seasoned officer". *Not acting like a rookie,* is how I read the reviews. He saw enough turmoil while he was in the service. He knows how to keep his head on straight.

The single guy has no marks on his record, but his reviews are basically "does his job". The evaluations from the men's superiors show two different approaches toward the job and toward life. The single one has a little more bravado about himself. The married one is more down to earth. Sounds like I have made up my mind. I ask the sergeant.

"So, what are your thoughts?"

"If it were me, I would rather have the settled down family man instead of the cocky single one. I have enough of them already."

"Then we agree," I say smiling.

"Yeah, but don't let it go to your head. Your men still can't come into Elko City limits and run roughshod over everything."

"Hey, if your people would just pick up their end, we wouldn't have to."

We always joke this way. Our inter-department relations will only get better.

We complete our paper work and take it to the personnel director. He is waiting for us as promised. He looks at our submissions and takes his form, makes a couple of marks on it and says, "Thank you, gentlemen. I personally think you made the best choice. He is a great kid and will do you proud, Lieutenant."

"You know him?" I ask cautiously.

"No, just from his first interview when he was hired on. I was impressed with him then. He has served his country well and deserves this. Would you like to call him, Lieutenant, and let him know? I will notify the others."

"I would appreciate it. Yes, I'll call him as soon as I get to my desk."

I walk the sergeant to the door and thank him for coming.

"I'll be calling on you for our next interviews," he responds.

"You got it, be glad to."

I go to my office and tell the crew we have a new team member. They both are pleased.

"Ray is a cool guy," Joseph says. "I've dealt with him on several cases. He makes a good complete report, and I didn't have to bug him for details, like some of the other deputies."

"Yeah, I agree. I like him. He does write a good report and always tries to follow up when he can. Like I did when I was on patrol," Gary adds.

"Good to hear. I'm going to call him right now."

Deputy Raymond Melendez works graveyard shift, so I will try his home. A woman answers. I assume it is his wife.

"Hi, this is Lieutenant Carson from the Elko Sheriff's Office. Is Raymond Melendez in?"

I can hear a soft intake of breath. "Yes, yes, he is right here, Lieutenant."

An obviously-nervous male answers.

"Hello, this is Ray Melendez."

"Ray, this is Lieutenant Carson. We chatted earlier today."

"Yes sir," is the answer.

"Ray, are you still interested in joining my unit as a detective?"

I get a resounding, "YES, SIR!"

"Ray, you got the job, but my name is Bob, not sir, okay? We are kind of informal here." I'm chuckling.

"Thank you…Bob, I will do a good job for you. Thank you for choosing me. I truly wanted this."

"I'm sure you will, Ray. I need to check with the patrol lieutenant to see how soon he will allow you to move to our unit. He tends to get crabby about this stuff, but two weeks is the norm."

We talk for a bit more and then I let the happy man go celebrate with his happy wife, who I can hear squealing in the background. Feels good when you can be a part of something like this.

Chapter Forty-Three

The Patrol lieutenant is as expected, crabby about losing another of his *best men* to me. Gary was the last one. *Two weeks and not a day sooner,* is his response.

Now that the Morrissey case is resolved, it is back to business as normal, whatever that means. Of course, there will still be the trials for Mrs. Howell and Dr. Wacko, which will require me to testify.

But I do miss the *thrill of the hunt,* like when I'm on a big case. I just don't have a big case now and neither do the guys. They only have the routine cases: burglaries, assaults, bad checks, the boring stuff. Occasionally we will have an armed robbery, but nothing lately. Which is a blessing. The county is a relatively calm place.

Gary sums up our mutual thoughts. "Now that the Morrissey case is wrapped up, I feel a letdown. It kept the juices flowing, you know. This normal stuff is okay but not as challenging as a high-profile investigation."

"I agree, Gary." I add, "But, I have an uneasy feeling we are not completely done with the case. Can't put my finger on it though."

Joseph looks at me. "I have had the same thoughts."

"Oh bull, you two and your *feelings.* What else could happen? Everyone is dead or in jail. It's done. Let it go." Gary snorts.

The two weeks pass and our new crewmember, Ray Melendez, comes on board. The military background is apparent—ram-rod posture, fresh haircut, crisp clothes, and even polished shoes. His smile is ear to ear. He tries to keep a serious look on his face but can't quite do it. Hope he stays this happy. I spend some time with him and then give him the basic guidelines, "Here are my rules…I want the job done. We both know how it can get out there. If you run into a situation that could come back on you, I want to know immediately. No surprises. I'll back you one-hundred percent if you're right and if you step on your dick, I want to know before someone calls the sheriff. I can't help if I don't know first-hand. Understood?"

"Absolutely, Lieutenant."

"Good. Now, time to start working this crazy job." I call in Gary and Joseph.

"I want each of you to spend at least a week with Ray and show him how you work your cases. Let him follow you around and Ray, you ask questions. They've been doing this job for a while so don't be afraid to ask, *why do you do that?* Make them talk so you can follow their line of thinking. Realize they may not have one and are just shooting in the dark. We do that sometimes."

The guys chuckle.

"Joseph shoots in the dark because his owl sees better then," Gary says.

"You're just jealous because you don't have an owl." Joseph sniffs.

Ray starts to open his mouth.

"Don't ask," Gary says. "You'll find out soon enough."

I send the three on their way. Three! I have three detectives working for me. When I started this work, I thought I was in heaven when *I* became a detective. Now I have a small army. Yeah, and a county almost as big as Texas to cover.

The next morning I'm sitting at my desk staring out the window. My mind won't settle. My damned *sixth sense* is haunting me. I know we're finished with the Morrissey case, except for the upcoming hearings and trials, so why do I feel I haven't seen the end of this?

I hear a loud *cough* coming from behind me. Spinning my chair around, there is Undersheriff George. He's standing right in front of my desk.

"Earth to Bob. You in there?"

"Uh, sorry George. Lost in thought."

"Come on, out with it. What's bothering you? I saw you when you came into the building. You had a vacant stare on your face, like you weren't looking at anything. What's up?"

"I can't get the Morrissey case out of my mind. Something else is there. I don't know, George. I can't put my finger on it."

"Just like Joseph. Your *feelings,* as you two call them, are not settled. Correct? As I've told Joseph in the past, let it go. What is going to happen, will happen. Go about your business and wait and watch. Can't do anything else. Can you?" He gives me a smile and leaves the room.

Okay, he's right. If I don't know what is going on, then I need to 'get back to work'. Just as I'm settling into the volumes of paperwork that have piled up while I've been catching criminals, my phone rings. Oh good, a distraction. Not like it's going to be a big case. It will probably just put me further behind in the damned paper work. It is the desk officer at the front lobby. "Lieutenant, there is a David Scott here to see you. He is a bail bondsman from Las Vegas. I told him he should go to patrol, but he insists on seeing *you*."

"I'll be right there." I sigh.

Sitting in the lobby is a balding, portly man in his late 50's. He is wearing a mismatched sport coat and slacks, horrible tie, and a plaid shirt. He's a bail bondsman? Most of them look like a Hells Angel member. This guy looks more like a used car salesman. He stands up as I approach and extends his hand.

"Lieutenant Carson, a pleasure to meet you. I know your reputation," he says in a flat mid-western accent.

"I didn't know I had one," I reply as I shake his hand. Fair grip. Eyes have bags under them. "What can I do for you?"

"I am a bondsman from Oklahoma. I know it is procedure to go through the patrol division to serve a warrant, but if I could talk to you, and explain why I am here, it would be appreciated."

"The officer said you were from Vegas?"

"No. I am from Enid, Oklahoma. I know Greg, from the Enid Police Department. I understand you two have worked together in the past. He said I should talk to you. I did just come here from Las Vegas. My subject left Vegas and came here to Elko. He is wanted for armed robbery and homicide in Oklahoma. If I could just explain why I'm here, please?"

I escort him to my office. He sits down and begins his tale. "Lieutenant, I'm trying to find this man and convince him to turn himself in; he's my sister's son. I'm afraid he would rather die in a gun fight with the police than go to jail."

Crap! Just when I was complaining about things settling down. *Keep your big mouth shut, Carson.*

"You are here more as a family member than as a bail bondsman?"

"Yes. I don't care about the bond. It is mine. I wrote it for my sister, but it is more important that he goes to jail, not the morgue."

"Obviously he jumped bail?"

"Before the ink was dry. 'I promise you, Uncle Dave, I'll be in court,' he told me. I knew better."

"Was the bond for murder?"

"No, just for armed robbery. The murder came as he fled town. He stopped to hold up a liquor store on the outside of town. The clerk pulled a gun and Wayne shot him. Before the clerk died, he named Wayne as the shooter."

"Tough on you and your family."

"It only gets worse. He is good for at least five armed robberies between Oklahoma and Las Vegas. No one else was shot, thank heaven."

"How did you locate him? Wait, I know, *he called his mother*, your sister, right?"

"Yep, they all have to call mom. They always do. She is so afraid he will be shot when he is captured, she begged me to bring him back. I told her I could only try, no promises." His weary eyes look down at the floor.

"Has he always been in trouble?"

"Ever since he was twelve or thirteen. Smoking and drinking, at school of all places. He has been in and out of juvenile probation and adult jails ever since. It was just fighting, booze, and drugs until the robbery.

My sister is an enabler to be honest. I gave up trying to tell her."

"Do you know where he is now?"

"He told her he was going to Elko, Nevada. I have his cell phone number, if you can trace it?" He hands me a crumpled piece of paper.

I call Buzz and give him the number. He has the resources and the talent to find the phone.

I ask what type of vehicle Wayne's driving, but the uncle has no idea. My phone rings, and I can tell from the area code the call is from Oklahoma. Well, well, I bet it is my old buddy Greg, from the Enid PD. I call to the guys and have them take Mr. Scott and get a written statement. As they leave, I answer my phone.

"Greg! A heads-up would have been appreciated, buddy."

"Oh shit, is he there already? I just talked to him last night. He was in Las Vegas. He must have driven all night."

"He did. What can you tell me about all this? And how's Gloria?" Gloria is the ex-wife of William Weaton. Greg took it upon himself to check in on her after we told her about her hubby being a suspect in several brutal murders. Just a few hours before we arrived, she had put two bullet holes in her apartment door when Weaton tried to get in. Greg is *still looking after her*.

"Oh, Gloria is fine. We're doing great, but Wayne Jackson is big trouble. Has been since birth, I think. I just sent the Enid warrant for *murder and armed robbery* to your office. He is also probably good for some hold-ups between here and Vegas. Bob, I wouldn't mind seeing you again, but I don't think you'll be asking me to come and bring him back. Wayne Jackson will be making the trip back to Oklahoma in a pine box."

"That's what his uncle tells me. You also think Wayne is that far gone?"

"Oh yeah. The only one more screwed up than him is his mother. She should have been institutionalized years ago. But we don't do that, do we? At least, not as much as we should."

"Sadly, I agree with you. If society could hospitalize and help the troubled ones, then maybe we would have fewer *Wayne's*." I may or may not be politically correct with this view, but that's how I see it.

"Be careful, Bob. This guy hates cops and he hates jails. The uncle is okay, but remember, he's family. He was dumb enough to post the kid's bail. I think he's an enabler, just like good old Mom. David thinks he can reason with Wayne, but I doubt it."

I tell Greg I will keep him posted. This sounds like a SWAT operation to me. Cop hater with disturbed background. We will see how this goes.

I call Buzz to see what he is doing with the cell phone number. "It is coming toward Elko. Because we don't have a lot of cell towers, I can't pinpoint his location, like they do in the big cities. He is moving north, toward the center of town. That's the best I can do. But since there's only one main route from the south, that helps. I'll keep trying to get a triangulation on him."

I join my guys in the outer office and ask the uncle if he is aware of any crimes Wayne committed in Vegas while he was passing through there.

"With the shootings, robberies, and violence in that

town, I have no clue. That's a scary place for a mid-west guy like me." He shivers just thinking about it. "I did speak to a patrol sergeant. He had so many reports, half of them could have been Wayne."

I've been to both Vegas and Enid, Oklahoma. One night's crime reports from Las Vegas would overwhelm Enid for a year. Us too. Different world.

Chapter Forty-Four

All five of us—Joseph, Gary, Ray, Uncle David, and I—are sitting around mulling our next move. We have no idea what Wayne is driving. The warrant Greg sent us has a good booking photo of Wayne. Ugly little shit, I must say. Deep set haunted eyes, scraggly hair, and beard. You can almost feel the anger, hatred, and demons that trouble him, just by looking into his eyes.

"Ugh, gives me the creeps just looking at him," says the usually compassionate Joseph. "We have to find him quick. I'm surprised he has made it this far." Obviously, Joseph feels the evil surrounding this man and knows we need to stop him, soon. As always, I am paying close attention to what Joseph is sensing.

"Maybe he doesn't want to die. Maybe he is just trying to find a place where he fits in. I'm just saying," Gary opines.

"Man, I thought being with Katie was good for you, but you're going to the bleeding-heart side. Don't let that juvenile counseling stuff get in your head," Joseph scoffs at Gary.

I step in. "Maybe Gary is partially correct. Wayne may not be thinking of *Suicide by Cop,* but he must realize the only place he's going, if he's caught, is to prison. In any event, he is likely to go down hard. I don't think this will be a *show me your hands, drop your weapon, and the bad guy complies,* kind of arrest."

211

Everyone nods in agreement.

David Scott, the uncle, asks in a pleading voice, "Can I at least try to talk to him? I promised my sister I would try to keep him alive." He sighs and then looks at me with those distressed eyes. "In truth, I know he won't listen to me or anyone. But I did promise her I would try."

"If you cared about him, why did you write his bond?" I am being a little harsh here, but this guy is the reason law enforcement officers are eventually going to have to face Wayne and try to bring him in.

That does it for Uncle David. "I didn't want to. My sister begged and begged me. No other bondsman in town would write it. They knew better. I did too. He was just involved in a hold-up. I didn't think he would actually hurt anyone."

"He had a gun, dude. That's what happens when people play with guns. Someone eventually gets hurt," Joseph admonishes him.

"David, you said Wayne would rather die in a gun fight with the police than go to jail. What made you say that?" I ask.

"The Enid Police told me the store clerk, before he died, said Wayne screamed at him, '*Son-of-a-bitch, why did you pull a gun on me? I just wanted enough money to get the hell away from here and my damn mother. Now I'll be hunted down. I will not go back! They won't take me!*' "

"I think he means it," David adds.

Buzz calls and says the cell phone signal has stopped moving. He tells me it is on the west side of Elko, somewhere around the I-80 highway and the airport. "He had to have passed by our office. Damn. I wish we had better tracking ability." Buzz complains.

"He's stopping for gas, I'll bet," I shout. "Keep on it, Buzz. We're headed toward the airport and the freeway."

The guys are on their feet and headed toward the door.

"Vests! Put on your vests!" I yell. "David, do you have any weapons?"

"No, sir, I don't ever carry one."

I pat him down. He's clean. I trust no one.

"Okay, you can come with me, but do what I say! Deal?"

"Yes, sir. I will."

Shit! Wayne did drive right past our office. He had to. If he came from the south and went toward the airport and I-80, he passed right by us a couple of minutes ago. We're in the city's jurisdiction, but I don't even know what we are looking for, so I'm not saying anything on the radio yet. Marked units flooding the area would only set Wayne off and put the officers in danger. They wouldn't know who or what they are looking for. Hell, we don't either. Our *plain wrappers* will hopefully give us an edge.

We are now passing the airport. There is a gas station at the airport but it's not noticeable from the road, so I know he hasn't stopped there.

Buzz comes on the radio. "I've tracked your signal, Lieutenant. He's still north of you and not moving."

"There is a mini-mart with a gas station just across I-80 on the right," Joseph radios.

In a minute we are there.

"Joseph, take the far side. Come around the back so you can cut him off, if he's here. Gary, stay behind me and cover this end. I'll get closer and maybe David can spot Wayne." Ray is riding with Joseph.

My mind is on full alert. My eyes are darting everywhere, and my heart starts beating faster. I cruise slowly toward the gas pumps. There are three cars parked in front of the mini-mart and two cars at the pumps. The car at the first island has a male pumping gas. The third island has one unoccupied car.

"That's not him," David whispers, as we pass the first car.

I ease up closer to the unoccupied car. It has Nevada plates. I can see the license plate frames are from a Las Vegas dealer. If Wayne came from Vegas, he could have stolen the car. Sounds right to me. As I pull toward the store entrance, a male in his twenties comes out of the store and heads for the car. It's him. I don't need David to verify this. He looks just like his booking photo.

David excitedly declares, "That's Wayne."

Wayne is walking hastily toward his car.

"That's him. Move in!" I bark into my radio, as I swing my car in front of Wayne's to block it. Gary cuts behind the pumps and stops behind Wayne's car. Joseph pulls alongside the pumps to the left of Wayne.

David jumps out of my car. "Get back here!" I scream as I exit my side, weapon in hand. The stupid son of a bitch is putting my men and me in danger.

David heads toward Wayne. "Wayne, it's Uncle David. Let me help you for once," he pleads, desperation in his voice.

Turning toward David, Wayne reaches for an automatic pistol concealed under his shirt.

"Police! Drop the gun, Wayne! NOW!" I shout.

"Wayne, give it up, please for your own sake. I'll help you. Please stop this now!" David begs.

Wayne looks at David, but he continues to drag the gun from its hiding place.

"Drop the gun now! It's over, Wayne," I demand. "David, get the hell behind my car!"

David starts backing up. Now Wayne looks at me. Turning directly toward me, he raises his pistol. Three rapid shots ring out. Wayne's body jerks, his head ratchets back, and gradually he slumps down to the ground, gun hanging from his hand. I move in and kick the gun away from his writhing body. My crew has now swarmed in.

"Who shot?" I can barely breathe. The threat has been dissipated but my heart is still racing as I look at them.

"I did, Lieutenant. I could see his finger tighten on the trigger."

"Excellent response, Ray. Three rounds, shows your military training. Didn't empty the magazine, stopped when the target went down. *Thank you!*" I slap his shoulder. "Welcome to the unit."

David is still behind my car. "I'm so sorry, Lieutenant. I just thought...I don't know what I thought." Tears run down his face. "I guess I wanted him to shoot me, not one of you!"

He comes over and looks down at Wayne. He slowly sinks to his knees, into the blood pooling around his dying nephew.

"Wayne, I am so sorry. I didn't want it to be this way."

Wayne looks up at his uncle. Blood streams from his mouth, "Fuck you and the whole damn family." He tries to spit on David but loses consciousness.

I check his vitals. He is out of his misery. Whatever it was.

Chapter Forty-Five

All hell breaks out now. We immediately call an ambulance and the Elko PD. It is their jurisdiction, after all. Sirens begin wailing all over town. Here they come. The first patrol officer on the scene does a quick inspection of Wayne's body. Then the ambulance, fire department, and more Elko PD arrive, along with a couple of our county deputies, who are checking on the situation. The coroner is responding.

The sergeant who assisted me on Ray's oral exam board comes up. "Lieutenant, I thought we had an agreement that you would keep your men from running wild in my town." He looks at Ray. "Congratulations, Melendez, on your promotion. I can see the Lieutenant doesn't believe in easing you into the job. What is this all about, Bob?"

I fill him in.

The city must do a shooting inquiry report, per our agencies' agreements. We do theirs and they do ours. It is a good system. It is fair and impartial. Also looks much better to the public. Ray gives his weapon to the Elko investigator for the ballistics testing. He will get it back when they make the 'justified shooting' determination. He will be on paid leave for that period. The Elko sergeant assures me he will be cleared quickly. It is an obvious case of justifiable 'use of force'. The coroner and the district attorney will have to submit their findings to the Elko Police Chief and to our sheriff. I tell Ray to plan on a couple of days off.

He is noticeably upset. "I understand. But I just started and get sent home already? I know that's the way it has to be, but, I'm sorry, Lieutenant, it just, I was so pumped to be an investigator..." He fades, blinking his eyes as he looks away.

"You know how government procedures work." I give him a smile. "But since you are getting paid and still technically in training, I want you in the office. You just can't go out on any cases."

The distraught look leaves his face. "Thank you, Lieutenant."

Isn't this the shits. The man is a hero, saves my life, and gets a *time out* for it. This is unfortunately part of the job. It is for the greater good. Checks and balances.

Undersheriff George arrives and comes over to me. I give him a weak smile.

"Wasn't our plan for the day," I say. I point to Uncle David who is giving his statement to the detectives. I fill George in on the events that led up to the shooting.

"Sounds like this was the only way it was going to end. Better sooner than later," he says, placing his hand on my shoulder. "At least you knew what you were facing, rather than having some patrol officer stumble onto him."

I solemnly nod in agreement.

We give our statements to the detectives and hang around as the crime lab does their job. Then we all go back to the office. We have sent David off to a motel. We will see him tomorrow. I tell my team I am proud of them. "No one else fired. That was good. In some places, every officer on the scene would have emptied their weapons at the suspect. I was just starting to fire when Ray did. I could see Wayne's body twitch as it was hit and his gun lower as he fell. When the threat was over, I relaxed on the trigger. I guess it was the same for you guys."

"It was close, man," Joseph admits. "Too close. I was just pulling up, but man! Ray! You were there! He was out of the car before I had it stopped. It was over before I was even out. Damn."

A disgusted Gary says, "I was behind Wayne's car. I couldn't have gotten a shot off if I'd wanted to, because *Uncle David* was also in my line of fire."

I look at Ray. "Thank you again."

Okay, that was closer than even *I* realized. Yes, I would have probably hit Wayne, but would I have stopped him, or would *he* have gotten a shot off? Unnerving thoughts. I will have to clean this story up before I go home and tell my *beloved inquisitor* about my day.

"Damn Uncle David!" I growl. "I shouldn't have taken him."

"We needed him, boss," consoles my shaman. "He was the only one who could positively ID the suspect. Wayne had to be stopped, like George said, the sooner the better."

"He put us all in harm's way. You may be right, Joseph, but I'm going to have to chew on this for a while."

"For what it's worth, Bob, I'd have done the same. If we didn't find him right then, he would have been long gone," Gary says.

219

Ray quietly says, "I agree, Lieutenant. You had no choice. The uncle had to be there."

"Thanks, guys. I can't say I feel any better about it, but thank you all." Then in a more formal tone, "Now it's almost time for us to go home to our loved ones. Moreover, we all know they will not be pleased with today's answer to 'How was your day, dear?' We all face the *moment of truth* when these things occur." I continue, "I've certainly learned, the hard way, the sooner the whole story comes out, the easier it is on everyone. Since I haven't heard from my wife, I can only assume she has not heard about a shooting at a local gas station. Otherwise, I would have received a call inquiring if I had been involved. Not much gets past her. How about you guys, any calls?"

They all check their phones and shake their heads 'no'. Our spouses do not know yet. We get to be the first to tell them. That helps.

Chapter Forty-Six

Quitting time comes and now we all must go and face our fate. I leave first. As I pull up to my home, I see Esther's car (she's Joseph's lady), Katie's car (she's Gary's resident counselor), and another vehicle. The cars are parked in my driveway and in front of my house. I don't think this is a Tupperware party. Do they still have those? Momentarily I debate if I should go back to work. No, I need to see what's up. Big brave cop—not.

I walk in and I can tell from the chattering, everyone is in the family room. Decisions, decisions. Which way should I go? Straight to the master suite and hide or—?

"Robert. Come in here and join us ladies," calls out my wife.

Crap. Well, go see what's up.

I walk into the room and see the above-mentioned ladies and one more. She is in her early thirties, a nicely dressed, attractive young woman. Must be a Tupperware party. (Yeah, right.) I go over to P.K., give her a kiss and a smile.

"Hi, ladies. What's up?"

I can be shrewd in a pinch.

"Robert, you need to meet Jackie. She's Ray's wife. We all thought she should be welcomed into our little group. We decided to get together today, after work."

"Hi, Jackie, I am pleased to meet you. I can't tell you how happy I am to have Ray on our team," I say as I shake her proffered hand.

Boy am I glad to have him!

"Jackie's mom watches her two kids, so we thought we could all just hang out for a little while after work, until you guys got finished fighting crime. How was your day, honey?"

"Do the guys know all of you are here?" I ask, trying to be nonchalant, while ignoring my wife's question.

"They all left messages for the guys to come over here after work. I didn't call you, because I knew you'd be here anyway." The love of my life smiles sweetly at me.

The doorbell rings.

"Oh, good they're here," says Esther.

"I'll get it," I quickly say. I beat feet to the door. The ladies who live and die every time we go to work are all here, and we just had one of those days they fear. Maybe I can just leave with the guys and…No, we have to face the music. I open the door and Joseph and Ray are there. Gary is just pulling up.

"Did you know about this?" I ask.

"My wife left me a message to come over here because she was meeting everyone's wife. Does she know?" Ray whispers

"No, no one knows, yet," I say in a hushed tone.

Joseph just winces and says, "Jeeze, this won't be pretty."

Gary has joined us. "What's up? Katie left me a text to come over here. Everything okay?"

"They are here to welcome Jackie, Ray's wife, into the group. Nice, but they don't know about today," I mumble, still in a muted tone.

"We need a good story; how can we spin this? You know how it will go," Gary says.

I take a deep breath. "Gary, didn't you listen to me? No, we all know how it will go. No matter how we spin it, eventually the truth will come out. Then we will be in the doghouse, big time. No, we need to be men and go in and tell them exactly what happened. There is safety in numbers, and if we hang out here long enough, maybe it will cool off somewhat." Did I say all that?

"Yeah you're right, boss," Joseph says. "We all know better. The truth will prevail."

Poor Ray looks at me. "Jackie was so happy when I got detective. She said she wouldn't have to worry as much."

"We have all gone through this, Ray. The women who love us will worry every day, but because they love us, they will always be there for us. That's why we need to be there for them. That means being honest with them."

Did I just say that too? Yes, I did.

"P.K. handles the truth better than the B.S. Doesn't like it but can deal with it. I love her even more for that. Now, let's do this!"

We do a high-five and Gary cries out, "One for all and all for one. There were four musketeers you know, not just three." We all just look at him and shake our heads.

We go in to meet our fate.

The four mighty protectors of Truth, Justice, and the American Way, *slink* into the house…it was a pathetic sight.

The men come into the family room, hug, and kiss their respective loved ones.

"Hey what's going on?"

"Why are you all here? Party time?"

"Hi, honey, the kids here?"

"No, they're at Mom's. P.K. invited me over to meet the other ladies of your group. They are all so supportive. What a way to start your new career. This has been a perfect day."

Then there is awkward silence. The hugging and giggling have died down. Mostly because the men in the room are noticeably subdued.

The Inquisitor narrows those eyes and looks into my soul, as only she can do. "You never said how your day was, *Robert*. How *was* it?" She is on to us, she smells blood, and is going for the kill.

All eyes are on me now. Without hesitation I say, "Joseph, why don't *you* tell the girls how the day went?"

"Oh, no. Not me, Bob. You aren't going to put this on me." The big guy is backing up toward the wall.

Gary pipes up, "Well, not much happened. Ray saved the boss's life, that's all. He was great, you would have been so proud of him, Jackie."

The women erupt. All are speaking at once.

I stand up and yell over the din, "Please, I will explain. Please, settle down. Joseph, get back over here and sit down with Esther. She's not going to hurt you."

"Don't bet on that," says the lady administrator in a cold, professional tone.

I tell a somewhat edited version of the day's action. Before anyone has a chance to comment, I hastily add,

"The guys and I already discussed that the first thing we would do, when we got home, was to tell our loved ones about the day's events. We are aware of how hard it is emotionally on each of you. You just threw us off when we walked in on this party. Nevertheless, we all knew what we needed to do. Hey, we are just dumb men, we got flustered. There! That's what happened. I am so proud of having these men on my team. Jackie, yes you can be quite proud of your husband today. Everyone did their job. Now can we have something to drink? You ladies are ahead of us."

I think we may have saved ourselves to fight another day. Maybe. We make an evening of it. We order pizza and need more beer. I have only a limited stock on hand; tonight calls for more. After calling in the pizza order, I go for my keys. Never have I seen so many men willing to go to the store and pick up provisions.

"I'll go," Gary offers.

"No, boss, I will. I'll even buy," Joseph counters.

Even Ray is on his feet.

The women just look and laugh. Can't fool them.

"Look at the big, brave cops; no one wants to stay behind." Esther chuckles.

"Why don't you *all* go?" suggests my wife. "Then we girls can discuss the day's events."

"Somebody needs to stay behind and look out for us," I advise.

"Oh, no!" says my little artist, who is now the pack leader. "You *all* go. Go on! Don't just stand there looking pathetic." P.K. is laughing so hard she almost spills her drink.

We all go, as instructed.

"It's going to be fine," I tell the worried males. "P.K. will actually put it all in perspective for your gals. Trust me." I say a silent prayer I am right.

"Maybe your owl could visit them, Joseph, and let them know it was all justified," Gary suggests.

"Hey, he's hiding out in the trees. He is smarter than we are. Knows better than to get involved in this."

Ray asks, "So just what is this owl thing with you, Joseph? You haven't told me yet."

Joseph tells Ray about his owl while we're driving. I hope he doesn't want to go back to patrol after hearing *this* story.

"That is so incredible. I've heard about spirit animals. My family has talked about the *ancients* and their special powers."

"That's Joseph. He's an ancient," snickers Gary.

"Shut up. Your only special powers are being able to stay on a bar stool longer than most," Joseph responds.

This keeps on all the way to the grocery store, the pizza parlor, and back home. We all get in on it, good therapy.

We devour the pizza, drink a few beers, and relax. Good bonding time for the team; our companions are definitely part of the *team.*

After everyone leaves, P.K. and I are tucked in bed and cuddling together. I ask, "So, leader of the pack, how were the ladies after we left?"

"Actually, quite good about it all. They were so amused with you brave men falling all over yourselves, it lightened the mood a lot."

"Glad to be of service. How was Jackie?"

"She feels you are great guys, who will always

look after each other. I told her the *cops and robbers* mentality would always be there. But by being part of a unit, none of you are alone, like Ray was, while he was on patrol duty."

"She buy it?" I ask.

"Of course. When the *Alpha Female* speaks, the pack listens. You do." She smiles.

I turn off the light.

"Come here, Alpha Female."

Chapter Forty-Seven

The next morning, we must deal with Uncle Dave and send him on his way. He is still falling on his sword about his actions yesterday. Aside from the fact he put all of *us* in harm's way, *he* could also have been shot. He is lucky to be able to *drive* himself back to Enid, Oklahoma. His nephew will also be going back, in a coffin. Enid. Shit, I need to call Detective Gregory at the police department in Enid and tell him he will not have to travel to Elko to extradite Wayne.

"Greg. How's it going, bud?" I say casually.

"Bob, what happened? Were you able to take Wayne into custody?"

"In a manner of speaking. He is no longer a flight risk."

"He's dead, isn't he?"

"Yes. David tried to talk to him and only agitated him more. One of my men had to shoot when Wayne turned the gun toward me." I relay the whole story to him.

"So sorry you guys had to get involved in this mess. His mother is wacko, and the kid never had a chance at a normal life. At least no one else got hurt. I'll notify the mother."

I give him the name of the mortuary that will have the body, after the coroner is finished.

"To be honest, I was looking forward to coming

out there. Get a change of scenery. Maybe Gloria and I will take a vacation and drop in on you and your wife, if that's okay."

"Absolutely. We would enjoy seeing you and Gloria."

Always good to talk with Greg. Personally, I would like to relax a little also. The last few months have been hectic. I now have another detective on my staff, and I could use a little change of pace.

Wait. I forgot. Be careful what you ask for—you just might get it.

Aw, that's just an *old wives' tale*. Anyway, P.K. and I are planning a vacation in a couple of months, but still something different would be—stop it. Do not bring a curse down on yourself.

I begin to get my paper work up to date. The caseload is low now, so Ray is getting plenty of assistance from Gary and Joseph. He does not seem to need much. He's sharp. I made a good choice.

George calls. "Didn't forget the management meeting this afternoon, did you?"

"Uh, no, what time was it again?" I stumble.

George is laughing. "I thought so. You've been busy. One thirty in the conference room. See you there."

Thank you, George, I did forget. The meeting will be a couple of hours of boring stuff. At least I will be able to brag about my unit's activities. We have done quite well, if I say so myself.

The appointed hour arrives, and I go into the sheriff's conference room. It's typical for such a place—large, ugly table, many uncomfortable chairs placed around it, sterile. There are a couple old photos of the Ruby Mountains on the walls. Honestly, the Rubys are beautiful, but there are plenty of other scenic locations in the county. This is characteristic of government offices. Put in the necessary furniture and hang some appropriate pictures and done. Oh yes, do not ever think of changing it...ever.

George and the sheriff are already there. Soon the patrol, jail, and civil department heads will show up. After we are all present, I get to speak first, as my unit has made all the headlines. The other administrators are polite and even give me kudos for our accomplishments. They are seething underneath. *Jealous are they.*

The jail division does not want to make headlines and neither does the civil division. Patrol, yes, they would, but usually anything patrol does creates negative press. It's the nature of the game. I keep it short, well kind of short; I do have a lot of stuff to brag, er, report on. As expected, civil and jail have nothing much to report, thankfully, as any jail news is usually bad. The patrol Lieutenant, however, starts to bemoan his shrinking staff and lack of experienced deputies. Hey, I only took one from you this month.

He does have a legitimate bitch. He's lost some experienced deputies and not just to me. He's had retirements, transfers, and deputies who have gone on to larger agencies. He has replaced these officers, for the most part, but now he has a younger, less experienced staff.

"Hell, I have trouble just finding an officer with enough experience to be a training officer for the new ones."

The crafty old sheriff looks around the table at all

of us.

"Perhaps some of you could spare an officer for a week or two to help out patrol. Get these rookies off on the right foot."

He stops at me and lingers, then says, "Just a suggestion. We do have our citizens' safety to think about."

Bastard. I've always liked you, too. Sure, the unit does a good job, no, a great job and now because we have another detective, I should *lend one* for the cause? He has a point, but that doesn't make me feel any better about it. I just got Gary and Joseph meshing with Ray. It would harm my plans for Ray. He needs to get all the experience those two can give him.

Wait a minute. Let me think this over. No, I open my mouth before the brain has fully engaged.

"How about I work some shifts with your new troops?"

I actually heard myself say that.

Wide eyed, the patrol lieutenant sits upright, "You'd do that, Bob? I think it's a great idea." He looks cautiously at the sheriff.

The sheriff leans forward in his chair. "That's the stuff, it's what makes us the team we are. Thank you, Bob."

He looks at the others. "I don't expect the same of you, nothing personal, but you have all been here as long as me. Bob's the youngster of our group."

The jail commander offers a deputy and so does the civil guy. The sheriff is pleased, and the patrol lieutenant is not crabby, for once.

After the meeting, George walks me to my office. "You sure of this?" he says. "I'm not worried about you, but your wife is not going to be thrilled."

"George, you're just worried your wife is going to give you hell, when her best friend tells her about this new plan to put me back on the streets. Don't kid me," I tease.

"Yeah, well, there's that too," he acknowledges.

He makes a valid point. Somebody must tell my wife. I guess the somebody had better be me. And damn soon, if I want to live.

Hi, honey, I'm home. Guess what I get to do?

No, that is not going to work. Take her to her favorite restaurant? Nope, will not work either. Better to bite the bullet. Go home and sit down with a glass of wine. Oh yeah, get her one too.

I go home a little early. When my beloved comes in, I have a glass of wine ready for her. We kiss and hug as always. Then, even before the usual *how was your day, etc.*, my partner for life looks deep into my eyes and says, "So what's up, *Lieutenant?*" Damn, she is good! She can read me.

"Why do you ask, my dear?"

"I know you, Robert. Home early, wine poured, what do you *not* want to tell me?"

"I got off early and thought this would be nice for us."

"I call B.S., my love. I know you too well, don't I?" She lowers her head and bores deeper into me with those *eyes.*

I hand her a glass and we sit down as I tell her the truth, the whole truth, and nothing but the truth. I do kind of gloss over the fact I volunteered. Instead, I *imply* the sheriff *implied* I should volunteer. She takes it well. Much better than I thought she would.

"Okay, you should know what you're doing. You've had lots of experience. Just a few shifts aren't too awful, I guess. When do you start?"

"I don't know yet. The patrol lieutenant will look at his schedule and get back with me."

Later in the evening she gets a look on her lovely face. Like a light just came on.

"What *shift* will you be working?" she inquires.

I was hoping that question would not come yet.

"Graveyard is when the new deputies work. It's the slowest, much less happening." I sit back and wait.

"You didn't mention that fact did you, Robert?"

"Blame me?" I counter.

"No. I do understand. I don't like it, but that is when the rookies should be out. Take care of yourself. We've just found each other, remember?"

Gently I take her in my arms and whisper, "And ever so grateful we did."

It was a good night after all.

Chapter Forty-Eight

In the morning, I tell my crew what I am going to do, *for them*.

"I'm going to work a few shifts on patrol to help out training the new deputies. It was either me or one of you," I announce.

Joseph almost spills his coffee. "Boss, why you? I mean I don't want to do it, but why you?"

"I volunteered so none of you would have to work patrol."

I smile magnanimously.

"What's the catch?" The shrewd Indian questions the wily white man.

"Actually none. It will give me a change of pace. Then you guys can work together on your own."

"What's P.K. think about it?" Gary asks.

"Not thrilled but understanding."

"Oh shit! *Understanding*. That is a heavy, deep place. What is this going to cost you?" Joseph shudders.

"Nothing, it's fine. She thinks I might get in less trouble on the street than I have in investigations."

"She has a point. You have stirred things up here, that's for sure," laughs Joseph. "I can't remember the last time patrol had to shoot anyone."

Ray speaks up. "Actually, graveyard patrol in the county is usually pretty tame, except for the usual bar fights and domestics, but that's about it."

"Do you even *have* a uniform?" inquires Gary.

"I thought my old Santa Clara County one would do. It looks pretty close to ours."

"You're kidding, right Bob?"

"Yes, I do have a brand-new official Elko County uniform. We all have to have one for ceremonies and I'll have you know, it still fits."

"Oh sure, make us feel bad," Joseph says as he pats his belly. "What is it, two months old?"

"Three actually."

Now, since everyone's sartorial concerns are satisfied, I get my schedule in order. I will be working eleven p.m. to seven a.m., and hope I get home in time to kiss my wife before she goes to her office. Of course, I will want to talk to my people each morning when they come in at eight. Keep informed and then get some sleep. I will want a little time in the evening with P.K. before I go back to work. There will be two days off each week. Monday and Tuesday. I can keep tabs on the office.

Whose bright idea was this anyway?

Tomorrow night will be my first shift. Of course, I will not be able to get any sleep before, so I will just tough it out the first night. Done it many times in the past. I was a little younger then. How many years has it been? Not that many, I'm sure.

The time has come, and I put on my uniform for the first time. Feels good I must say. Always felt proud in whatever uniform I have worn. I pick up my gun belt. Same one I wore last time I was in uniform. Soft, pliable old leather. At least I won't have the rookies' squeaking leather. That's embarrassing, squeak, squeak, every step you take. Humm, belt's a little tight. I seem to need an extra notch or two. Okay, I got that handled, feels secure now. I snap my weapon into the holster, and I'm ready.

"Wow, baby, come here," says my wife as I step in front of her. "You could give me a ticket anytime." She gives me the *look*. "Be careful, hotshot; remember who is waiting for you."

Love that girl.

Shortly thereafter, I walk into the patrol unit's briefing room. It's been awhile since I walked into one of these. A few folding chairs and a bulletin board on the wall. That's all you need. Oh, and deputies too. They are straggling in, coffee in hand.

The patrol lieutenant is here. "I just had to come and thank you for doing this, Bob. The sergeant will do the briefing, but I wanted to be here."

"Go to bed, old man," I joke. "It's past your bedtime."

"Yeah, it is. Have a good night."

Sergeant Andrews, who is handling the briefing, is feeling a little awkward but handles it well. I make it easy on him.

"Keep your eye on me, Sarge, it's been awhile. Point me in the right direction and I should be fine."

I am introduced to Deputy Boyer, a new hire. He has finished his P.O.S.T. (Peace Officer Standards and Training) Academy and has just completed his mandatory six months of working at the jail. This is his first night on the streets.

He is so nervous he is about to shit himself. First night on patrol and who is his FTO (Field Training Officer)—a lieutenant. Cannot say I blame him.

I extend my hand and tell him we are going to have

a good night.

"Uh, yes sir, Lieutenant." He hesitates as he shakes my hand.

"Call me Bob. We're partners. What's your first name?"

"Carl, sir."

"Carl, knock off the *sir*. We are going to be together for eight hours. Let's be casual, okay?" I smile.

"Okay, Bob," He replies.

Carl is about six feet tall and has a good strong build. Sandy hair, well-tanned, looks like a farm boy. I, on the other hand, am five foot ten, thinning hair, and medium build. The gun belt holds in the beer-belly.

Sergeant Andrews continues the graveyard shift briefing for the night—wanted persons known to be in the area, any happenings to watch out for on our beats, the usual stuff. With the briefing finished, Carl and I go to the parking lot and find our assigned car.

This is where the fun begins. Carl has not been in an Elko Sheriff's patrol car yet. He went to the regional police academy and then straight from there, to duty in the jail. For complete disclosure, I have not been in an Elko Sheriff's patrol car yet either. My assigned unit is an unmarked SUV. My last patrol vehicle was in Santa Clara County. They are pretty much the same, but each patrol car has its own uniqueness. Not to mention *a couple of years* have passed and the technology has changed. Where is Buzz when I need him?

Therefore, Carl and I sit in the parking lot and play with the lights, siren, switches, and everything else we can find. We are jumping in and out to see what switch did what. Satisfied, we are now prepared to go on patrol. I look in the rear-view mirror and see the patrol lieutenant and Sergeant Andrews laughing like hell.

I jump out. "You jerks were just watching and enjoying all this. You could have offered help!"

"You were doing just fine, Bob. Have a good night," the lieutenant says, in a rude, high-pitched, singsong kind of voice. What a jackass. Well, I guess he has the right, seeing as I have stolen two good officers from him.

As we begin patrolling our assigned beat, I ask Carl how familiar he is with this area of the county.

"Very familiar. I grew up here. My family has owned a ranch here for years."

"Good, knowing the area is always a help. You didn't want to stay in ranching?"

"No. I've wanted to be a police officer since I was little. The ranch is okay, but I wanted to be out in the world. I enlisted in the army and did a tour in Afghanistan. After that, ranch work is kind of boring."

"Having done a combat tour myself, I can understand you feeling that way. You'll find police work is somewhere in-between," I comment.

Before the briefing, Sergeant Andrews showed me Carl's file. Good grades in junior college and excelled at the police academy. Second highest in his class. "That's why I assigned him to you, Lieutenant. I knew you would give him a good start."

It is a weeknight, so our radio is rather quiet. Most of the citizens are in bed; they have to work tomorrow. We do the initial sweep of our beat area, then start checking on businesses that could be targets for a burglary. Nothing is going on so far. I can show Carl how we old-timers did patrol checks on businesses. We would shine our spotlights all around the property, buildings, and on the roof. I caught a burglar on the roof of a closed business once. Having already pulled off the cover, he was trying to squeeze into a ventilation duct. He was half in and half out when I hit him with the light. He panicked and got himself stuck in the shaft. We had to roust the firefighters out of bed to bring their ladders and pull him out. I thoroughly enjoyed it. They did not. Hey, what is the difference— kitten in a tree or burglar on a roof? Same principle. Oh yeah, no front-page photo for saving a burglar. The Police Department did get a brief back page story about capturing the would-be thief.

I am driving—too soon for Carl. The night air is beginning to get nippy. The change of seasons this California boy hates has arrived. There is no snow or ice yet, just the cold mountain wind buffeting the town.

I decide to make some traffic stops, more for his benefit than to meet a quota. Oh yes, *quotas.* There are such things, despite what some administrators of law enforcement agencies say to the press. Patrol officers are sometimes told, two per shift average, or it may be implied, *you are on the public streets for eight hours, statistically you will encounter at least X number of violations in that period.*

There is truth to the fact you *will* see traffic violations every shift. Stopping the driver is a positive step for public safety. My personal *attitude* toward a traffic stop reflects the offender's *attitude.* I start out low key and almost conversational in tone. If the driver maintains the same low-keyed attitude as mine, the *enforcement contact* will go well. Minor violators may even receive a warning and be sent on their way. An adversarial response from the driver will usually result in not only a citation for the observed offense, but, if the driver's attitude escalates to the yelling and swearing form of reaction, then the ticket may take more than one page to list all the violations I find. *It is all about attitude.*

Carl is doing well. He asks sensible questions and is alert. What I do notice, quite favorably, is that he is not a typical gung-ho rookie. For some of them you need a choke chain. Because of his combat experience, he keeps his eyes open, checks the surroundings, and is aware of what is going on around us. He's going to be good at this job.

The vehicle stops go well. I let him watch and listen while I do the first few stops. Then, after the citizen has driven off, we discuss the finer points of the stop. Carl is getting it. Next, I have him approach the vehicle and make the initial contact with the driver. I cover the passenger side of the car, listening and watching. Poor guy is nervous as hell. So was I, my first time taking the lead. He does very well, and I tell him so. I make suggestions and he listens. The traffic is getting lighter as the hours pass. We do some more driving around our assigned area. Carl shows me his folks' ranch. He wants me to drive up the road to the house. I explain to him that two a.m. in the morning is *not* a good time to be in a person's front yard with a police car. You could scare someone.

Then we get our first radio call—bar fight. *These are never good.* We are the closest unit, and any back-up unit will be at least twenty minutes or more behind us. If the bar is calling for us, there must be a problem they cannot handle. Our arrival is always bad for business.

We pull up to the joint. It is a joint. It is not one of the finer watering holes of the county. I have been here in the past, when I needed to do a follow up on some case I was working. The place is a real dive. The owner is an ass, but he looks like a ferret, squinty beady eyes, pointy little nose, and skinny neck. He's at the door motioning us to hurry. Approaching the door, we can hear breaking glass, furniture, etc.

"So, what's going on, Joe?" I inquire calmly.

The owner is visibly agitated. He has a black eye and a bloody hand wrapped in a dirty bar towel.

"Those bastards are wrecking the place. My bouncer is lying inside, on the floor. We couldn't control them."

Our closest back-up is still over ten minutes away.

"Let's take a look," I say to Carl. He appears calm. That is a good sign. He scored high in defensive tactics, I remember from scanning his academy grades.

We enter the bar and see two gentlemen, probably ranch hands, going tooth and nail at each other. They are both over six feet and at least two hundred pounds apiece. The place is a mess. Anything that was breakable is broken. They are rolling around on the floor banging away at each other.

"Knock it off! Sheriff's Office!" I yell as loud as I can.

Unbelievably, they stop fighting. One lays back on the floor into the broken glass and blood and the other man sits up.

"Damn you, Joe." He curses at the owner. "Why'd you call the cops? We was just having us some fun."

Carl and I handcuff them quickly before they get a second wind. One of them is so big it takes two pairs of cuffs to get his arms behind his back.

The bouncer is now conscious and only has a bloody nose. We call for an ambulance. The combatants have minor cuts, nothing too serious looking. Just a couple of country boys having fun. The bar is destroyed. Joe, the owner, is furious at them and says it will cost a fortune to replace everything.

One of the fighters says, "Joe, the crap you had in here was falling apart anyway. It's time you got some new stuff. We done ya a favor."

I had to hold Joe back from attacking the man.

Our back-up units finally arrive. I have them take the *good old boys* to jail. Assault and battery charges will do for a start. Carl and I will do the report. We clear off a place at the bar, and Carl fills out the paper work. Always let the rookies do the report. They still think it's fun. The bouncer and Joe both refuse the ambulance. Their choice. Finally, we finish the report and as we are leaving, I stop at the door and casually say to Joe, "You know, you really ought to keep this place cleaner. What would the health department say?" I cannot quite hear his response as we walk outside.

We get back into our patrol unit and Carl is laughing nervously, "I can't believe they stopped when you told them to. I thought we were going to have a battle."

"So did I. You never know about drunks. They may try to kill you or like in this case, behave. You were great, Carl. Calm and controlled. Good job."

He smiles and says bashfully, "I was scared. I was ready to go at it with them, but man, they were big! Do you think we could have taken them?"

"Yes. Don't underestimate the tasers. Unless those

bad guys were strung out on drugs, we should have been okay. The tasers would have given us the edge we needed, hopefully. No guarantees, you know." I give him a half-hearted smile.

"I understand."

"Now, are you getting hungry? We are allowed a meal break you know."

"Yeah, I am. I couldn't eat any dinner; I was too nervous."

"Understandable. Let's go to the old all-night coffee shop close to the highway. Used to be a popular place for the long-haul truckers, until the corporations put in the huge truck stops with fuel, food, motel, hookers, and just about anything else the drivers wanted."

Carl says the local kids still go to the coffee shop at night.

"I like the food. Been there at all hours. We can be called out at any time, you know," I add.

"How many detectives do you have?"

"Four counting myself. The newest one just came from patrol, so that's why I'm here. To help out your boss."

"I'm sorry you had to do this, Bob. But I'm glad to have you for an FTO. You're more interesting than some of the instructors at the academy."

"You don't have to feel sorry for me. I'm enjoying this. Being back in uniform and prowling around the county for a change. Not to sound like an academy instructor, but patrol is the heart of law enforcement. This is where we have our biggest influence on the public. Joe, the bar owner, notwithstanding."

Carl snickers. "He's always been an ass."

"Oh, you know Joe. Been there before?"

"Sure, all of us kids have. He was sloppy about ID's. Probably still is. Maybe we should visit him after he gets the place back in shape." Carl chuckles.

"Good idea. The kids won't be happy, but bar checks are good tools."

Pulling into the parking lot, I can't help but wonder, how many times in past years have I walked into an all-night diner? Given the odd hours I would hit one, usually in uniform; the customers would be sparse, a few revelers getting some food after a late night out, travelers, and some working stiffs like me. Someone who had to be out at this ungodly hour.

Scanning the place to take stock of the clientele, we sit down at the counter. The waitress comes over, coffee pot in hand. I like her. Fifties, I would guess, heavy on the make-up, medium height and build, clean uniform. A face that has seen it all but still pleasant, and like a bartender listens to the whines and stories of the customers. I like the late-night servers; they see all, know all. She looks at me, her brow furrows, her eyes narrow. "Who did you piss off? In uniform and on patrol? Must have been a doozy."

"No, I volunteered for this. Patrol needed a little help with the new troops."

"Well at least you got Carl. He's always been a good kid. Congratulations, son, glad you got back from Afghanistan in one piece," she says as she pours our coffee.

There is a table of young people, in their twenties I would say, in the back of the place. I hear one of them shout, "Carl, you son-of-a-gun. You made it." Everyone from the table comes over to us. They are high-fiving

Carl and slapping him on the back. He introduces me, and they all assure me Carl is a good person.

After they go back to their table, I say to Carl, "You're known around here and respected. That will serve you well in the future. Great start."

We had no more action; the rest of the shift was calm.

At seven a.m., we are pulling into the parking lot.

"See you tonight?" I ask.

"Oh, yes sir, I mean Bob. I didn't want to ask if you were coming back or not."

"You're stuck with me, son, if that's all right with you?"

"Absolutely. See you tonight." He extends his hand. "Thank you for making my first night a good one." I feel my throat tighten as I shake his hand.

I go home and regale my spouse with the night's adventures. "Good boy, no gun play, I'm proud of you." After calling and checking with my crew at the office, I go to bed. I am tired but still wired. Eventually, I fall asleep. Around five o'clock, my wife's lips on mine, I wake up. I slept. Now I am awake. I throw my arms around her.

"Come here. I missed you."

"I missed you," says the sexy ocularist.

Do not want to bore you with details, but eventually we had some dinner and I went back to work.

Didn't I just leave?

Chapter Forty-Nine

We are patrolling on a weeknight again, so it's quiet, for the most part. We back up another sheriff's unit at a domestic dispute. We resolve the problem by getting the male to find another place to spend the night.

After Carl and I leave the location, we start back toward our patrol area or *beat*. I decide we should check on good old Joe's place. Yep, the lights are on and he's open for business. There are a couple of cars in the lot. Hope it's not the same boys from last night. We then cruise around the back roads that run to the various ranches and farms. All is quiet. Good.

On the way back toward the more populated area, we are again approaching Joe's bar. I don't know what the business's name actually is. There is just a blinking half-lit neon sign proudly proclaiming, *BAR*. We are about two hundred yards from the bar when an older pick-up truck darts out of the parking lot and swerves onto the highway in front of us. The truck is not maintaining his travel lane. In other words, wandering from side to side. It is also exceeding the posted speed limit. In fact, it is pulling away at a rapid rate of speed.

I smash down the gas pedal, flip on the roof top red-blue lights, and begin pursuit. The truck has already gotten a lead on me. It will soon be heading into the business district. The road makes a slight right bend and

I can't see the truck's tail lights any more. I am flat out and there is no sign of the truck. The road ahead is dark except for the lights from the all-night diner. Their glow spills onto the roadway and I can see a dense cloud of dust in front of me. I hit the brakes and start rapidly slowing. Suddenly, there is a resounding thump across the front of our patrol car. The car convulses violently, something slaps against the windshield, hard, which causes a definite cracking noise to echo through the unit. The final sound is a tremendous metallic ripping noise crossing the roof. Shit, what just happened!

I slide to a complete stop. Nothing in sight. Carl and I get out on our respective sides. There is an eerie quiet. I see nothing but the dust swirling around us. My emergency lights are not on. Damn. I know I had them on. Ducking into the car, I can see the indicator lights on the switch panel are lit. Stepping back out, I look at the roof. No lights. In fact, no light bar. Nothing but a lot of black marks running toward the rear of the car.

Carl is pointing toward the road behind us. "Look. What did we hit?"

Our light bar is lying about twenty feet behind our car. Farther behind our patrol car is a large black power cable, hanging about a foot off the pavement. Son-of-a-bitch. Where did that come from?

We advise dispatch of our situation. Our unit is disabled. Other units are dispatched to our area. Carl is putting out flares to stop any traffic. Looking at the cable, it is still attached to the pole near the diner. On the opposite side of the road, it doesn't appear to be attached to anything. Using my flashlight, I follow the cable into the open field. Sure enough, there is the faint glow of tail lights. As I get closer, I can see the pick-up has struck a pole. It's about fifty feet from the road. He must have lost control and careened into the field. Unfortunately, he found the pole.

Truck hits pole, pole breaks, cable drops onto road and along we come…Wham!

I radio Carl to stay and handle traffic control, while I check on the driver of the truck. I approach the pick-up truck and see the driver's door is still closed. There is a male slumped against the collapsed steering wheel. The windshield is cracked, and his head is covered in blood. No seat belt, of course.

He is dead. After an impact like that, without seatbelts or airbags, if he *had* survived, he would have been a vegetable.

Our other units arrive and then the ambulance. No need for the ambulance. The coroner is called. We determine the offending cable is for telephone, not electricity. Then the telephone company repair crew shows up. They are the only happy people here. Overtime for them.

I can now take stock of the damage to our patrol car. Cracked headlights, shattered grill and the scary part—a large crack through our windshield, at eye level. Thank you, Lord, the windshield and its corner posts did their jobs. If that cable had continued through the window we could have been decapitated. Carl is taking this all quite well. "Never saw this in Afghanistan."

The patrol sergeant comes toward me as clean up continues. "Ahh, Lieutenant, you know we try to take better care of our cars than this." He then laughs. "Glad you two are all right. Especially Carl. We need him on patrol. Well, you too, Bob. FTOs are scarce."

"Your compassion overwhelms me, Sarge. Am I going to be put on desk duty, I hope?"

"No such luck. Go get another car and get back to work." He snarls, in a joking way.

A tow truck is sent for our poor car. Sarge says he will drive us to get another car, but first we need to go across the road and have breakfast. He insists. "You are cutting into my regular schedule. My guys know better than to interrupt my mealtime. Makes me cranky."

We go to the diner, and the same waitress as last night comes rushing up. "You two okay? I saw what happened. I was so relieved when you all got out of the car. I was on the phone to 911 because I heard some car screeching and then all I saw was a cloud of dirt. Then you must have hit the cable because the phone went dead. What are you boys having?"

Nothing much fazes her.

After getting another patrol car, Carl and I go back out to finish our shift.

"Carl, how are you going to spin this incident for the mother of your children?" I jokingly ask.

"Well, last night's shift was no problem. I told her how I got to write citations. I did mention the bar fight, but I told her how you just yelled at them and they stopped fighting."

"And how about tonight?"

"Well, it's no big deal. We saw a drunk driver and he hit a pole and the wires scraped our car. No big deal. Right?" He looks at me. "What are you going to tell *your* wife about tonight?"

"We were chasing a suspected drunk driver and he hit a telephone pole and the lines hit our light bar."

"How is that any different than what I said?"

"It's all in the delivery," I reply with authority.

Seven o'clock in the morning comes and we part company until tonight. I go home, and my sweet wife has a fresh donut for me.

"Oh honey, a donut. I haven't had one in years," I say amusingly as I kiss her good morning.

"Since you're back on patrol I thought it was appropriate. Now tell me all about the heroics you two got into last night."

"Pretty dull except for the possible drunk driver we tried to stop. He wound up hitting a telephone pole and the falling phone lines hit our light bar as we were skidding to a stop. Poor fool killed himself. He was going way too fast.'

"That was it? No gun play?"

"No ma'am, none. Darn it."

I'm let off with my explanation and P.K. goes to her office. I go to bed after a quick check with my unit.

"Go to bed, boss, we're fine," Joseph admonishes.

A deep sleep, an evening with my wife, and I am back at the station. Another shift, but it's good. I am enjoying this. Would I want to go back to patrol again? No thank you.

I let Carl begin the drive tonight. The grin on his face is huge. He of course wants to go anyplace where people might know him. I tell him there will be plenty of time for that. We old-timers tend to get jaded. Now and then, it's good to see the pride and enthusiasm of youth.

We work on car stops. I advise my partner that during a stop, we make sure anyone we *light-up* has a safe place to pull over. This is rural country. Some roads have no real shoulder. You don't want to make the citizen pull into a soggy field. Worse yet, you don't want to have to wade into the soggy field. Being a country boy, he has a better grip on this problem than some city kid would.

The shift goes quietly, as it should. Carl makes some traffic stops and does well. We make bar checks, yes even on Joe. He is so appreciative of our concern for his well-being. Yeah right. We finish the night shift. Just a routine patrol, for a change.

As I enter my castle and make my way to the queen of my realm, I notice the morning newspaper laying on the kitchen counter. On the front page is a large photo of a sheriff's car, *my sheriff's car*. You can see the damage to the front, the cracked windshield, and the smashed light bar behind us.

Who took that? I'm dead.

I hear a sound behind me and spin around.

"Hi, my lovely wife. How'd you sleep?" I'm speaking very rapidly.

"A lot better than I would have if I'd see that picture last night." She comes over and grabs my shoulders and shakes me. She has to reach up to do it, but she gives me a hell of a firm shaking.

"Robert, you didn't tell me it was that bad. No big deal you said. Scraped the light bar you said. You guys could have been DECAPITATED." Then she hugs me, tears running down her soft full cheeks. "I know what you do is dangerous, but I'll never get used to it. I think I liked it better when you were with your guys."

Wonder if Carl's wife has seen the paper?

Chapter Fifty

Next evening Carl is pulling into the parking lot just as I arrive. I wait for him.

"So how did your morning go? See the paper?" he asks.

"Oh yes. It was laid out waiting for me. You too?"

"Uh huh. My wife was standing at the front door holding it when I drove up."

"You resisted the temptation to just keep driving?"

"We talked it out. She's better now, but I guess the wives never get use to this life, do they?"

"No, they don't. It's tough on them. There is no good way to handle the dangers of our job. If you minimize it, you can bet somehow they will hear how it went down. If you tell the whole ugly blow-by-blow of what happened, they will still be distraught. They deal with it and say a silent prayer when we leave for work."

Carl and I continue working together for the rest of the week. I agreed to two weeks, and the first week is over. Carl is doing quite well, but he will not be on his own for some time yet. He will be partnered with a deputy who has a longer amount of time on the force than Carl. Not perfect, but better than when I started eons ago. We were cut loose much too soon back then.

After tonight, we'll get two days off. Carl is looking forward to the time off, but I will be in the office, can't stay away. Tonight, Carl is driving and we're on a street near the Elko City city limits. I'm looking around at the area and I have a thought.

"Turn left at the corner."

"That's city jurisdiction, right?" he asks, perplexed.

"Yes, but we do serve the whole county. Besides, I want to check out something. I go back to my *old* job in a couple of days you know."

He brightens up. "Doing some investigative stuff, right?"

"Yeah, I just thought of something when I noticed where we were. Pull into the condo complex up on the right."

Carl turns into the parking area. "What are we looking for?" He's all eyes now.

"We just found it. The red Cadillac parked over there. She's baaaack. I just had a feeling. Pull behind it."

He stops the patrol unit behind Jeanie's Caddy. The cold night air hits me in the face as I exit the patrol car. Damn, I hate the winter. I walk over to the Cad and shine my flashlight through a side window. Fast food bags and drink cups on the passenger side floor and a few cardboard boxes stacked in the back seat. I walk to the front of the car. The hood is warm, not hot, but warm.

My deductive reasoning tells me she pulled up stakes in Vegas and came home. Looks like something serious happened if she drove all night. It is now almost four a.m. I may be overanalyzing this, but I sensed she was not an honest person from the first time I interviewed her. That's why I dropped a hint to Dr. Davis when I met him. I'm thinking maybe he listened to me. I'll be having my crew do some checking when I get home.

It is now seven a.m. One more week and back to my normal life, spending my nights with my fine-looking wife and not with Carl. Nothing personal, Carl.

After sending P.K. off to her office, I call my office. Joseph answers.

"I was going to call you, Bob. The dentist who moved to Las Vegas called asking for you yesterday. He wants you to call him."

"Dr. Davis, I am guessing."

"How did you know?"

"Deductive reasoning, Dr. Watson. Actually, I saw Jeanie is back in town, after she drove all night."

"I never did trust her. I know you don't. Did she cook the doctor's books?"

"My guess. I'll call him back right now. Give me his number."

"Hey, boss, you need some sleep. Want me to do it?" Joseph offers. "No, never mind. I know you too well. You will do it. Call me if you need anything done. You do need to sleep sometime today. George isn't going to be happy if you wreck any more patrol cars," snickers the smart ass.

"Just give me the phone number, Joseph," I reply in a crusty tone.

I immediately reach Dr. Davis. He is already at the office. Those dentists begin work at an ungodly hour in the morning. Longer days, more money, I guess.

"Thank you, Lieutenant, for getting back to me so soon," the doctor says. "I started thinking about what you were *actually* saying to me, when we were discussing Jeanie. You mentioned Donald wasn't particularly business orientated. You are correct. I began to check the books closely, as I had been trained to do, when I took business administration in college. The more I checked, the worse it became. She is using a non-existent supply company to embezzle from us. It took me quite some time to figure it all out. I confronted her last night. I told her she and I would be talking with Donald this morning. Jeanie has not shown up for work yet today."

I explain to him, "She won't be showing up at the office today. She drove to Elko last night; I found her still warm car in the parking lot of her condo." I'm stifling a yawn. I'm tired but this is getting my juices flowing.

"What should Donald and I do? Is this for the law enforcement in Elko or the Las Vegas police?" he asks.

"Was she doing this while she was here in Elko, with Dr. Morrissey?"

"Oh yes. That's evident. She started this scam early on, right after she got the job. I told Donald this morning. He feels like a fool."

"He should. If she was embezzling here and in Vegas, then both agencies should be involved. It started here, so we will take the lead. I'll contact Las Vegas Metro Police and have one of their financial investigators call you."

"Thank you, Lieutenant. I've been so busy getting settled and all, I probably would have let it go, at least for a while. But your comments kept coming back to me. 'Why would he say that?' I kept asking myself. Thank you again."

"I had to let someone there know what I suspected. You seemed to be the only one with any common sense."

Next, I call Preston in Las Vegas. We keep in touch, so he knows all about my *patrol escapades.*

"What did you wreck now? Or did you give the County Manager's wife a ticket?" Preston jokes. "Aren't you about done with your punishment tour?"

"Funny. Actually, I have need of one of your fine officers to do some work."

I tell him about the case. He will have a Metro investigator handle it and contact the doctors.

"Get some sleep," are his parting words. My mind is racing. I knew Jeanie was up to something.

I try to sleep. No use, I can't, so I get up and get dressed.

"Why aren't you in bed?" Gary asks as I shuffle into our office.

"Days off. Somebody has to watch you guys." I must be a sight—bleary-eyed, need a shave, old sweat shirt, and worn Levis.

"Can't sleep. *The Jeanie thing.* We need to get the evidence and arrest her before she disappears." I collapse into my office chair.

Joseph shakes his head. "Not surprised. I thought you would come in sooner or later today. What do you need us to do?"

I relay to them what Dr. Davis told me, then I call him again. I need whatever information he has on the phony company Jeanie used. He faxes me pages from their books and invoices from the company.

'A and J Wholesale Supply LLP' is the name on the invoices. Wow, how clever. Couldn't stand for Anna and Jeanie, could it? The only address is a post office box in Salt Lake City, Utah. No phone number. Dr. Davis has not found any listing for such a business in Nevada or Utah. He sent along copies of the cancelled checks. They were deposited to a checking account located at a bank in Salt Lake.

Using the mails for fraudulent purposes—a federal offense.

Engaged in criminal activities crossing state lines—a federal offense.

I don't have time for the inter-agency formalities.

Time for an FBI Andy call.

Andy is of course his usual, disgustingly helpful self.

"I'll get right on it, Bob. Send me what you have. Say hello to your lovely wife for me."

Damn, he can be annoying. But in all honesty, the FBI is a great resource for us locals. They can do in minutes what would take us days, or longer, to accomplish. He will be able to get the PO box info and all the data from the bank on the checking account. He'll get *stats* for this, look good for his boss, and only make a couple of phone calls. The mighty FBI.

There is nothing more to do now. What time is it? Eleven twenty. Hey, I can go have lunch with my wife. I haven't seen enough of her lately.

"*What* are you doing out of bed?" Eyes flashing, the little blonde demands, as I open the door to her office.

"Days off remember? How about lunch? I've got tonight to sleep, with my wife."

Chapter Fifty-One

Ah yes, Jeanie. Not done with you, my dear, not even started. The next task I will assign my unit is to set up the *Buzz Wagon* and keep a watch on her while we gather evidence from bank records.

Come on Andy…Time is wasting.

Back to work, I have things to do, criminals to catch, all that fun stuff. Quick shower and down to the office. My team is already there. All of them, including Buzz.

I lay out my plan to apprehend Jeanie. Buzz is to prepare the surveillance van, now officially known as the *Buzz Wagon,* for action. The four of us will divide the shifts. We need to keep a full time watch on Jeanie's condominium so she does not disappear before the warrants arrive.

"What about me? I can watch too. It's my van after all," Buzz snivels.

I sigh. "Buzz, you are the *Raison d'être* for the van. You always need to be available in case we have any problems. You cannot stay in there 24-7. Unless you want to?"

"All right, I guess, but all of you remember what I've taught you and don't mess anything up," the geek warns sternly.

"Raisin what?" asks Gary.

Joseph looks disdainfully at Gary. "Buzz is the

reason for the existence of the van."

Gary cocks his head. "Is that Native American language?"

"No, west coast boy, it is French." Joseph sniffs.

"Hey, I didn't take French. Give me a break."

I take charge. "School's out. Buzz, you and I will take the first shift. Get the van and call me when you are ready."

I check my phone messages and YES, Andy has called. He says he has received the bank info and is perusing it. He will call when he has a clearer picture of what Jeanie was doing. He goes on to say it looks like she was laundering the dentist's money into her own bank account.

We pull into the parking lot of the complex and locate the Cadillac. It is in a reserved spot, marked for Unit 123. I have Buzz park in the rear of the lot, get out, and walk around until he spots Unit 123. Jeanie would recognize me. She has not seen Buzz yet. He comes back and slips into the van.

"It's the third door on the left side of the pool." He points toward the swimming pool area. Perfect, we are already located where we can watch that door. We get into the back of the van and pull the curtains. Buzz gets the equipment on line and within minutes, the area around Jeanie's door is on the monitor. Nothing to do now but wait and watch.

There is little activity. No one is using the pool today. The nights are now colder since winter is approaching, but at mid-day, it is still comfortably warm. From the soft layer of steam rising from the pool, I would say it's heated. This is quite the upscale place. It's a weekday so maybe the residents are all working. Jeanie must be planning her next move. She must know the doctors are calling the police on her.

I'm getting thirsty, so I reach into the cooler and look for a water. There is nothing inside but bottles of *green tea*.

"Buzz, I told you to stock the cooler. This stuff is not fit for human consumption."

"It's healthy and good for you, plenty of antioxidants and nutrients." He is defensive.

I call Gary and tell him to bring water when he comes for his turn.

"Green tea! Yuck," Shouts Gary into the phone. "I'll die if that's all there is to drink. Besides, it makes you pee more. Last thing you want on a surveillance." So true, but we will not delve any further into that subject.

Gary relieves me at five o'clock. He has a supply of water and cola and has brought along some sub sandwiches. Buzz opts to stay longer. His choice. I take Gary's car and go back to the station. Nothing yet from Andy so I go home.

Oh yes, I had received a cell phone call from my wife, wondering what I was doing out of bed and where was I? We have a long overdue quiet night at home together.

Yes, I took time to check in on Gary. He was fine, and Buzz was hanging in. Once the novelty wears off, he will go home. Joseph and Ray will relieve them.

The next morning, I check in with Joseph. He says it was all quiet during the night. There were lights on in Unit 123, but no one came outside.

I get to the office just as Andy calls. He has the proof from the banks. Jeanie has indeed been putting the dentist's money into a bank account in Salt Lake City, the one she set up for the bogus wholesale company. Then she transfers the funds into her own personal bank account in Elko. That makes it a Federal crime. Interstate blah, blah, blah, of funds etc. etc. Andy is thrilled. Almost seems to be a sexual thing, he is so elated. Feds love that kind of talk.

Fine, Fed Boy, take the credit. Just because I called it in the first place, and put it all together, go ahead and crow.

I next call the D.A. She has been in touch with Las Vegas Metro's Financial Crimes Unit. With their information and the bank records Andy has obligingly e-mailed to us, she says we have enough to issue a warrant and she will contact a judge immediately.

"The Feds can do what they want. *We* have an intrastate embezzlement in Las Vegas and Elko. I'll call you as soon as I get the warrant signed."

Yeah, lady, let's do this.

Gary, Buzz, Ray, and I prepare to go to the condo area and relieve Joseph. Until we know for sure Jeanie is inside, we will not move in. Buzz, Gary, and I will go to the van. Ray will hang out nearby with Joseph. I know Joseph is not going to miss the action, even though he could use some sleep.

As we settle in the van, Andy calls. Cautiously I answer.

"What's up, bud?" I innocently ask.

"If I know you at all, I'm sure you are getting ready to arrest Jeanie. Therefore, I wanted to let you know there is another name on the bank accounts. Jeanie Martin and Anna Jacobs, both show the address in Elko you gave me for Jeanie. I assume you received the bank records I sent?"

"Yes, thanks Andy, and yes, we are getting a warrant ready. Unless you have a jet at your disposal, we will probably do this without you. No hard feelings?"

"None at all. I always like the locals to do the hard work of arresting and booking. We can file *our* charges later. They won't be going anywhere." He is laughing but I know he means it. Jerk. However, I still like him.

Another quick call to the D.A. She will add Anna Jacobs to the warrant.

All three of us are now in the van. Buzz is at the control panel and I sit in the chair alongside. Gary looks and sees a seat near the back door. It looks like an ottoman.

"I'll sit here; I don't recall it being here before, Buzz. When did you get this?"

"I brought it on my way in this morning. It is a camping toilet. Seemed like a good idea if we are going to be doing much of this kind of surveillance."

Gary jumps up, hits his head on the roof. "Damn, a toilet, why didn't you tell me?"

"I just did." Buzz laughs.

"Sit down, Gary; it's got a lid on it. Jeez," Buzz admonishes.

It is another mild, unclouded day, and some residents are already in the heated swimming pool. As we are dutifully surveilling the area, a nicely shaped woman in a two-piece suit climbs out of the pool and languidly stretches out on a chaise lounge. Gary is being extremely vigilant and to be honest, she has not escaped the attention of either Buzz or myself. Other people come and go from the pool and the condos as we watch.

Come on, Jeanie, make a move and show yourself. I do not want to sit here all day. Her vehicle is here but we don't know if Anna has a car or if they have skipped out already. Joseph said the lights were on all night in the condominium. Might have left them on and slipped out. I do not want to show our hand and spook them until I have the warrants.

The three of us are getting bored by now. Just staring at some magazines Buzz brought along, computer and electronics periodicals, of course. We *are* bored.

Suddenly, Buzz sits up and says. "She's moving."

Chapter Fifty-Two

"Who? Jeanie?" I drop the magazine and look at the screen.

"No, the lady in the bikini." Buzz announces. "She is leaving the pool and going toward the condos."

My cell rings. It's the district attorney. She has the signed warrants of arrest for both Jeanie Martin and Anna Jacobs and warrants to search their dwelling and vehicles.

"Great," I say. "Now I just need to see Jeanie… Whoa, wait a minute."

"What's going on?" the D.A. asks.

"Uh, the lady in the bikini is going toward Jeanie's condo," I say as I watch the woman head to Jeanie's door, Unit 123, and open it.

"Lieutenant, are you trying to catch a criminal or girl watching?" She is getting indignant.

"Actually both. The woman just entered Jeanie's condo. She must be Anna. I think it is time to move in. Get the warrants to us, now. I can have a patrol unit pick it up from your office."

"No, I'll bring it myself. I'm leaving right now."

"Okay, Joseph and Ray will meet you in the parking lot."

I call Joseph and Ray and update them. They have been around the corner waiting at a Starbucks. Tough assignment for them. At least they had a real bathroom.

"If that is Anna, why didn't someone see her come out of the condo?" Gary asks. "She was already in the pool when we took over from Joseph. I'm sure of it."

Joseph answers his cell. "Yes, Bob, anything happening?"

"Yeah, you and Ray go to the entrance of the complex parking lot and meet the D.A. She will have warrants for Jeanie and Anna. And...while you were in the van, did you see a woman in a two-piece suit go to the swimming pool?"

"I did see a lady in a two-piece suit, but I don't know where she came from. A UPS truck pulled into the parking lot and stopped right in front of me. The truck blocked my view of the condominiums. I slipped out of the van and walked out in the lot, so I could keep an eye on Unit 123. That's when I saw the woman walking to the pool area. She put a towel down on a lounge and got into the pool. Nice, uh looking lady, huh?" Joseph comments somewhat shyly.

"We all agree. However, the problem is, when she got out of the pool she went into Jeanie's condo. She must be Anna. Let me know when Bates arrives. We will move in then."

"Oh crap, sorry, boss, but I couldn't see because of the truck."

"It's okay, Joseph, no problem. We hadn't counted on good old UPS to spoil our view."

While we are waiting, Buzz rewinds the recording and sure enough, the big UPS truck pulls right in front of the camera's field of vision. When the big vehicle finally does leave, there is Anna, in the pool. No harm done this time, but it is something to consider for our next stakeout.

I have called the sheriff's dispatch to inquire if there is a patrol unit, with a female deputy, on duty. Fortunately, there is one not too far away. The dispatcher advises the Elko City Police also have a female officer on duty. I request Elko to lend her to assist us. Imagine trying to do this a few years ago.

In about fifteen minutes, Joseph calls to inform us the D.A. has arrived. I have him bring her to the van. We let her in, and I send Gary to find the maintenance man. We have been observing him making his round of the complex. Chances are he will have a master key.

Bates gives us the warrants and we show her our set up, along with the recording of Anna going into the condo.

"All right, she has a nice figure; I'll give you a pass on that. But she's no spring chicken," the female prosecutor proclaims. "Now what's our move, Lieutenant?" She is trying to contain her excitement. Apparently, she has not been present for an arrest before.

"As soon as Gary gets the maintenance guy, we will move in. Ray will cover the back of the unit. There is a small fenced-in patio for each unit. Therefore, that means a back door. The rest of us will hit the front. Hopefully we can con the maintenance person into knocking on the door. Before you ask, Buzz, yes, you grab your video camera and follow us in."

"I knew that," Buzz says defensively.

"No, you didn't. I heard you sucking wind ready to whine, '*Can I go too*?' Right?"

"Well, it *is* part of my job, Lieutenant."

Gary comes up with the maintenance man. He is pumped to be of service to law enforcement. It will be his moment of glory. He will tell this story to the bar crowd tonight.

"They're bitches anyway. Good riddance!" he spits out.

The female officers have arrived, and we all group around the van doors and go over the plan. Then it is time to move out.

Ray moves to the rear of the building and the rest of us quickly head for Unit 123.

The window drapes are drawn shut. We all stand to either side of the door.

The maintenance man has his master key out. Then, per my instructions, knocks loudly and calls out, "Maintenance! It's Chris from maintenance!"

From inside we can hear a muffled, "Just a moment."

I ease Chris to the side and get ready.

We hear the door unlocked from the inside and slowly it opens. Jeanie cautiously peers around the door, hair uncombed, dark circles under haunted eyes; she is a mess. Putting a foot in the doorway, I smile. "Jeanie, good to see you again. You are under arrest." Looking past her as I push the door fully open, I see Anna, now completely clothed. "Anna Jacobs, you are under arrest." The team enters the unit, and the lady officers quickly secure the two women.

We send Chris on his way thanking him for his service to the community and close the door. The D.A. reads the warrant to the arrestees. I advise them of their rights. They begin to shout over me.

"You said they would never find us. The dentists thought you moved to Vegas and didn't know about this place!" Anna is screaming at Jeanie.

"Shut up, bitch! This was all your idea in the first place. I should have stayed with Dr. Morrissey and dumped you. He was too stupid to ever figure it out," Jeanie spits back.

"You weren't smart enough to keep Dr. Davis out of the books. What do you mean, *stay with Dr. Morrissey*? Did you sleep with him? You did, didn't you? You slut!" Anna starts to lunge at Jeanie. The female officer yanks the handcuffed woman back.

Ah, a woman scorned is a woman scorned, no matter the circumstances.

I speak up. "Ladies, ladies. We have much to do here, and I'm going to have to ask you both to sit down and be quiet."

That did not happen.

Therefore, the D.A. instructs us to send them both to jail. We can do our search, per the warrant, with Buzz videotaping it all. The prisoners are transported to jail, separately. Gary and Ray will each ride along with one of the female officers. At the jail, my team members will do the booking.

Gary gives a 'why me?' look. I casually reply, "Seniority".

Joseph looks up and just smiles.

Chapter Fifty-Three

With Jeanie and Anna out of the way, we can continue our search of the premises and vehicles. There is a plethora of incriminating evidence located in the condominium—bank statements, printed forms for the phony business, and even a copy of the order to the printers for the forms, signed by Anna. Their computer yields a host of e-mails back and forth between Anna and Jeanie. Spelled out in black and white with incriminating details, is their swindle. My team takes the documents and computer but leaves the crime lab crew to see what else they can uncover. Anna also had a vehicle parked in the lot. However, neither car had anything of apparent evidentiary value inside. We did have them impounded, just in case.

D.A. Bates looks around the room and smiles. "Lieutenant, I am so proud of how you and your team have handled this difficult case. You know it's my job to keep you within legal guidelines, so we can successfully prosecute. I am quite confident with the evidence in this entire matter."

After that praise, back at the office, my team is enthusiastically writing their reports of the operation. Yeah right, not the fun part, but the whole case rests on our reports being written properly. Buzz is searching the computer to see what other secrets it may hold.

Crap, I work with Carl again tonight. Two days off

aren't enough, if you are doing two jobs.
****

I walk into the briefing room and find Carl already there. Grabbing a cup of coffee, I sit next to him. No one else has arrived yet.

"This is our last week, Bob. I want to tell you how much I've appreciated having you for my first FTO. I've learned a lot and had some fun too." He extends his hand. The boy's a class act. He will do well.

As I shake his hand, I take hold of his shoulder with my other hand and say, "Carl, you are going to be fine. I consider it a privilege to have been your FTO."

"Ahhh, I'm going to get tears in my eyes," comes from behind us. It is the sergeant.

"Stuff it, Sarge," I yell, without turning.

"Seriously, Lieutenant Carson, I've enjoyed you being here. Your presence has bumped up the morale of the team. They're impressed someone from management would come back and work the streets. And do it well—shattered patrol car notwithstanding."

"Yeah, thank you, Sergeant, but I don't consider myself management. More like the lead investigator. But thanks again. I have enjoyed it—shattered patrol car notwithstanding."

After the nightly briefing, Carl and I begin our patrol. I let him drive. He's interested in what I found out about the red Cadillac we saw two nights ago…I tell him the basics of the case. I do advise him not to say anything until it hits the papers.

As we drive alone, resting my head against the seat, I reflect on my journey to this point. From a police officer in California to a lieutenant in Nevada, rural Nevada at that. Yes, it was a fluke that I could make that jump in rank, but it worked out for me. Elko was losing trained deputies to the larger law enforcement agencies, and no deputies in Elko wanted to be detectives. Something to do with the hours—on call, any day, any time. George was the lieutenant then. When he was appointed Undersheriff, he had only Joseph as an investigator. A very inexperienced investigator. The fluke was…while personnel rules mandated promotion from within for most positions, a department head could be selected from outside the agency. Having previously worked with George on a cattle rustling case, he put me on his short list of candidates. George knowing my old partner Charlie, and my boss in California, didn't hurt either.

Long story short, I took the job. Best decision I ever made. Met the love of my life and married her, got lucky on some high-profile cases, and now I have a unit with three detectives and a geek. Life is good.

My thoughts are interrupted by dispatch advising that Elko City Police and Fire are responding to a 911 call on Silverton Avenue. All the dispatcher could determine from the hysterical female caller was something had happened to her mother.

Silverton Avenue? I've been there. Who lives there? That's the street where Diane Morrissey lived.

"What were those house numbers, Carl? 1130?" I ask my partner.

"1130 Silverton. Want to go?"

"No, it sounds like a medical call. We don't need to add to the congestion. I had a case on Silverton Avenue, the dentist's wife I told you about. She lived at—*she lived at 1131.* That's just across the street. Holy shit! 1130 is where Mrs. Howell lives."

"Let's go, Carl. She's out on bail for murder." I'm fully awake now.

"Maybe she tried to kill her herself again," Carl offers. "You said she wasn't too stable."

Before I can answer, the radio advises the call is a shooting. An elderly female is the victim.

"Step on it, Carl!"

We come screeching up to a gaggle of emergency vehicles with multiple flashing lights bouncing off the darkened, up-scale homes.

I tell Carl to stay with the car as I head toward Mrs. Howell's house. The ambulance crew is wheeling someone out on their gurney. I run up to them. There is an oxygen mask on the person and IV's have been started. I take a quick look at the face. Yes, it is Mrs. Howell, blood coming through the bandages on her chest. She doesn't look good.

"We're losing her," shouts one of paramedics as they rapidly load her into the ambulance.

I head toward the front door. An Elko officer says, "I'm sorry, Lieutenant, but this is a crime scene."

"It may be *my* crime scene. I arrested the vic for murder." Poor guy doesn't know what to do.

"Bob, come in. I was just going to have you notified." It's the Elko City sergeant. He tells me Mrs. Howell's daughter, who has been staying with her mother while she was awaiting trial, called 911 when she was awakened by loud noises. She was upstairs and when she got to the top of the stairs, she saw her mother lying on the floor at the bottom of the stairs. The front door was wide open.

Her account matches that of the first officer to respond. Mrs. Howell was found lying on the floor, inside the front door, near the bottom of the stairs. No weapon has been located. He said it appeared Mrs. Howell was shot at least three to four times in the chest.

The sergeant and I talk with the daughter. She's wrapped in an old flannel robe, her hair disheveled, and her eyes are red and swollen from crying. She has calmed down somewhat since her 911 call and she is able to answer our questions, between sobs and wiping her eyes. She keeps saying, "I'm sorry."

"That's all right, just take your time. We know this is difficult for you," the sergeant says, as he hands her another tissue.

She tells us her mother doesn't sleep very well and will stay up all hours of the night just wandering around the house. We ask her about any weapons in the house. Since her mother's attempted suicide, she is certain there are no weapons in the house. The daughter has no knowledge of any threats against her mother.

"No one ever calls here. After Dad died, her only friend was the lady across the street. Now she's gone. Mother would never have hurt Diane on purpose. I think she has suppressed what she did. She keeps saying—*what a shame Diane had to move to Las Vegas. I miss her.*" The lady looks at both of us. "Who would have done this?"

The sergeant responds. "We will find the person responsible, ma'am."

We leave Mrs. Howell's daughter in the care of the responding officers. I take the sergeant outside. "I might know who did this. Let me check it out. I'll call if I need assistance."

As I run back to the car, I'm calling Joseph on my cell. "Call Gary and Ray and have everyone meet me at

Louise's old house."

I direct Carl to where we're headed. I radio dispatch to send me two marked patrol units and, of course, the Sarge. Louise's house is in the county jurisdiction, so this is our case now. I instruct the patrol units to hold back several blocks away while I check out the residence.

I have Carl ease our car up the street and cut the headlights. The night time talk shows are over, so the citizens should be in bed. All the houses on the street are dark except for the occasional outside light. Good. As we get closer, I can see a car in the driveway. That's what I thought. The house is still on the market and the perfect place for her to go. Leaving our car two houses away, Carl and I turn down our personal radios and softly edge up the driveway. There is a typical late-night quietness about the neighborhood. The car in the driveway has a license plate frame that proudly proclaims, *this vehicle is a rental*. The massive house is dark except for a faint glow emanating through the front drapes. We silently move across the front yard and around to the side. From this position, we observe a bright light coming from a window near the back of the house. We try not to make any sound. We move up to the window, being careful not to stumble in the pitch-black yard. The window has no covering. Inside, sitting at the kitchen counter is *Louise,* dressed in a name brand jogging suit (what else?). She has a wine glass filled with red liquid in her hand and a bottle of wine on the counter in front of her. She is alternately crying and drinking. Alongside her on the counter is a small revolver. From my vantage point it appears to be a Smith and Wesson Chief's Special. That particular weapon has a five-shot capacity. I leave Carl to watch her. He is to give me a heads-up if she moves off that stool. I go to the front to use my radio. Joseph is on the street and Gary and Ray are minutes away. My team.

I lightly push down on the front door latch. It's locked; of course it is. But there's a realtor's lockbox hanging from the handle. Louise would still have her own key. I get an idea. I look at the realtor's sign on the lawn. Yes, just as I remember, it is the fire captain's wife. That's perfect. She may not answer her phone at one-thirty in the morning, but *he* will. I tell dispatch to call the Elko Fire Captain and request his wife give us the key code for the lockbox at this address.

In what seems like forever, but is only a couple of minutes, the dispatcher advises the key code. Joseph, Gary, Ray, and the sergeant are now with me. I have the marked units quietly move in. I send Ray to cover the back yard. Another deputy is sent to be with Carl at the window.

Sarge covers the front, while Gary, Joseph and I go to the door.

I enter the numbers we were given. Doesn't open. Damn! Try again, Lieutenant, you are a little tense. The second time the box magically opens, and YES, the key is still in there.

I put the key in the lock and turn it. Then slowly pushing down on the latch and holding my breath, the latch goes all the way down. We're in. With drawn weapons we enter the premises. Thankfully the door didn't squeak when opened, and the only light is still coming from the left side of the darkened house. We move toward the light, picking our way through the large pieces of furniture in the shadowy living room. I hear a soft bump and Gary sucks wind. Wonder what massive piece of furniture he hit? Next, we pass through a dining room and then up to the brightly lit kitchen.

Louise is still sitting at the counter with her back toward us, drinking and sobbing. The pistol is still to her right side on the counter. I motion for Gary to get the gun and for Joseph grab her left side. I will take her right arm.

I nod, and we move in. Just as we are about three feet from her, she jolts upward and spins around. The wine in her glass splashes across her chest and the glass flies from her hand, shattering on the floor. Joseph and I grab her arms and Gary secures the gun. It's over in a second. She is in handcuffs before she can react. Gary states the pistol still had one round left unfired.

"Louise Davis, you are under arrest for attempted murder."

Louise struggles and begins to cry hysterically. "No. No. That woman had no business trying to kill *me*. *I* didn't deserve to die. She always hated me. Why would she want to kill *me*?" She is bawling and starts to go limp. We get her into a chair.

She looks at me. "Is she dead, is she dead? I want her dead!"

Between the booze and her emotional state, she is a wreck. We call for an ambulance to take her to the hospital. She will need to be in restraints for now.

While we are waiting for the ambulance, I pull Gary aside. "What did you run in to? I heard you groan."

He looks downward. "The arm of a big fucking sofa, crotch high."

"Well, since you aren't talking in a high pitch tone, I guess you're okay."

"Thanks for the concern, boss."

The paramedics come and take Louise away. Gary goes with them. When she gets to the hospital, Elko PD will take over. The crime did occur inside the *city* limits.

Then as if on cue, the Elko sergeant who was at Mrs. Howell's house comes up to us.

"Gee, thanks, Lieutenant. Another fine mess you made for us to clean up. How do you manage to get people shot in the city limits, wind up with the arrests, and we city officers have to do all the paperwork?"

"I don't want you guys to feel left out." I grin.

"You sure you were never in the FBI? You operate like them."

"Honest, just a local boy like you."

Chapter Fifty-Four

I look at Carl and say, "Well our work here is done, let's go get some breakfast."

Gary, Joseph, and Ray all stop what they are doing and stare in disbelief at me.

"Uh, Lieutenant, there is a lot of evidence to be collected here. You can't leave...well I guess you can do what you want; you're the boss, but?" Gary is trying to find the right words.

Wise Joseph speaks up. "Don't forget he is on patrol tonight. His shift is not over, and his crew is on the scene. But I still don't think it's fair." He snorts.

"Sorry, guys, but patrol's function is done here. Carl and I have to finish out our shift." I am enjoying the moment. They will get back at me later—I know that—it won't be pretty.

"You going to be in the office at eight in the morning, Lieutenant, or are you going to bed?" Joseph asks with trepidation.

"You share all the evidence you collect here with the Elko investigators, and I will be in the office after seven when I'm finished with patrol. I will expect to see all your bright and smiling faces at eight o'clock, sharp," I say in my most authoritative tone. Then I break into a smile. "You guys try to get some sleep when you're done here and come in tomorrow when you feel like it."

"You really are going to the office?" Gary asks.

"Just long enough to fill in the Undersheriff and the D.A. Then I am going home to bed. I'll see you all tomorrow."

Carl and I go to breakfast. He cannot stop talking about the night.

"Wow. What a night! I don't suppose you would consider coming back and working with me again, would you? I've learned so much in just two weeks."

"Nothing personal, Carl, but I'm beat. I need a rest. I would work with you again anytime; you are a quick study and fun to be with, but together we seem to attract more action than all the rest of the units combined. It's been fun, partner."

Seven o'clock comes and the shift is over. As we part, I give Carl a *guy* hug. "You will do just fine. Keep your head on straight and remember, you can call me anytime you have a question or a problem. Once a partner, always a partner."

He hugs back and says, "Thank you, Bob, I'm very grateful for the time we worked together. You don't know how much it's helped me. I was starting to wonder if I was cut out for police work. Now, I'm ready."

I walk over to my office, choking up a little. To be a part of helping a rookie get off on the right foot is very rewarding. The sun is up, and a new day is upon us. The warmth feels good, or maybe the warmth is coming from inside.

I enter my darkened office and just sit at my desk. I settle into my chair and reflect. It has been quite a two weeks. Exhausting at times, but I have never been one for routine or boredom. Opening the window shades to let in the light of day, I call Undersheriff George. Fortunately, the patrol sergeant has already briefed him on the night's activities.

"How did you know Louise Davis was in town and where to find her? You are beginning to scare me with your insight. You're rivaling Joseph. And don't give me that 'elementary, my dear Watson' crap either." Boy, George is in a mood this morning.

"Well it is elementary actually. I spoke to her husband, and he said she came back to Elko to get the house sold. See, George, elementary."

"I heard about calling the fire captain's wife to get the lockbox code. That was a stroke of genius, my man. Well done. Now go home and get some sleep."

"After I call the D.A., I will." I yawn.

"No. I will advise the district attorney, and you go home. That's an order."

"Yes, sir! Thank you, George."

I arrive home and into the warm embrace of my beloved. Sexy as ever, this morning dressed in a cute peach colored blouse and blue pants. Damn, I'm sure glad night shift is over.

"How was your last shift, baby?" she asks, embracing me.

"You mean I get to be the first to tell you about something that happened? I half expected reporters at the door."

"Robert, what did you do this time?" I love how P.K. always thinks 'I' did something. Even if it is usually true.

"Louise Davis shot Mrs. Howell."

For once, my wife is speechless. I can see her mind is spinning trying to make sense of what she just heard.

I fill her in on the details. She is still trying to grasp it all.

"Because Mrs. Howell tried to poison her, Louise thought she could *shoot* her?"

"That's about it, yeah," I say as I drink some orange juice that has been set out for me.

"That's just crazy. She is crazy!" P.K. is incensed.

"Yes, I would say *certifiable* now."

"And you thought I would find Elko too boring? There have been multiple murders, robberies, embezzlements, and God-knows what else since I've been here. This place is giving Reno a run for its money."

"Honestly, honey, I'm not arranging this for your entertainment. I'll still bet on Reno in the long run." I raise my juice glass.

We talk about it a little more, then after I am in bed, the ocularist goes to her office. After she's gone, I realize I did not tell her about *how* we captured Louise. You know, the creeping through the darkened house, sneaking up on a drunken, distraught, armed woman. Well, too late now. I will address that if it ever comes to light. I know it will, someday, probably sooner than later.

I am still wound up. As I lay there, I start to think about Doctor Davis. He was the only one of the whole bunch involved in the Diane Morrissey case who seemed normal. The first dentist I ever actually liked. I would go to him for dental work, and I hate dentists. Now his wife is a murderer. She will go to prison or at least to a mental institution.

What a convoluted case—Mrs. Howell, who was trying to poison Louise Davis, poisons Diane Morrissey accidentally. Dr. Andresen poisons Diane Morrissey, to scare her into leading a healthy life. Louise Davis shoots Mrs. Howell, for trying to poison her. On top of all that drama, Jeanie is robbing the two dentists blind.

Chapter Fifty-Five

I should call Dr. Davis and update him on what has transpired. I just do not know what to say to him.

"Hi, we have Jeanie and her partner in custody, for the crimes they committed against you and Dr. Morrissey, and by the way, sorry about your wife being a murderess." No, that is not going to work. Maybe I will chicken out and just call Dr. Morrissey instead. However, Dr. Davis was the reporting party. Thinking about it, he has probably been notified his wife, Louise, is under arrest for murder. He may even be back in Elko. Wait, what day is it? My life has been a whirl the last two weeks, especially the last few days. When did we arrest Louise? It was night before last, *Yes.* It *was* night before last. Louise's husband will know by now.

I call Elko PD and talk to the detective in charge of the case. "She is wacked out, Bob. Apparently, she went over the edge. They have her on suicide watch in the psych ward at the hospital. I have officers there 24-7. She has not made any phone calls, says she does not want to talk with anyone. She will converse with the doctors and nurses, but never mentions what she did. One of the shrinks says he will try to encourage her to discuss the shooting. We have notified her husband, and he's at the hospital. She even refuses to see or talk to him."

Now I call Dr. Morrissey. The valley-girl sounding

receptionist is the usual gatekeeper, "Doctor is with a patient. May I take a message?"

I *clearly* identify myself and say I am calling the doctor with information regarding the police report he filed.

She mumbles something unintelligible. "Oh the Jeanie thing. I'll tell him right away." At least, I *think* that is what she said. In less than two minutes, the doctor comes on the line.

"This is Doctor Morrissey." He sounds anxious.

"Doctor, this is Lieutenant Carson, Elko Sheriff's Office."

"Yes, Lieutenant, what can I help you with?"

"I wanted to inform you we have arrested Jeanie Martin and Anna Jacobs on the embezzlement charges, filed by you and Doctor Davis."

"My word, so soon. I thought she would be long gone by now and would never be caught. Thank you for such quick work. Uh, you said Anna somebody, who is that? Was she also involved in stealing from us?"

"Yes, she was Jeanie's partner all along." I let that sink in. "They lived together in Elko."

"You mean, like lived together as in, well you know…" He is getting the drift.

"Yes, doctor, I would say so. It would appear they have been together for several years."

He swallows hard, sounding as if he is trying not to barf. He is taken aback with the information. I am enjoying his discomfort.

He tries to talk but does not seem to know what to say. Sputtering and stumbling a bit he finally says, "Excuse me, I'm just somewhat overwhelmed. What do we need to do now?"

I explain to him the D.A.s in Elko and Las Vegas will be in touch with him shortly.

"Have you seen Chuck, Doctor Davis?" he asks quietly. "I know what happened up there."

"No, I wanted to talk to you first. I know he is here, and I will go see him. I just can't imagine what he is going through. How is he handling it?"

"He's not well. I wanted to go up with him. He said no, that we need to try and keep the practice going. We still don't know how much harm Jeanie did to us financially. Our new CPA is going over all the records, starting from the day she was hired."

"Doctor, did you have a CPA while Jeanie was with you?" I am sensing I might have another conspirator here.

"Yes. Yes, we did. Now we are using a Las Vegas firm since our records are here. Chuck said we should use a new CPA. He thought the old one should have noticed some irregularities in the past. That was going to be our next step."

I smell blood. "Who *was* your Elko accountant?"

"You know I'm embarrassed to admit, I never met him. Jeanie handled it all...Oh no, no, no! What a damned fool I have been. She said she could get me a good deal with an accountant she knew. I am such a fool."

Yes, doctor, you are...Serves you right.

"Get me the name and I will check into it. This case may not be over yet."

He checks his files and comes back on the line.

"It was AJ Bookkeeping and Accounting. There is a post office box in Elko on the billings."

"Doctor, I will bet AJ stands for Anna Jacobs.

Jeanie's partner. Give me the PO box number and I'll check on it."

"She was scamming me from the start." He begins a tirade of swearing but then abruptly stops. Softly he says, "I had it coming, didn't I? She saw a mark and I went for it all the way."

"No comment, doctor. I will follow up on this and keep you advised. I will try and see Doctor Davis and fill him in." This is my professional tone now.

"Chuck, oh God, what is going wrong with the world? I didn't care for Louise, but Chuck seemed to love her. I found her a bit too overbearing. She certainly was beside herself, after she learned that woman had wanted to poison *her,* instead of Diane. Chuck was worried about her but then she seemed to come to terms with it all. I guess what she did was decide to get revenge. This is still about Diane; will no one let her rest in peace? I miss my wife. If I had been a real husband instead of the self-involved *Dentist of the Year,* she might still be alive. Excuse me, Lieutenant, I have to go…" The line goes dead.

A check of the file we have on Jeanie and Anna confirms the PO box for AJ Bookkeeping and Accounting is theirs. Boy did they have a scheme going. Wonder if any other clients were taken in? I let Buzz know what I just found out. He tells me he has already located the AJ Accounting files in the computer we confiscated from the twosome.

"I was just going to call you. Sure looked wrong to me. The dentists were the only clients, but from what I have seen, between the phony billings for supplies and the accounting charges, the women were doing quite well. Jeanie was still getting a good salary, too."

"And a new Cadillac to boot," I add.

After advising the D.A. of our new information, I decide to go to the hospital and try to see Dr. Davis. I don't want to, but I feel an obligation to talk with him. I am the one who found his wife. Given the mood she was in, there was a distinct possibility she would have shot herself or at least tried.

Arriving at the hospital, I am advised Dr. Davis is at the hospital chapel. His wife still does not want to see him. I ease into the dimly lit quiet chapel, which feels completely multi-denominational. It would be soothing to anyone of any faith, or even those looking for faith.

The doctor is sitting in a pew near the rear, slumped back, just staring ahead. I let the door click shut so he knows someone is there. He straightens up and turns toward me.

"Doctor Davis," I begin. "I don't know what to say, except how sorry I am."

He sluggishly rises to his feet and comes toward me. He is beyond tears now. I don't know how long he has been here, but he is clearly in desperate need of food and sleep.

"Lieutenant." He seems to be gathering himself up. "Thank you for not shooting Louise. I know that could easily have happened. She's still alive, thanks to you. She is my wife and I love her. I don't know what will become of her. I hope she will respond to treatment and come around."

He starts to hold out his hand, and then just throws his arms around me. Shaking and crying, "Why? Why? I keep asking myself, what could I have done? What should I have done?" His voice is quivering. "Why didn't I see what was happening to her?"

The poor man is ready to collapse. I get him settled in a pew and sit next to him. I begin to talk. I am not sure what I am saying, or how long we are there. Eventually he gets himself centered. I coax him into going to the cafeteria and get him to eat a little. He is going to go to a hotel and try to get some sleep. He has decided he will be available when Louise is ready to talk with him, but will not continue to stay at the hospital, hopelessly waiting for any news. We go to Louise's floor and tell the nurses where he will be staying, if they should need him. You can see the relief in the staff's eyes. They already have one seriously disturbed patient on their hands, and they did not want another. Chuck has been here for almost twenty-four hours. The nurse hands him a phone message that just arrived. It is from the dentist he'd worked with in Elko. The note says Chuck is more than welcome to come and stay with him. Dr. Davis looks overwhelmed.

"Why don't you give him a call?" I suggest. "Being alone now is not a good idea."

Chuck calls and after talking with his old associate, he tells me he will go to stay with him.

"Good move, doctor. Need a ride?"

I drop Doctor Davis off at his old partner's house. I hope he will get through this. Of all the people involved in the 'Diane Morrissey case', he was the only one I liked. Dr. Morrissey, on the other hand, I hope is being tormented by guilt-ridden emotions over his thoughtless, self-centered deeds. Diane Morrissey, the innocent victim and one of the nicest ladies in Elko, whose horrible murder started this whole case, has been buried, exhumed, autopsied, and re-buried. She deserves to rest in peace now. Jeanie and Anna are *in-*

residence at the County detention facility. Dr. Asshole-health nut is on bail awaiting trial. Poor Mrs. Howell is dead, her troubles finally over. She can also rest in peace.

Emotionally drained with all that has happened in the last few days, I need to unwind. As I enter our home, I feel a wave of release flowing over me. I go toward the family room and see a glass of wine sitting on the table next to my chair. Alongside, in her chair, is my cherished wife.

"My love, you have had a hard day. Come in and relax with me." She pats my chair and holds up the wine for me. God, I love that woman. We talk for a long time. I am unwinding.

"You're finally done with this case, aren't you?" asks P.K. "There are not many players left; between the deceased and the incarcerated, only the two dentists are still left standing."

"Yeah, never in my wildest imagination would I have believed that finding one body would morph into a case with two homicides in the first degree and one negligent homicide. Not to mention the illegal dispensing of drugs and two embezzlements. This case is one for the books."

****

"Has everyone turned in their reports from the last few days? I need to see them before the D.A. does."

All nod in the affirmative.

I go to my office and check on their reports, and then I complete mine. A few details need refining, but mainly, all the cases are in the hands of the District Attorney's office.

Jeanie and Anna's cases will require court

appearances by me, and of course, appearances by the two dentists. Andy will get his two bits worth in somewhere along the line.

Doctor Andresen will get his turn before the bar of justice. One hopes he will lose his license *forever*...The creep.

Finally, Louise may or may not be tried criminally. That will all depend on her psych evaluations. I will be on call for those hearings also.

Chapter Fifty-Six

A few weeks later, I'm sitting at my desk poring over crime reports looking for any commonalities, clues that might tie one case to other cases. Being totally absorbed in the details of the reports, it startles me when my office phone rings. It rings all the time, but this time is sounds different. It's odd, almost ominous. I focus on the phone. The area code is 408, so the call is from California, Santa Clara County to be exact. That's my old stomping grounds. I don't recognize the number.

"Lieutenant Carson," I answer in a business-like tone.

"Bob, Tom Green here. Morgan Hill PD. The one who sacrificed himself, so you could go on to greater things." Tom was my replacement at Morgan Hill. Good guy. I worked with him when he was just a reserve officer. Last time I talked with him he had become the lead investigator for the department. He may be Chief by now.

"Tom. How are you? Good to hear from you. Take over the Department yet?"

He laughs. "No, not yet, still chief investigator, but quite happy with that. You wouldn't recognize this place now. San Jose had no room to grow so it just spread south, and we are now one big city. How are you doing? I've seen quite a bit of Elko stuff recently in the news. You've been busy."

"Yeah, for a while we were. One case turned into several. Now hopefully we are back to just one case at a time. What can I do for you, Tom?"

I'm getting an uneasy feeling in the pit of my stomach. I almost feel that I should just hang up and not talk with him.

"Okay, here goes. I have dreaded calling you until I had all the answers; I still don't, but I'll give you what I have." His voice is quivering.

The last time I heard from Tom was near the close of the Weaton Case...I discovered the murdered woman, after a truck had dragged her lifeless body directly in front of my patrol car. I had only seen the silhouette of the truck and heard a scraping sound. A short time later I found her body. The truck was never located—no cameras back then, middle of the night, no real description of the truck, only a few officers on the road at that time of the night. The All-Points Bulletin turned up nothing. Years later, at my request, Tom had taken the victim's clothing, which had been residing in the Morgan Hill PD evidence locker, to the coroner to test for DNA. When the crime was originally committed, DNA testing was unheard of. Now, it is the norm in major cases. The results were negative for anyone's DNA except the victim's. At that time, I was checking for a connection to William Weaton. He fit the M.O. for the crime and I'd always believed he was responsible for it.

I ultimately tracked him to Oregon, where I shot him, while trying to take him into custody for several other homicides. On his deathbed he stated he did not commit the murder of the woman in California.

Subsequently, I learned he was not in California when the incident occurred.

I have never felt I was finished with that case. It's haunted me. I was only a patrol officer at the time and as such, was not able to do any follow-up on the case.

When I became a detective for the county, I had a similar occurrence involving a trucker. I identified that trucker as Weaton and pursued him for several years, before the encounter in Portland.

Now here comes Tom Green with something he doesn't want to tell me. It must be about *my case*. *My Case* is how I have referred to it—all these years.

"Bob," he begins. "Last night, around two thirty a.m., one of our patrol officers found a floral wreath sitting on the side of a street. It was one of those big funeral pieces on a tripod. There was a typed note attached to it that said:

'I am sorry. I never intended for this to happen.
I live with what I did to you.
You know I always loved you.'

"The officer picked up the whole arrangement and brought it into the station. He thought it fell from a vehicle or something. This morning when I reviewed the patrol log, I saw the location where he found the flowers." Tom pauses; he sounds emotional. He continues. "Bob, it was right where *you* found that lady's body. How many years ago? It was the same location, I swear. The whole area has been developed now, the gas station is gone, the street has been widened, but it was the same place. I even got out your old report to be sure. When I looked at your report, I saw the original date of the murder. It is today's date. So many years ago, but the same date. The officer even found it at about the same time you located the body. He swears it was not there forty-five minutes prior, when he had driven past."

I swallow hard. "I don't know what to think, Tom."

He continues. "I found a florist's sticker on the tripod under the wreath. The florist is local. The owner says he remembers the person who ordered the wreath. She picked it up yesterday. The florist offered to deliver it, but the lady said she would handle it. The florist had never seen the woman before. Said she was in her fifties at least, looked like she had led a hard life. Paid cash. The woman carried the wreath out to an older Chevy SUV parked down the street. The florist thought it was odd. He didn't notice the license plate. Just an older, dirty beige SUV. The florist does not have surveillance cameras in his store, and I couldn't find any on the street that covered the area.

"I checked what video cameras there are in the area and the nearest cross streets. You can see a Chevy Tahoe, about eight or ten years old, in one shot but the sun glares onto the windshield so no hint of who was driving. I checked all the cameras in the area where the flowers were found, and one of them shows a similar vehicle going down the street at about two fifteen this morning. The vehicle was picking up speed. It was probably after she dropped off the flowers. I'm sorry, Bob. That's all I could find out."

"Did you talk with the victim's family?"

"Yes, I did," Tom answers. "Shocked it was a woman. The family had no knowledge of the victim having any relationship with a woman. They acknowledged she did not seem too interested in the local men. I tried to calm them by saying maybe she was finally feeling guilty and trying to make amends. Where *has* she been all these years? Why is she just now showing up?"

"Maybe in prison on another charge or she just got religion. After the recent cases I handled, who knows what goes through a person's mind or what affects them."

"I'm sorry I don't have any more information for you, Bob. This kind of re-opens your old case. I will be following up on it. Do you have any ideas?"

I think for a moment. "No, not for now. You have covered everything. But three hundred and sixty-four days from now I will be in Morgan Hill and waiting on that street—for her."

"I will be with you, Bob."

And so, dear soul, who I never met until I found your lifeless body, I hope somehow you are aware you may be cold but not forgotten.

A word about the author...

RJ Waters has lived the life this book portrays. Using his imagination and real-world experiences in law enforcement, he transforms his knowledge into an intriguing, humorous, believable novel. Waters and his wife, Penny, live in Las Vegas.

Thank you for purchasing
this publication of The Wild Rose Press, Inc.

For questions or more information
contact us at
info@thewildrosepress.com.

The Wild Rose Press, Inc.
www.thewildrosepress.com

To visit with authors of
The Wild Rose Press, Inc.
join our yahoo loop at
http://groups.yahoo.com/group/thewildrosepress/